THE REDEMPTION OF
DON CALOGERO

THE REDEMPTION OF DON CALOGERO

R. D. CROFT

Matador
9 Priory Business Park,
Wistow Road, Kibworth Beauchamp,
Leicestershire. LE8 0RX
Tel: 0116 279 2299
Email: books@troubador.co.uk
Web: www.troubador.co.uk/matador
Twitter: @matadorbooks

ISBN 9781788037655

British Library Cataloguing in Publication Data.
A catalogue record for this book is available from the British Library.

Printed and bound by CPI Group (UK) Ltd, Croydon, CR0 4YY
Typeset in 11pt Adobe Garamond Pro by Troubador Publishing Ltd, Leicester, UK

Matador is an imprint of Troubador Publishing Ltd

Dedicated to the memory of
Pip Appleby (1931–2016)

For whom the humble; was king!

A verray parfit gentil mann

The line dividing good and evil cuts through the heart of every human being.

Aleksandr Solzhenitsyn, *Archipiélago Gulag I*

Greater love hath no man than this, that a man lay down his life for his friends.

Gospel according to St John 15:13

What you are about to read is:

At best, implausible;

Somewhat farfetched;

Totally unbelievable;

It could not possibly happen!

Could it?

Surely not!

Not in a million years!

Of course it couldn't!

By the way:

Has anyone seen Laozi recently?

I

HABEMUS PAPAM

I:I

'It is just after six o'clock on 24 June and you are watching the early evening news on BBC News 24. My name is Stuart Anderson.

The headlines:

The Roman Catholic Church has a new leader. At just after three this afternoon white smoke was seen coming from the chimney above the Sistine Chapel. This was the signal that the cardinals, meeting in Conclave, had finally agreed on the election of a new pope to replace Thomas XV, who so unexpectedly resigned last month. We'll be live in St Peter's Square in a few moments.

In other news:

The chancellor has announced that he cannot guarantee a fall in the basic rate of income tax in the Budget, due in the spring of next year;

Britain's trade deficit with the rest of the world rose to a new high in February by £2.5 billion to £17 billion; we'll have detailed analysis later in the bulletin;

The Liberal Democrats have announced that they will not be putting forward a candidate in July's Brixham North by-election, although the reasons for the decision have not been made clear;

And in sport: it has been another woeful day for the English cricket team as they lose the third Test to Bangladesh by an innings and 265 runs.

First: let's cross to our correspondent in Rome, Chris Buttler, who can bring us up to date with today's momentous events in a very wet and windy Eternal City. Chris, I hope you've managed to stay dry.'

'Not a chance of that I'm afraid, Stuart, the weather has been absolutely dreadful here during the afternoon. It would not be any form of exaggeration to say that most people here are soaked to the skin, but the rain has done little to dampen the enthusiasm of the tens of thousands who have flocked to the piazza, to witness the formal announcement of the name of the new pontiff and to catch a glimpse of their new spiritual leader. We shall not have official confirmation of the new pope's identity for another hour or so, but it is rumoured that it is to be Cardinal José Ignacio Garcia, who is currently Archbishop of Andalucía in Spain. He's just forty-one years old and only the third Spaniard to be elected pope; the last one being the notorious Alexander VI, otherwise known as Rodrigo Borgia. He's the youngest pontiff for over five hundred years, and is also one of the tallest at nearly six feet four inches in height.'

'Pardon me for interrupting, Chris, but what more do we actually know about the man? It is not a name I have heard before.'

'Yes, it has come as something of a surprise for a lot of people. Interestingly, while he had many supporters across the Catholic community, it was felt that he was a pope for the future not necessarily the present, but the cardinals obviously did not agree. It would appear that they have chosen him in spite of his relative youth and inexperience. Having said that, he does have a massive following in Andalucía where he is credited with bringing hundreds of young people, many of them families, back into regular contact with the Church.

He is also something of a celebrity in that he can often be seen riding his racing bike through the streets of Sevilla. As a much younger man he was considered a promising cyclist and even, on one occasion, took part in the Vuelta, otherwise known as the Tour of Spain, although admittedly with one of the minor teams. I very much doubt whether he'll be allowed to ride his bike on the notoriously busy roads here in Rome, Stuart – far too risky!

On a serious note, it could well be that the new pope will have his work cut out for him – he has something of a reputation as a reformer and moderniser. It remains to be seen how well some of his more radical ideas go down with conservative elements within the Catholic establishment; but at this stage there is no doubting the anticipation that is felt both here in the Eternal City as well as in the wider Church. As we say in the press: watch this space!

Back to you in the studio, Stuart. We'll return when the proclamation is made from the Basilica's balcony.'

I:II

VIS: VATICAN INFORMATION SERVICE
CARDINAL JOSÉ IGNACIO GARCIA
ELECTED AS POPE,
TAKES TIMOTHY AS NAME

Vatican City, 24 June (VIS) – Cardinal José Ignacio Garcia has been elected as Supreme Pontiff, the 271st successor of Peter, and has chosen the name Timothy. He is the third Spanish Pope and the first Timothy in the pontificate.

At 7.15 pm the Cardinal proto-Deacon Alberto Stromboli made the following solemn announcement from the Loggia of the Vatican Basilica:

'*Annuntio vobis gaudium magnum;*
Habemus Papam;
Eminentissium ac Reverendissium Dominum,
Dominum Ioseph Ignatius,
Sanctae Romanae Ecclesiae Cardinalem Garcia,
Qui sibi nomen imposuit Timothy.

(I announce to you with great joy,

We have a Pope;
The most reverend and eminent Lord,
Lord José Ignacio,
Cardinal of the Holy Roman Church,
Who has taken the name Timothy.)'

At 8.00 pm the new pope appeared at the Loggia on the Vatican Basilica and having blessed the vast crowds gathered in the piazza he said:

'My dear brothers and sisters in Christ,

I thank you from the bottom of my heart for your warm welcome, especially considering the inclement nature of today's weather. My brother cardinals have been moved to elect me as the new Bishop of Rome – your bishop: I hope a bishop for all the people. As you will have just heard, I have decided to take the name Timothy. You may wonder why I have chosen this name. From what we know, Timothy was a relatively young man when he had leadership thrust upon him, but he still had a lot to learn. I have a lot to learn but, with your support, love and prayers, I hope that I can become half the man he was. I believe that, by working together in love and brotherhood, we can build a New Jerusalem where there is no space for conflict, dissent or abuse.

May the Blessed Virgin watch over and protect all of Rome and our wider family of Faith.'

The Holy Father ended by imparting the apostolic blessing.

II

FIVE YEARS LATER
EFFUGIUM?

II:I

Although it is early in the morning it is clear, to even the most lethargic weather watcher, that it is going to be another blindingly hot day in Rome. One could almost believe that the Eternal City is being assaulted by an infernal alliance consisting of Ra, Helios and Apollo, all pooling their formidable powers and resources to create heat of an almost Gehenna-like intensity. The daytime temperature has not dropped below 40°C for over two weeks, and news broadcasts are full of horror stories about deaths attributed to the abnormal climatic conditions. Nobody can remember the weather in early May being as hot or unforgiving as it has been. In the centre of the city there are only a few earlybird tourists and pilgrims in St Peter's Square, endeavouring to avoid the inferno that the plaza will become later in the day. Overhead a few hardy pigeons attempt a couple of desultory circumnavigations of the cupola above St Peter's Basilica, but the effort proves too much; and now they line the colonnades perched on statues of long-dead and largely forgotten saints, seeking shelter from the rising sun, and watching as a street washer truck sluices water ineffectively across the sizzling cobbles.

Inside a spacious bedroom, in an apartment high up overlooking the square, a florid, portly, balding man lies in an antique Italian walnut bed, allegedly dating from the mid-nineteenth century, but in reality having been purchased relatively recently from a rather low-budget online website specialising in reproduction furniture. On one wall hangs a huge tapestry of the *Adoration of the Magi*, by Gentile da Fabriano but, rather like the bed, it is not all it seems: it is merely a seventeenth-century copy, the original now residing in the Uffizi in Florence. Given the provenance of the bed and the tapestry, it may well come as no surprise to learn that the Louis XIV armchairs, set around an elegant centre table, and the exquisite Persian carpet beneath it are also both imposters; one could hardly walk daily on a gift from Shah Abbas II to Pope Urban VII.

The only authentic furnishing, in this otherwise immaculate but rather misleading setting, is a square formica-topped table dating from the early sixties, located close to the bed, on top of which there is a small revolving fan that is attempting to direct some small cooling breeze towards the inert form enmeshed in the crisp white cotton sheets. The man snores gently, a sheen of fine perspiration coating his upper lip. Cardinal Basil Alfonso Cuella, Secretary of State to the Vatican and former Archbishop of Valencia, second only in power and influence to the pope, is not known for his early rising. While many of his contemporaries have started the day with Mass, followed by breakfast and are already at their desks in the Secretariat offices, the good cardinal slumbers on, oblivious to and unappreciative of their efforts. What he does not know is that in precisely thirty-seven seconds his bedside telephone will ring, and his life will be forever transformed.

The phone peals. On the eighth ring he finally manages to pick up the receiver.

'Cuella!' he barks.

'He's disappeared.'

'What?'

'He's gone. He's not here. I can't find him!'

'Who's gone?'

'The pope. The pope's gone.'

'What do you mean? Who's speaking?'

'Monsignor Tardelli. The pope is not here. I can't find him.'

'Where the hell are you?'

'His apartment. We were waiting for him to come to Mass at San Giovanni but he did not arrive. I came back to the apartment to see if anything was wrong but it was empty.'

'What time is it?'

'Seven thirty. He's always in the basilica by ten to seven. He's never late. I've searched the flat three times. I've looked everywhere. He's gone. What are we going to do?'

'Get a hold of yourself, man. Calm down. Have you checked with Jackson?' Peter Jackson and Tardelli are the pope's two private secretaries.

'I've phoned Monsignor Jackson on his mobile and his landline but there is no answer.'

'Surely Giovanni will know where he is?' Giovanni is the pope's personal manservant.

'The pope gave him a week's holiday. He's somewhere in Milan, with his family, visiting relatives.'

'Good God. Well then, what about the sisters? Surely they should be there getting breakfast?'

'They've not turned up either. The whole place is totally deserted. Shall I ring the convent and find out where they are?'

'Yes, ring me back on my mobile if and when you get

a reply. Whatever you do, don't tell anyone at the convent that the pope is missing. It will be all over Rome within half an hour if you do. I'll be with you in fifteen minutes. In the meantime get security to mount a thorough search of all the rooms and corridors in the building. Get on with it.'

Not waiting for a reply Cuella slams down the phone. It's probably all a storm in a coffee cup, and there is bound to be a perfectly reasonable explanation, but it's a lousy way to start the day, especially when later on there are meant to be celebrations, admittedly low-key ones, marking the fifth anniversary of Timothy's pontificate.

For a man weighing 110 kilos the good cardinal can move remarkably quickly when the need arises. Normally his butler, Alberto, would assist him in dressing but today there is no time. It is an emergency. On goes the black cassock but the wretched scarlet buttons take an absolute age to do up; then the scarlet fascia gets twisted three times before he wraps it securely around his amble girth. The language that accompanies these processes is rich, varied, extremely colourful and is most certainly not for the ears of children or those of a sensitive disposition. At last the pectoral cross goes over his head and the scarlet zucchetto is fitted snugly on his balding pate. Black slip-on shoes are engaged and he heads rapidly for the door. No time for ablutions this morning; people will have to take him as they find him.

Cuella bustles down a labyrinth of austere bland corridors never normally seen by members of the public. He is a man of generous physical proportions – to be honest he is morbidly obese – so he waddles rapidly along, rather like a constipated duck experiencing occasional bouts of painful flatulence. He pointedly ignores the salutations of people he passes in the passages; he is a man on a mission and so cannot begin to contemplate delays or procrastination. It takes him only five minutes to reach the papal apartments, during which time he has a call from Tardelli. The Mother Superior of the Order of Elena the Servant, who supplies the pope's domestic support staff, is evidently distraught. The rooms of Sister Carmen and Sister Elvira have been checked, but both are empty; the beds have not been used. The mother superior is not even sure whether they returned home from the papal apartments last night. A search of the convent has been ordered, and two sisters have been dispatched to trace the route usually taken by their colleagues on their way to work. He is also told that Obest Karl Alexander Geisinger, Commandant of the Swiss Guards, who are responsible for the safety and protection of the pope and security within the Apostolic Palace, is on his way to the apartment. Mario Antonetti, Inspector General of the *Corpo della Gendarmeria*, who heads the equivalent of the Vatican police force, will join them as soon as he can.

Arriving at the papal residence, he finds Tardelli in the most dreadful state; the private secretary is obviously taking the disappearance of his boss to heart. The worthy monseigneur is a small, pasty-faced individual, who can sometimes act as if challenged by his diminutive stature; it could easily be said that he suffers from, what is sometimes called, short man syndrome. While he is an outstanding administrator and a gifted linguist, Tardelli is also more highly strung than a Steinway grand piano. He is beside himself, pacing up and down, wringing his hands and giving more than a passable impersonation of a headless chicken. Cuella nods in his direction.

'When did you last see the pope?'

'About seven last night. He was complaining of a headache and said that he would forgo supper and have an early night. It was extremely unusual for him not to attend night prayers in the chapel, but I put it down to all the stress he has been under recently.'

'Did anything out of the ordinary happen yesterday?'

'Not really. It was a very quiet day. There were no major meetings and, as I remember, only one visitor all day.'

'And who was that visitor?'

'It was Father Callum Flanagan from the Mission to the Islands.'

'How long did he stay?'

'I think he arrived about four. I'm not sure what time he left – it will be recorded by the Guards downstairs.'

'I'll get Geisinger to check when he gets here. Are you sure there was nobody else?'

'As far as I know Flanagan was the only visitor but I cannot be totally sure. I was not with the pope all day. I had a dentist appointment after lunch and was away for most of the afternoon.'

'Right, go back to your office. Make it look as if everything is perfectly normal and keep your mouth firmly shut. If anyone turns up wanting to see the pope say that he is indisposed today. He has been affected by the heat and this has been exacerbated by the fact that he has been working very hard recently. Make it sound like a short-term problem, which I earnestly pray to God it is. Go!'

Tardelli bustles away, apparently glad to be relieved of any further responsibility, and Cuella begins a systematic search of the rooms. He starts in the bedroom. It is an austere, monk-like cell with no pictures on the walls, the only 'ornamentation' being an unpretentious crucifix above the bed. The bed is in pristine condition; it has obviously not been slept in. The closets contain all that one would expect from a papal wardrobe, but there is no evidence of underwear, socks or handkerchiefs, and there are only a few pairs of formal dress shoes. He moves to the bathroom and checks the cabinet over the hand basin, knowing that is where the pope keeps his prescription medicines for high blood pressure and elevated cholesterol – strange he needs them given that he is a fit, relatively young man. Nothing; they are not there. In the study the shelves still contain the works of theologians and philosophers from Aquinas to Zimmer, but there is one significant work missing. Timothy's most prized possession is a leather-bound, limited first edition of Graham Greene's *A Burnt-Out Case*, containing a hand-written, dated dedication to José's father by the author. It is not there. He finishes in the drawing room, where the pope receives friends and personal guests. There, on an occasional table in the centre of the room, he sees a large family bible, and on top of it is the *Annulus Piscatoris,* or Fisherman's Ring, one of the most powerful symbols of papal authority. There is no way in the world that the ring would ever leave the sacerdotal finger. Cuella feels sick to the pit of his stomach. All the work he has put into securing his position and future within the Curia is about to come to naught. There can be little doubt now that the pope has gone, but why on earth would the man 'do a runner'? What possibly could have motivated him to do such a ridiculous thing? But the plain fact of the matter is that when a new pope is elected he appoints a new secretary of state. To all intents and purposes it is not inconceivable that Cuella's career, within the upper echelons of power in the Vatican, is at an end; more to the point, how on earth is he going to manage the fallout from this unholy mess?

Geisinger arrives, closely followed by a perspiring Antonetti. Colonel Geisinger, in keeping with tradition, is a Swiss national whose family have been associated with the Guards for centuries. He is a dapper little man who, even though he is wearing a dark blue three-piece suit, looks remarkably cool given the rapidly rising temperature outside and the intense heat that the situation inside has generated. Geisinger's greatest quality is the ability to melt into the background, an exceptionally valuable trait given the delicate nature of his occupation, but whether he is capable of decisive action is quite another matter. It has always been his belief that the pope must be protected but not necessarily seen to be protected.

Antonetti is different. He is a tall man in his mid-forties, with jet black hair beginning to show flecks of grey around the temples. Dressed in beige chinos and a blue blazer, over a brilliant white open-necked shirt, it is easy to understand why, when he enters a room, he immediately becomes the centre of attention. Perhaps, not surprisingly, he has a formidable reputation as a 'ladies' man. Normally a swarthy, avuncular fellow, well met and hearty, today his complexion is white from stress. Perspiration drips from his face. He is out of breath and has quite possibly been running to get to the apartment. Geisinger and Antonetti barely acknowledge each other; their mutual loathing is well known throughout the Vatican, although few know the reason for the feud. Perhaps the only person really in the know is Frau Geisinger, but that is totally another story!

Geisinger begins: 'Your Eminence, I came as soon as I heard the news, but it is impossible, totally impossible.'

'Not impossible, Geisinger, it's a bloody reality. I've checked the rooms. He's gone. One of his secretaries is not answering the phone. The sisters who worked as domestics have disappeared, and he gave his butler a week's vacation several days ago. The whole bloody thing looks like a well-thought-through plan to disappear. I thought we had CCTV in the corridor outside?'

Geisinger turns even whiter. 'We did until last Monday. The pope told me to disconnect it, because he wanted to make sure that if people desired private access to him they could do it without fear of being taped. After all the problems we have had recently, it did not seem an unreasonable request at the time. That's why there have been fewer security patrols this week. And, of course, one of the first things Timothy did when he was elected was to get rid of the two korporals who used to stand guard outside the apartment. If you remember it was because he said that he did not want to live like a bird in a gilded cage. It's all a terrible mess.'

'Why was I not informed about the CCTV?'

'The pope insisted that it should be an "understanding" between us. I came to the conclusion that he was expecting a number of visitors who would very much prefer to remain anonymous.'

'Who, in God's name?'

'He did not tell me.'

'And you didn't think fit to ask?'

'It did not seem to be my place.'

'Incredible!' Cuella turns away in disgust and casts his eyes across the room. 'Right, there must be an appointments diary somewhere. Get someone to check the computer. I want to know all those people who had access to the pope yesterday and I want it by eleven o'clock. Tardelli says that he only had one visitor, but at the moment the monseigneur is about as reliable as Italian State Railways. Make another fingertip search of the buildings. I don't suddenly want to find out that he has been lying comatose in some isolated corner for the last twelve hours.'

Cuella turns to Antonetti. He is not polite. 'You, Antonetti, get your fat arse over to Jackson's apartment and see if you can find anything that sheds light on this blasted shambles. I'll set up a meeting with the cardinal bishops for midday at the secretariat, and I want you there and I want answers.'

Cuella storms off. Geisinger turns on one of his subordinates.

'You heard what the secretary of state said,' he says resignedly. 'Search the building again.' It is blindingly obvious to him that heads will roll and that, in all probability, his will be one of the first skulls which will be thrust roughly, and without mercy, into the lunette.

II:II

An hour later, just after nine o'clock, Antonetti and two gendarmes are standing in the living room of Monsignor's Jackson's first floor, two-bedroom apartment, which is located on the corner of Borgo Vittorio and Via del Falco only a short distance from St Peter's Square. The flat dates back to the eighteenth century and is situated at the confluence of two quiet cobbled streets. Even though it is close to the Vatican it is a relatively quiet part of the city. Most of the houses have wood shuttered windows although nearly all are closed, most probably to guard against the wretched heat. It has been a bit tricky gaining access to the apartment as the Vatican police have no jurisdiction in the City of Rome, but the caretaker is finally persuaded to give them the keys when Antonetti explains that the pope is anxious because his trusted private secretary has not turned up for work. There is concern that he may be sick or in some form of difficulty.

The room is in semi-darkness, but even in the half-light it is possible to see that it is crowded with books, papers and files crammed onto every conceivable surface. One of the gendarmes throws open the shutters and light floods into the room. Bookshelves surround them. It is obvious that Peter Jackson is not only Catholic in spiritual terms but also in literary terms as well. Minette Walters and Patricia Cornwell lie casually, almost provocatively, atop Gustavo Gutiérrez and Karl Barth. In the middle of the room there are a couple of moth-eaten sofas and a dusty coffee table, containing yesterday's newspapers and six dirty coffee mugs; two of them have lipstick around the rim. The only concession to modernity is a huge 55-inch flat screen television set into the corner of the room. The power has been switched off at the mains. *Not only widely read,* thinks Antonetti, *but environmentally conscientious as well;* or is it that the occupant knows that he will not be returning anytime soon.

They search the rest of the flat. The kitchen is a bombsite. The sink is crammed with dirty dishes, glasses and cutlery; scraps of uneaten pizza on greasy plates occupy the kitchen table, together with a couple of half-consumed bottles of cheap red wine. Nor does the main bedroom contain many surprises. Like his master, Jackson sleeps in something akin to a monastic cell; the whitewashed walls are bare with only a simple crucifix hanging above a cast iron bed. This intrigues Antonetti. His own bedroom is rich in lively colours and subdued seductive lighting. He often 'entertains' in his bedroom, and so the creation of an 'appropriate' ambience is fundamental to the success or otherwise of his 'enterprise'. Is the total absence of decoration and colour in the two bedrooms, he has visited today, a reflection of a desperate nightly struggle between the spiritual and the carnal, imposed by the rigorous, and perhaps unreasonable, demands of enforced celibacy? It's an intriguing thought, is it not?

The guest bedroom is a revelation. It is a mass of plastic clothes hangers, cardboard boxes, tissue paper and plastic bags; all of which, at some stage, had contained ladies' clothing of various types, styles and forms, from dresses, slacks and shoes to some exceedingly 'interesting' lingerie. Discarded on the bed are two plain blue uniform dresses; the two Sisters of

Charity have obviously kicked the habit and indulged in an extreme makeover, not only in terms of fashion, but of lifestyle as well. The items appear to have been purchased from online stores of somewhat questionable provenance. One might be forgiven for wondering what the delivery men made of it all, especially if they knew that the supposed recipient was one of the pope's closest spiritual advisors!

Antonetti beckons the two gendarmes back into the living room. 'Right, gentlemen, there is nothing here but I want you to stay and take this place apart. It's not a crime scene, so you do not have to worry about contaminating or disturbing evidence. I have no real idea what you are looking for, but I want you to find out as much as you can about Jackson and what he got up to. Examine all the books to see if there are notes or papers inside; check all the files; hack into the computer; examine the phone records and go through the garbage. Build up a picture of the man. See if you can find any clue as to where the four of them might have gone, because gone they have. And, if you breathe one bleeding word of what and why you are doing these things to anybody, I shall personally ensure that my boot relocates both your scrotums to the general vicinity of your cervical vertebrae. I trust I have made myself totally clear?'

It is immediately apparent, by the looks on their faces, that the bold gendarmes have received and understood the message. They know better than to mess with their superior officer; he has a formidable temper when roused, and they have both been on the receiving end of a tongue lashing from the chief in the past.

Antonetti continues: 'Right, I am going downstairs to interview the caretaker, and then I shall be going to report to that bastard Cuella and his henchmen. You will stay here until I return, and you'd better have something for me, because it is highly unlikely that I shall be of a sunny disposition when I get back. *Hai capito?*

Oh yeah, they understand: they really do understand!

*

The caretaker is an elderly, pot-bellied man with a couple of days' growth of grey beard on his saggy, well-weathered cheeks. Fraying red braces hold up a pair of shabby black trousers, and his threadbare checked shirt stretches alarmingly against the thrust of his enormous belly. His rheumy blue eyes peer blankly at Antonetti as they talk in the dark, filthy kitchen of his ground floor flat.

'How well do you know Monsignor Jackson?'

'Hardly at all, he keeps himself to himself. Most of the time he's not here.'

'When did you last see him?'

'A few days ago. He came down to pick up a few packages which had been delivered for him earlier in the day, when he was out.'

Antonetti thinks for a few seconds, and then asks, 'Have a lot of packages been delivered recently?'

'Come to think of it, yes there have.'

'When he came down to collect his packages, was he alone?'

'Yes.'

'Was he alone last night?'

'How the hell should I know?'

'Did you hear anything? After all, his apartment is directly above yours. Was there movement?'

'Suppose so.'

'What the hell does that mean?'

'Whatever you want it to mean.'

'Was there more than one person in the flat?'

'Might have been…'

'You're not exactly helpful, are you?'

'You're Vatican police, right? You've got no right to ask me questions. Piss off and leave me alone.'

Antonetti takes another moment to weigh his options. He could pin the man to the wall and threaten excruciating physical pain but, the caretaker is right, this could result in a huge political storm, especially as the local authorities in Rome are not exactly among the greatest supporters of the Vatican security services. His choices are severely limited, but he is only too aware that he will shortly be facing Cuella, who will expect him to have made some form of progress. There appears to be only one option.

'How much?'

'What do you mean?'

'Stop buggering me about. How much to loosen your tongue and engage your short-term memory?'

'Make me an offer.'

'One hundred…'

'Make it a five and I might even throw in a cup of coffee.'

Antonetti considers his response, but he really has no choice; the caretaker has a firm and unyielding grip on his *testicoli*. 'OK, but I have not got that much on me now. You'll have to wait.'

'How much have you got?'

Antonetti empties his wallet. It contains 220 euros in notes. He throws them on the table.

'I'll take it as a deposit,' he says, 'but I want the rest by this evening. Understood?'

'Understood. Now, what happened last night? How many people were there in the apartment?'

'Two nuns or sisters arrived just after seven, and an hour or so later Jackson turned up with a religious man I have never seen before. He had a large black beard and was very tall, but it was dark, that was all I could really make out. Three other people also arrived: two men and a woman. Again, I can't help you with who they were. Then there was a lot of noise and banging and scraping on the floor. About quarter to nine they all came downstairs with suitcases, got into a large silver minibus and drove away.'

'Was it a taxi?'

'It might have been, but as I said before, it was dark so I really cannot be sure.'

'Is that it?'

'What more do you want?'

'But you are sure that it was about quarter to nine?'

'Yes, it was half-time in the football on TV. Coffee?'

'Piss off!' Antonetti is seriously not amused.

'I want the rest of the cash this evening or I'll make a complaint to the state police.'

'You'll get your dough, but even bloody Judas gave better value for money.'

Antonetti leaves; at least some of his suspicions have been confirmed but at a price. He heads back to the Vatican. There is still time to call into the security HQ before the meeting. He fervently hopes that they have met with a modicum of success, otherwise the conference with Cuella is going to be something of an ordeal.

II:III

VIS: VATICAN INFORMATION SERVICE
CANCELLATION OF PAPAL AUDIENCE

It is with deep regret we announce that today's Papal Audience, due to be held in the Papal Audience Chamber at 1200, has had to be postponed. It had been hoped to use the event to celebrate Pope Timothy's five years of service to the Mother Church. However, the Pope is unwell and will be unable to attend. His Holiness has had a particularly heavy workload recently and this has been undertaken during the hottest start to the month of May since records began. It is stressed that his condition is not serious but his medical staff has advised that he needs to rest. He has been flown to Castel Gandolfo for a period of recuperation in more clement climatic conditions. Further statements will be issued in due course.

His Holiness wishes to apologise to all those who have made such strenuous efforts to attend the Audience and stresses that it will take place at a later date.

II:IV

Before going to the meeting with Cuella and the senior cardinals in the Mediaeval Palace, Antonetti heads for the Governatorate building, which is located in the middle of the Vatican Gardens behind the towering basilica. It is a massively impressive four-storey, triple-fronted edifice, set amidst perfectly manicured lawns and ornate flower beds. It is here that the Central Security Office of the *Corpo della Gendarmeria* is located. Antonetti wants to see if progress has been made piecing together the events of the pope's previous working day, and to ascertain who precisely had access to him. In a room in the basement of the Governatorate he meets up with Antonio Mascola, who is in charge of security at the many and varied entrances to the Vatican itself. Antonetti does not even bother with a greeting.

'Got anything?'

'Good morning to you as well, Mario. You'll like this. Think we've worked out what happened. Watch this. It's from the entrance on the Porta Angelica. It was taken around three thirty yesterday.'

Mascola taps a command into his laptop and a grainy CCTV image appears on the screen of the computer. It shows perspiring sweaty holidaymakers, many in brightly coloured T-shirts and dresses, wandering in and out through the open gates in the white hot heat. The window shutters on the terracotta-coloured eighteenth-century houses are thrown wide open, in a vain attempt to make the most of whatever cooling breeze is wafting through the boiling streets. A couple of colourfully uniformed Swiss Guards are preening themselves and posing for pictures, unashamedly showing off their masculinity to admiring young female tourists.

'There,' says Mascola, pointing at the screen.

The image shows a short, heavily bearded, corpulent priest in a wheelchair propelling himself across the cobbles. A large, wide-brimmed hat keeps the worst excesses of the sun from his face. Negotiating the rough surface of the street is obviously not easy but he turns down offers of help from concerned passers-by, and is seen heading in the general direction of the Palace of Sixtus V, which houses the papal apartments.

'Meet Father Callum Flanagan, Head of the Mission to the Islands charity. You can see that he arrived in a wheelchair at about four thirty. There's nothing else from inside the Palace because the bloody machines were switched off, but now – take a look at this. As you know, members of the clergy and religious orders are allowed access to the museums after tourists have left. Just look what happened at around half past seven. It's from the public entrance on Viale Vaticano.'

Mascola types new instructions onto the keyboard and the screen comes to life again. This time the playback shows the entrance lobby of the museum. The area is deserted but earlier in the day it would have been pulsating with life. Now it is empty and dark, save for a priest pushing a man in a wheelchair, and a solitary, bored guard manning the reception desk. The person seated in the chair is also a priest and has a luxuriant dark beard. He is sporting a homburg hat, appears to be wearing tinted glasses and is hunched over, apparently staring at a book on his lap. Antonetti gazes at the screen. He clearly recognises the man pushing the wheelchair but he can't believe it; he just can't believe it. It is not possible.

'It's Jackson!' he gasps. 'It's bloody Jackson!'

'And if the man pushing the chair is Jackson?' asks Mascola.

'It can't be!'

'Look how he is hunched over,' says Mascola. 'He's obviously a tall man. Is he doing that to play down his height? Think about it, Mario. Think of the audacity of it all. How else could you get an extremely tall man out of a place where his is the most recognised face in the building? It's unbelievable but I just can't think of another alternative.'

Antonetti wants to argue; he wants to disagree; he wants to come up with another explanation, but he can't. Logic and his own eyes confirm Mascola's hypothesis. The two policemen gaze at the monitor, and watch as Jackson exchanges some form of greeting with the guard; the external door is unlocked and the wheelchair is pushed through the entrance into the early evening half-light. It disappears almost immediately.

Ladies and gentlemen, thinks Antonetti, *I am here to tell you straight that the pope has left the building* – but how the hell is he going to explain it to Cuella and the mob?

II:V

A ntonetti takes the lift from the ground floor of the Apostolic Palace to the top storey of the building. When the doors open he turns right, and walks along marvellously frescoed corridors towards the offices of the Vatican Secretariat, which are very modest in comparison with the opulence of the hallway. He is ushered into a meeting room with plain white walls and a battleship grey carpet. It is dominated by a large oak conference table littered with papers, files and documents. At the far end of the room about a dozen cardinals are huddled around a coffee machine. When he enters, their muted conversation stops, and they turn to look at him. Even though he knows all of them well, he immediately feels as if he is the prize exhibition at a freak show. The men stare at him with unashamed curiosity. Geisinger has not been invited; he is still overseeing the new search and, anyway, if the pope is no longer on the premises, his responsibility ends at the gates of the Apostolic Palace. Antonetti's role as head of the gendarmerie means that he will be in charge of tracking down the runaway pontiff; although once outside the confines of the Vatican City the task will become increasingly complex.

Cuella enters and the clerics begin to seat themselves around the conference table. Antonetti is directed to a place at the far end directly facing the secretary of state. He stares up through an avenue of bishops, cardinals and archbishops to Cuella who, so far, has not acknowledged his presence. The head of the *Corpo della Gendarmeria* is, quite clearly, the *lepus in lumina*. While waiting for the ordeal to get underway he looks at those seated around the table. In all truth, they are an unprepossessing bunch. If the Good Lord had been required to rely upon them to spread the Gospel to the four corners of the Earth, he might well have been sorely disappointed. They might well be leaders of curial congregations, pontifical councils, commissions or tribunals but, collectively, they have the presence and personality of a glint of goldfish. They open and shut their mouths to order but have very little real or original to say. Cuella knows this and that is the reason why they have been promoted, or one could say translated, to positions of immense power and influence within the Church. There will be absolutely no assistance forthcoming for the hapless policeman from the chaps in purple.

Cuella begins: 'What I am about to tell you must not go outside this room. I must ask you to maintain total confidentiality, much in the same way as you do every day within the sanctity of the confessional. There is no easy way to say this but the pope has disappeared. He did not turn up at Mass this morning and subsequent searches have failed to find him. One of his private secretaries, Peter Jackson, is missing as are two of the sisters who are on his domestic staff. I have asked Inspector General Antonetti to join us in the hope that he will have made some progress in ascertaining what has happened to them.'

The red and purple goldfish are gaping. Their mouths flap open and shut, like fish out of water fighting for air. One might have expected that there would be exclamations of surprise and a whole host of thought-provoking, probing questions, but there are none. These men did not rise to the top of their profession by being original thinkers or creative problem solvers. They have acquired advancement through unquestioning obedience, mindless compliance and trusting that any difficulties facing them would, at some stage in the future, simply disappear. Their only immediate consideration, considered in the privacy of their own thoughts, is what this might mean for them and their futures. Most had not liked Pope Timothy anyway. They had elected him because they wanted a 'frontman', a public face of the Church, someone good at PR. They had not been prepared for his desire to initiate reform and passionate commitment to challenge long-standing traditions and practices, both within the Curia and the Church as a whole.

'General Inspector,' Cuella continues, 'before we hear what, if any, progress you have made, have you ruled out the possibility of kidnap?'

'Not totally, Your Eminence, but given developments in the last couple of hours I think it is highly improbable.'

'And what developments are these?'

Antonetti brings the meeting up to date, relating his conversation with the caretaker and describing his subsequent meeting with Mascola. There are gasps of astonishment from around the table when he tells the prelates how the pope appears to have exited the building; it is almost impossible to believe. Towards the end of his briefing, there is a loud knock at the conference room door. Cuella motions Antonetti to be quiet and then, incredibly for someone as senior as the secretary of state, goes to open the door himself. It is one of his private secretaries. There is a mumbled conversation, inaudible to the rest of the men in the room, then Cuella returns to the table ashen faced and sits at the head of the conference table with his head in his hands. There is silence for what seems like an eternity. Finally he speaks: 'Is there any more, Inspector General?'

'Not at this stage, Your Eminence. However, I have two men searching Jackson's apartment and I would hope to have more information by the end of the day.'

'Thank you, Antonetti. I was going to allow you to leave to pursue your enquiries further, but I have just had some appalling news which I think you should hear. We will shortly be joined by Herr Hans Blumenthal from the Financial Information Authority. Until he arrives, I suggest that we spend the time in quiet prayer, and beg the blessed Virgin Mary to intercede for us before the throne of the Almighty, because gentlemen, we face the greatest crisis since Martin Luther nailed his ninety-five theses on the door of the *Schlosskirche*.'

Hans Blumenthal is a German banker. He was employed by a previous pope, who was concerned about the large number of financial irregularities across the whole of the organisation. His job is to oversee all aspects of the Vatican's financial management, from top to bottom; right down to maintaining a rigorous oversight of the monetary dealings of the post office and the single local supermarket. The main function of the Financial Information Authority, however, is to exercise tight supervision over the national and international transactions stemming from the Institute for the Works of Religion, otherwise known as the Vatican Bank, in order to ensure that money laundering and other such dubious practices do not take place. The bank does not exactly have an unblemished history in this regard. It would be satisfying to report that Blumenthal breaks the mould of the stereotypical Teutonic banker, but he does not: he is methodical, precise, formal and a stickler for rules and regulations. Blumenthal does not have a sense of humour.

He arrives wearing a charcoal grey three-piece suit, white shirt, dark blue tie, horn-rimmed spectacles, and carrying a black leather monogrammed laptop case. His hair, slicked down with Brylcreem, is greying at the temples, while his sky blue eyes convey all the passion and *joie de vivre* of a rather ancient depressed Galapagos turtle. Cuella motions him to take an empty seat next to him. HB, as he likes to be called, sets up his laptop never taking his eyes from the screen. When all is ready he sits back and looks intently at Cuella. In the five minutes he has been in the room he has not said a word.

Cuella breaks the silence. 'I think everyone will know Herr Blumenthal,' he says, 'so I don't think that introductions are necessary. Please begin, Herr Blumenthal.'

Blumenthal clears his throat. 'You will all be aware that financial management within the broad organisation that is the Vatican is very complicated indeed. Perhaps it is not surprising in an organisation that is many centuries old, and which has undergone massive changes over the years. However, it does mean that, despite the best endeavours of several recent popes, the potential for abuse remains high. My job is to monitor the monetary and commercial activities of all the Vatican agencies, most particularly the Institute for the Works of Religion, to ensure that financial improprieties do not take place.

'I have to tell you now that I have failed. My officials

and I have just become aware that in recent months a considerable amount of money, running into many millions of euros, has been channelled into a single charitable account at the Vatican Bank-headed Mission to the Islands. Most of the money has come from the Extraordinary Section of the Patrimony of the Apostolic See which, as you will know, is under the jurisdiction of the pope and his financial advisors. After formal trading hours yesterday, a substantial sum was transferred to an account held with Credit Suisse in Zurich. Normally all such transactions are made during office hours. This means that they are subject to our personal and professional scrutiny, before funds "leave" the building. The extremely unusual process that was used last night meant that the transaction was not seen until this morning, by which time it was too late to do anything about it.'

'What do you mean by substantial?' interjects Cuella.

'Twenty-five million US dollars,' replies Blumenthal. Now there are more exclamations of incredulity and sharp intakes of breath from those around the table. 'The payment should have been authorised by my team before it was made, but it was not. There is an urgent investigation at the bank to try to work out how this could possibly have happened, but we have not been helped by the fact that we are unable to locate the manager responsible for the transaction, Benito Pedulla. He was the supervisor on duty last night but, I regret to inform you, he has not been seen since about half past seven last evening; he does not appear to be at home and he is not answering his phone.'

Antonetti wonders if this is mere coincidence or whether there is a more sinister element to the equation. 'May I ask how the payment was authorised?' he asks.

'The Mission to the Islands is a charitable body which is administered by a board of eight trustees and, as you probably know, the pope is the patron of the organisation. For a payment of such size to be made there has to be approval from at least three of the trustees, each of whom has a secret authorisation code. When three codes are entered into the relevant online account, a transfer of funds can be effected, but only after an additional password has been entered onto the system by the authorising authority at the bank. Last night that authorising authority was Pedulla, and currently we don't know where he is. We would very much like to find him to ask why he authorised the transaction in such an irregular manner.'

'And who are the trustees?' asks Antonetti.

'As I say there are eight trustees, who are spread right around the world. Most have been involved in missionary work on islands from the Caribbean to the Pacific. There are only four based in Rome: Father Callum Flanagan, who is head of the organisation, Monsignor Peter Jackson, the pope's private secretary, Monsignor Adriano Fullcini, who is the Rector of the Island Mission Seminary in Trastevere, and Bishop Francisco Pereira, who originally was based in Cape Verde but is now living here in retirement. We are contacting them as we speak, to find out if they used their codes last night. Unfortunately we are unable to identify individuals from their password and authorisation code details. Bishop Pereira is an unlikely candidate because he has been seriously ill recently and has spent a considerable amount of time in hospital.'

Antonetti asks the blindingly obvious question. 'Does the pope have a password, or access code, which would give him entry into the account?'

'Most unusually yes, but it has always been a cause very close to his heart and so, while it is not common for a pope to have direct access to an account, it is also totally understandable.'

'So Flanagan, Jackson and the pope could have initiated the transfer?'

'With Pedulla's assistance, I'm afraid so yes.'

The room goes very quiet. One of the gaping fish asks a question: 'Is there no chance to get the money back from the Swiss?'

'Unfortunately not. I have a close friend who works at Credit Suisse in Zurich and he made some discreet enquiries because, as you know, the Swiss are not always forthcoming when it comes to giving out such information. The sum was forwarded, less commission I expect, almost immediately to another bank, but he was not prepared to tell me where or which one. My perception is that, if fraud and money laundering are involved, then it may well have been transferred into a shell company offshore and will have been forwarded through several tax haven jurisdictions by now,' says Blumenthal resignedly. 'Of course, there may be a perfectly reasonable explanation, but we do need to see the pope and his financial advisors as a matter of urgency. In the circumstances, and given the delicate nature of the situation, I thought it would be best to consult with Cardinal Cuella before taking the matter further. I was not really expecting such a large distinguished gathering, including the *Gendarmeria*.' He gestures in the general direction of Antonetti, who, with a slight bow of his head, acknowledges the recognition.

'But the pope's disappeared...' utters Cardinal

Castiglione without thinking. If Cuella could reach he would kick him as hard as he possibly could, but it is too late, the damage has been done.

'Disappeared? What on earth do you mean?'

Cuella stares hard at Castiglione and then intervenes. 'I'm sure that I can rely on your discretion, HB.' Blumenthal nods, perplexed and bemused.

'The pope did not arrive at St Giovanni in Laterano this morning. You probably know that he has made a point of cycling there, with his bodyguards of course, every weekday before seven in the morning to take part in Mass with the congregation. He regards it as part of his obligation to the people of Rome. This morning he did not show up. Nor was he in his apartment when we searched it half an hour later. Antonetti believes that he has left Rome, accompanied by one of his private secretaries and two of the sisters who look after him. We have issued a press release saying that, due to overwork and also the heat, the pope is indisposed and will be resting from his duties for a brief period. It will buy us a couple of days, but in that time we shall have to come up with a more permanent solution. At this stage I have absolutely no idea what that might be!'

Blumenthal has lived through banking collapses and economic crises, and in the process has witnessed unbelievable criminality and mind-numbing incompetence. He is not easily shocked, but Cuella's revelation leaves him dumbstruck. His recent discoveries take on a whole new significance, especially the disappearance of Pedulla, if the pope really has 'absconded' with his staff and twenty-five million dollars.

While Blumenthal has been thinking, Cuella is drawing

the meeting to a close. 'I emphasise once more that nothing said in this room should be repeated outside, even to fellow cardinals and bishops. Go about your daily business. Give every impression of normalcy. Pray for guidance. When there are developments, I shall call another meeting. Antonetti, report to me in my office at six this evening – I want to know if you unearth anything at Jackson's apartment. HB, can you come along with me and we shall consider how to handle the situation from your end.'

Cuella turns his attention to the cardinals: 'Go in Peace…'

'… to Love and Serve the Lord,' mumble the cardinals, shocked to the very core of their being and, no doubt, in need of a stiff libation to calm their shattered nerves.

II:VI

A ntonetti returns to Jackson's apartment to see if the search has yielded any results.

'Found anything?' he snaps at the two miserable gendarmes.

In truth they have found very little. There are traces of hair clippings in the bathroom, and an empty pack of Garnier Belle Color Golden hair colouring in the bin, but there is no real way of knowing which of the four (possibly seven) escapees has undergone a transformation. However, they have found a discarded pack of anti-malarial tablets. This is interesting, because it may give some clue as to possible destinations to which the absconders might be heading; but, having said that, it only really narrows the choice down to scores of countries containing over half the world's population. One of the gendarmes has been checking through all the books, but without finding anything of any interest, beyond Peter Jackson's apparent attraction to graphic erotica. The computer in the lounge has had its hard drive removed; this has been taken back to HQ to be interrogated. Next to the phone they find a business card for a local taxi company. It may well be worth checking to see if they used that particular firm last night; but, Antonetti muses, there is not really a lot to go on. He had hoped for a great deal more.

'Might be something here,' exclaims the gendarme who

is hunting through the books. He holds up a colourful leaflet, which has fallen out of a leather-bound edition of Dante's *Divine Comedy*, advertising a private train service called the *Seine Tiber Express*. The company offers a luxurious overnight sleeper service to Paris, in 'deluxe' compartments including, somewhat unusually, an ensuite shower room and toilet. The carriages, the leaflet boasts, have been fully refurbished to the highest standards existing anywhere in the world, even down to the specially made 'feather down soft beds'. The whole ambience is one of elegant sophistication. Is this how the miscreants have escaped from Rome?

Antonetti has been wondering how the seven might have left the city. If their intention was to leave the country, then they would obviously need new identities and travel documents, but, given the resources available to men who were at the top of the Vatican hierarchy, this would probably not have presented an insurmountable obstacle. Indeed, they might well have multiple identities by now. So how would they have effected their escape? The quickest option would be by plane but, by the time they would have been able to reach the nearest airport, it would have been late at night, so there would only have been a limited number of flights available. Plus, the chances of being recognised would have been considerably higher in the confines of an airport, or on a half-full plane. Driving could have been a distinct possibility, but much would depend on the distance they intended to go, together with the risk of being the subject of a random stop by the traffic police. Antonetti had originally discounted trains; while it would have been easy to remain undetected in a large, bustling mainline railway station, once on the train anonymity would have been much more problematic. He had considered overnight sleepers, where it would be possible to lock oneself away in a compartment, but all three nightly services to other European capitals left before seven thirty in the evening, and the caretaker had seen them at quarter to nine.

'Does it give a timetable?' he asks the gendarme who is studying the leaflet. The policeman turns to the back page.

'There are three trains a week on Monday, Wednesday and Friday, departing at ten o'clock at night and arriving in Paris at eleven fifteen the following morning.'

Today is Tuesday. They could easily have caught the train last night. It could be the first real break they have had. Antonetti springs into action.

'Pascal, get onto the taxi company. Check if they sent a minibus, or people carrier, here last night and, if they did, find out where it took them. Paulo, contact the people who run the *Seine Tiber Express*. See if they are prepared to give us the passenger manifest for last night's train. We know they will not have travelled under their own names, but find out if a block booking was made for four men and three women. I know it's a long shot, but if we look at the allocation of the accommodation, we might be able to work out if the seven of them were put in adjoining compartments. I'm going back to the office. Let me know how you get on as soon as you have any news. *Affrettatevi!*'

II:VII

It is now eight o'clock in the evening, and Antonetti is seated opposite Cuella in the secretary of state's private office. At least he now has a little positive news for the cardinal. The Palazzo Taxi Company did indeed send a minibus to the Via del Falco, between half past eight and nine o'clock last night, and it took a group of people to the Roma Termini. It had been booked earlier in the day by Peter Jackson. Antonetti thinks it is a pity that Jackson did not book the taxi under his newly acquired, assumed name.

The news from the railway company is less encouraging. No block bookings for seven people had been made, and it is not possible to determine, from a study of the allocation of the compartments, whether the group travelled together or were spread throughout the train. However, from the sixty passenger names on the manifest, it is possible to rule out a number of the train's customers. The group might have been travelling under false documents, but they could not possibly have transformed themselves into the eight Chinese, Japanese and Indian passport holders who boarded the train, at Pope John Paul II railway station, just before ten o'clock the previous evening. Nor can they, even with an advanced transformation, be one of the eighteen passengers aged in their sixties and older. That still leaves over thirty possible candidates.

'So is it reasonable to assume that they are now in Paris?' asks Cuella.

'I think so,' replies Antonetti. 'The train did stop in Bologna, Milan, Lausanne and Dijon, but only a couple of people got off in Lausanne and Dijon. The problem we face is that it is getting on for ten hours since the train reached the Gare de Lyon. They could be absolutely anywhere by now. The train arrives on the return journey late tomorrow morning. I have checked with the company. The staff on board will be exactly the same as for the trip to Paris last night, so I am going to head for the station tomorrow morning to interview the crew. I'll take photos of the sisters and Jackson to see if any of the staff recognise them. I'll also find out if I can get descriptions of the three other people who were with them. We still have no idea if Pedulla and the others were part of the party. If we're lucky we might get a breakthrough on a couple of the identities, which will at least take us a step or two further forward, but it's going to be a hell of a job trying to work out what they did after they left the train in Paris.'

'You have to find them, Antonetti,' says Cuella quietly. 'The chances of keeping this thing quiet for more than a couple of days are virtually non-existent. You heard what that dolt Castiglione said in the meeting with Blumenthal. If necessary clear your desk, go to Paris and see if you can find out what's happened to the wretched people. I want a full report, on your visit to the station tomorrow, by lunchtime.' And with that, Antonetti is dismissed with a cursory wave of the hand, rather like an errant schoolboy being sent from the headmaster's study, after a particularly painful interview.

Cuella waits until the policeman has left the room,

then goes over to an elegant rosewood sideboard, pours himself a huge brandy, downs it in a single go, and hurls the glass across the room. It hits the wall at speed, missing a priceless Canaletto by a matter of inches, and shatters into a thousand pieces – rather like the secretary of state's dreams and ambitions.

As Antonetti walks across St Peter's Square, watched over by 140 mutely sympathetic saints on top of the semicircular colonnades, he mulls over the events of the day. The real loser in all this has been poor old Geisinger, who has been exceptionally careless in not keeping a closer eye on the pope. For an instant, he remembers Frau Geisinger's naked body writhing underneath his in coital ecstasy, clawing his back with her long sharp nails, and moaning like a wildebeest on heat. God she was good; she was so very, very good and, better still, exceptionally grateful. Mind you, being married to an anally retentive automaton, with all the excitement and imagination of a slowly decaying banana, cannot be easy for the poor woman. For a few seconds he is lost in the moment, then professionalism returns, and he liberates the thought from his mind; the image disappears.

No, as far as he can see, Antonetti is on a winner. He has not 'lost' the 'Boss'. In addition, he has managed to glean some useful information in a relatively short time. If sent to Paris, on a totally impossible wild goose chase, nobody can possibly blame him if he does not succeed in his quest. If he does accomplish something, then his star will be firmly in the ascendant. He might get a proper job in a proper police force, rather than chasing pickpockets and handbag snatchers most of the time, which is all his piddling little constabulary seems to do. He can't possibly lose – or can he?

II: VIII

Perhaps unsurprisingly, given its location in one of the most gloriously beautiful and historic cities on the planet, Roma Termini is a monumentally impressive building. The roof of its huge cantilevered entrance hall resembles some sort of gigantic pterosaur, spreading its protective wings over the travellers below. The cavernous concourse, with its highly polished marble floors, is littered with high class boutiques, upmarket cafés and major brand retailers. Tannoy announcements echo around the vast interior, directing passengers to one of the twenty-nine platforms, where trains wait to take the 150 million passengers, who use the station every year, to destinations across Italy and Europe. Antonetti goes to Platform 26 where the *Seine Tiber Express* has recently arrived from Paris. The train is a real throwback to the golden age of railway travel. Royal blue carriages stand at the platform, ornate gold-painted signs on the sides giving the different names of each carriage, such as *Tiberius* or *Charlemagne*, as well as the different designations of the coach, for example Wagon-Lit and Carrazzo Ristorante.

Antonetti makes himself known to the train manager who, dressed in a sharply pressed royal navy blue uniform with gleaming brass buttons, resembles a character from *Murder on the Orient Express*. He is taken to the lounge car, with its chintz armchairs, thick luxuriant carpet, well-stocked bar and even a small piano. They sit at one of the mahogany tables, and Antonetti accepts the offer of an espresso.

'I am here on an enquiry of the utmost delicacy,' he begins. 'May I rely upon your total discretion?'

'We are well used to such things,' says Pierre Flambert, the train manager. 'Anyone involved in the hospitality industry will tell you that, especially if you're dealing with wealthy clients or celebrities, then one needs finely honed diplomatic skills. It is often necessary to look the other way, or be somewhat economical with the truth.'

Antonetti begins: 'We are trying to discover whether certain people associated with the Vatican travelled on this train to Paris the night before last. It is a matter of paramount importance that we discover their whereabouts, but I'm afraid I can't divulge the reason for our enquiries.'

'I understand,' replies Flambert.

'Do you recognise any of these people?' Antonetti shows Flambert the pictures of the two sisters and Peter Jackson.

'I'm not sure about the women. They look familiar, but this one, if it is her,' he points to the photograph of Sister Carmen, 'had different-coloured hair. It was more blonde than this.'

'That would check out,' says Antonetti. 'What about this man?'

'Oh yes, I certainly recognise him. He was travelling with another gentleman. They shared a compartment in *Charlemagne*. His companion was extremely tall, and had a rather large beard. Strangely enough, I thought I recognised him, but I couldn't work out where I had seen him before.'

'Can you put a name to them?'

'Let's go to my office and I'll check the manifest.'

Antonetti is taken to an incredibly well-equipped but compact office located at the rear of the train. Flambert fires up a large laptop which is sitting on a glass-topped desk facing a wall lined with four flat screen TVs. They show: the view from the front of the train; a map of its current location; a table showing staff currently on the train and where they are working, and finally a twenty-four-hour news channel. On a stand by the window he sees an array of phones and communication devices, together with a microphone which is probably used to make announcements to the passengers on the train. Behind the desk there are shelves of files and manuals containing policy documents, technical specifications and timetables. There is not one paperclip out of place. The office is immaculate.

Flambert smiles ruefully. 'You should see my office at home,' he grins, 'it's absolutely nothing like this!' He turns back to the screen.

'Here we are,' he says. 'The man in the photo is Peter James Franklin. He was accompanied by Hugo Joachim Taveras. They were in *Charlemagne D*. The young ladies are Blanca Concepcion Diaz and Irene Adriana Espada, and they were in *Marie Antoinette B*. I can't really help you with the other three you mentioned. I don't recollect seeing any of them once we left Rome. Unusually for a train, we offer full room service, as a lot of our clients place rather a high price on their privacy, therefore we ensure that there is no real need for them to go to the restaurant car, or any of the other public areas on board, if they don't want to. I can check to see if they ordered food to be delivered to the compartment, but there is no record of them reserving a table in the restaurant. They disembarked at 1120 and 1127 respectively yesterday morning.'

Interesting that the group did not get off the train together, thinks Antonetti. They were obviously aware of the dangers involved in travelling en masse. Flambert then takes him to meet the attendant who was responsible for the *Charlemagne* carriage on the Paris-bound journey, but he is able to add very little. He gives a perfect description of Jackson, but says he did not see the other man at all, who, on both occasions he entered the compartment, was in the bathroom. The attendant remembers taking them a couple of plates of antipasti, and a bottle of quite reasonable Chianti, about an hour after leaving Rome. He returned to pick up the empty plates and glasses sometime later. Beyond that, he has nothing more to add.

Antonetti thanks Flambert profusely, and heads back to his office in the Governatorate building. The discovery of the new identities is a real breakthrough, but, in a sense, it creates more problems than solutions. It might be possible to find out if the group stayed in a Parisian hotel, but this would have to involve the local authorities and it would be necessary to give good cause for the enquiry, which, in itself, might prove problematic. Antonetti cannot really envisage Cardinal Cuella being too happy about publicising to the French judiciary, not to mention the police, the fact that the Head of the Catholic Church, with its millions of worldwide adherents, has absconded with a couple of attractive nuns and twenty-five million US dollars. Then there is also the added problem that, if they have gone to the trouble of arranging multiple identities, there is every chance that they will not use those names again, at least for the next stage of their journey. Having said that, a few days in Paris, all expenses paid, would be a very attractive little diversion from the otherwise mundane job of policing the Vatican City.

At that moment his mobile phone rings. It is Cuella.

'Any news?' he bawls. The secretary of state does not waste time on the niceties of mutually respectful social intercourse.

'We have four positive identifications and names to go with them. I can confirm that they travelled to Paris two nights ago. I suspect the other three were with them, but at this stage we still do not know their new identities. The problem is, what do we do now? I just can't see that we will get the support of the French authorities without telling them why we are interested in these people, but I do have a few contacts in the local *sûreté*, who I know could be relied upon to act with discretion. Do you still want me to go to Paris and see what I can find out?'

There is a pause. Cuella is thinking. If Antonetti goes, he will almost certainly end up dealing with minor functionaries in the *Préfecture de police de Paris*. There are bound to be awkward questions asked, meaning that the chances of mobilising a thorough investigation will be limited. If Cuella goes himself, then he will be able to operate through his own 'political' connections at a much higher level, and there will be a much greater chance of confidentiality being maintained. Anyway, he loves Paris and has not been for such a long time. What he has in mind will only take a couple of days at the most.

'Antonetti,' he growls down the phone, 'are you still there?' The Inspector General replies in the affirmative. 'You stay here and head the investigation. I shall take care of the Paris end of things.' With that he cuts the connection.

The following morning, a casually dressed Cuella is comfortably ensconced in a luxurious leather seat on a specially chartered Citation Bravo executive jet, glass of prosecco in hand, travelling at over four hundred miles an hour, heading directly for La Ville-Lumière. It's a lousy job, but someone's got to do it.

II:IX

Cuella's chauffeur-driven Mercedes hire car pulls up in front of a plush apartment block, on the Square Lamartine in the Sixteenth Arrondissement. He gives instructions to the driver to take his cases to his 'hotel', in the Avenue George Mandel, and to pick him up from there at eleven the following morning. He heads inside. Taking the lift to the fourth floor, he walks along an elegant corridor, and rings the doorbell by an ornate front door. After a few seconds it is opened by a incredibly handsome man, probably in his late forties, wearing a crisp white shirt, immaculately pressed black trousers and highly polished, black patent leather shoes. Maurice Jean-Paul de Lange, Bishop Emeritus of Limoges, radiates presence. He is a tall man with an impressive crop of chestnut hair, deep brown eyes, an aquiline nose and a strong, prominent jaw. If he is surprised to see the Secretary of State at the Vatican, arriving on his doorstep unannounced, he does not show it.

'Basil, my old friend, what an absolute delight to see you,' he says. He pauses. 'But, if this is an official visit, then, do please come in, Your Eminence.'

Cuella smiles. 'It is unofficial and strictly off the record. Good to see you again, Maurice. It has been far too long.'

De Lange is a fascinating man with a fascinating back story. He graduated from the *Institut national des langues et civilisations orientales* in Paris, leaving as the top scholar of his year, fluent in Chinese and Vietnamese. A period followed in the Faculty of Oriental Studies at Oxford, where he completed a postgraduate degree in Modern Chinese Studies. Rooming in Oriel, it is possible he subconsciously imbibed the views and philosophy of John Henry Newman, because by the time he left the sanctuary of the college he was well on the way to a life-changing experience, having set his heart on a life of service in the Catholic priesthood. When he confided his intentions to his family in Bordeaux, who remain to this day one of the oldest Huguenot families in France, they cut him off immediately and have had nothing more to do with him ever since. They will never be able to forgive his conversion from the glorious sunlit uplands of rigid Calvinism to the clutches of the bells, smells and rosaries of contemporary Catholicism.

Leaving France, he entered the Pontifical Roman Seminary, not far from the San Giovanni Basilica in Rome, where he proved himself a profoundly serious theological scholar. After ordination, he rose through the ranks of the clergy until, at the ridiculously early age of thirty-seven, he was appointed Bishop of Limoges in central southern France. It appeared that nothing could stop his progress. He was tipped for great things. Could he possibly become the first French pope since Pierre Roger de Beaufort, otherwise known as Pope Gregory XI, who was pontiff from 1370 until his death in 1378? After all, Pierre was born in Maumont in Limousin, only about 100 kilometres from Limoges! Coincidence – surely?

But nearly all men, as St Paul tells us, have a thorn in the flesh. In Maurice's case it came in the form of a middle-aged, good-looking, blond, lithe, witty, urbane, sophisticated police officer, who was serving with the *Police nationale* in Limoges. Gustave Henri Fournier blew Maurice to pieces. He had never seen anyone so wonderfully beautiful in his whole life. Gustave was utterly irresistible, and it was not long before the pair embarked on a passionate affair that was, eventually, to lead to the good bishop's downfall. Had de Lange been a merchant banker, a doctor, a lawyer or even, increasingly commonly, a military officer, his infatuation, as long as it did not interfere with his work, would not have mattered one iota. But Maurice was none of these, nor was discretion a quality he possessed in relation to his private life. Word of the affair got out among the conservative, narrow-minded, entrenched, one could even say bitter, members of the cathedral congregation. It was made clear to Maurice and, more importantly, to the Bishop of Amiens, who at the time was leader of the Conference of French Bishops, that it might be best if de Lange's considerable talents were used elsewhere in the service of the Lord. So the star-crossed, outcast lovers moved to the flat in Paris. Gustave picked up a job with the *Préfecture de police de Paris* in the General Information Department, involving the oversight of case records and other administrative documentation. It is he Cuella has really come to see, but Maurice is the point of access.

Basil enters a large, light room with sizeable windows overlooking the square below. It is full of oriental furniture and artefacts. The walls are adorned with silk paintings, which extol the harsh beauties of the Chinese countryside. There are Southern Officials armchairs, a Hundred Eye chest, black lacquer cabinets and two Shoji screens, one showing a huge wave threatening a desolate shore underneath a forbidding sky, and the other displaying a cherry blossom tree in full bloom. Draped across the floor are rich, vividly coloured oriental rugs and carpets. The only concession to Western modernity and comfort is a large, right-angled leather sofa. Otherwise, one could easily be in some senior colonial official's house in the Far East at the turn of the century. On the far side of the room French doors lead to a large terrace with intricate wrought iron railings, and flooded with gloriously coloured plants and flowers.

'These all come as a result of the job?' he asks.

'Yes,' replies de Lange. Although he does not possess a formal job title, Maurice is, to all intents and purposes, the pope's 'fixer' in the Far East. If problems arise in terms of the maintenance of theological orthodoxy, or if, to put it delicately, a senior cleric undergoes a 'personal crisis', de Lange is sent to provide succour and support to the local diocese. At a broader level, he has even managed to make some progress in raising the profile of the Church in China, where, for legal and political reasons, the domestic Catholic Church is not formally under the authority of the Vatican. However, recently the Chinese authorities have been willing to make some concessions, mainly because they appreciate the fact that de Lange speaks their language, and is so obviously immersed in their culture and traditions. Strangely, given that he lacks discretion in his private life, his diplomatic skills and qualities in dealing with recalcitrant priests and hard-nosed government officials are the stuff of legend in Asia and beyond.

'Drink?' asks de Lange.

'A whisky would be most welcome,' replies Cuella.

'Irish or Scotch?'

'I prefer Irish if you have it.'

'Bushmills?'

'Excellent. Could you make it a large one?'

'You arrive without warning, dressed incredibly casually – by the way it suits you – and now you're hitting the bottle. Things must be bad,' observes de Lange.

'Horrendous. I am in desperate need of your help. But first, tell me, are you still seeing the pompous old faggot who caused you so much trouble?'

A voice emanates from the terrace garden. 'Yes, Eminence, he is still an item with the pompous old faggot; but I resent the notion that I somehow caused him trouble.'

The pompous old faggot enters the room, cradling a voluptuous Persian cat in his arms. Contrary to the description, he is not all that old, and is probably only a few years more mature than de Lange. Blonde haired, blue eyed and with a smooth tanned complexion, he is almost the complete opposite physically of his friend in terms of skin tone and colour. But there can be no doubt, even to a committed heterosexual like Cuella, that the man is gloriously beautiful.

'Good afternoon, Basil,' he says. 'I do hope you are not allergic to cats. Hercules here has proved himself to be remarkably attracted to men of the cloth.'

'No, fortunately I have no such aversion to our feline friends,' the cardinal says pleasantly, shaking the man's hand vigorously and stroking the cat at the same time. 'It's good to see you, Gustave. You mustn't take the ramblings of an old man to heart.'

'Proverbs 21:23?' says de Lange.

'I shall control my tongue, and keep myself out of

trouble from now on,' promises Cuella good naturedly, taking a sip of the neat Bushmills.

'Is it too early to ask why you have arrived in such a fashion?' asks de Lange.

'I need your help. With other people I have had to get them to swear to secrecy, but in your cases I know that total discretion will go without saying.'

'Mysterious,' says Fournier. 'Don't tell me someone's been caught with their hand in the till, or up the cassock, yet again?'

'Closer than you think, Gustave. Last Monday, the pope left the Vatican and has not been seen since...'

There is a brief pause. 'But I thought there was an announcement that he had been taken ill by the heat, and had been sent to Castel Gandolfo to recover?' says de Lange.

'That's what we told the press to buy time; but the pope has totally, utterly and completely disappeared. So has his private secretary, the head of Mission to the Islands, two nuns from the Order of Elena, somewhere over twenty-five million dollars from the Vatican Bank and, quite possibly, a banker and his wife from the same wretched, corrupt, sickening organisation.'

'Have you involved the police?' says Fournier, ever the professional.

'Antonetti from the Vatican *Gendarmeria* has done most of the work so far, but there is a limit as to what he can achieve without raising suspicion. He searched Jackson's flat, and managed to deduce that the pope and his entourage took the *Seine Tiber Express* on Monday evening, arriving here mid-morning on Tuesday. After that, we have absolutely no idea. They might still be somewhere in Paris, or they could easily be on the other side of the world.'

Realisation dawns, and Fournier looks at Cuella in disbelief. 'And so you want me to find out?'

'If at all possible, yes. I'd like to know if they stayed somewhere in Paris, and, if they left the city, how they did it. Did they hire a car, or move on by plane or train?'

'And, you say that they arrived on Tuesday?'

'Yes.'

'And today is Thursday?'

'Yes.'

Fournier stares at the Secretary of State to the Vatican. 'Totally impossible, the timeframe is far too short. They could easily have changed their names and so now have new identities.'

Cuella gets the list of the known names from his pocket. 'This may be a start. We know at least some of their changed identities, and anyway, *'Impossible n'est pas français'*.

Fournier snorts in disbelief. 'They only arrived two days ago. There is no way, without approaching hotels directly, to find out where on earth they might have stayed. Do you know that there are over two thousand hotels in Paris?'

'I am sure you will try to do your best, Gustave. Why don't you start with the airport hotels? I need you, Gustave, for the good of the Church, you understand.'

'Maurice?' Fournier looks pleadingly at de Lange.

'It's a needle in a haystack, Gustave, but I really would appreciate it if you could try.'

'Lunacy,' mutters Fournier. But he leaves with as much good grace as he can muster, and the two clerics are left alone.

De Lange walks over to the terrace window and looks out over the bustling square. It is a glorious, sunny day and ordinary Parisians are going about their ordinary business while, in the apartment high above the square, extraordinary affairs are being discussed.

'I really wish that I were surprised,' he says.

'What do you mean?'

'The last time I saw José Ignacio he was terribly miserable.'

'José Ignacio? The pope was miserable? When did you see him? Why didn't I know about this?'

'There is much you do not know, Basil. José and I have been friends for many, many years and, before you ask, not in "that" way. I spent the summer in Sevilla before I entered the seminary, and he was wonderful, pointing out the pitfalls, the challenges, the obvious privations, as well as the enormous joys and privileges that a vocational life could bring. He confirmed everything I knew or expected, and, by the time that the summer was over, I was convinced that I was on the path God had chosen for me.'

'When did you see him? Where?'

'Last summer at Castel Gandolfo. Pardon the vernacular, but I was secreted in through a "back passage". We spent a weekend together talking, sharing, laughing and crying. He was desperately unhappy, and a lot of it he blamed on you.'

'Me?'

'He had started his pontificate with such high hopes, such aspirations, such dreams of change and modernisation…'

'Modernisation… pah!' Cuella is not impressed. He is not a reformer at heart. 'If he wanted so-called modernisation, why on earth did he choose me to be his secretary of state?'

'Simple: because he believed you when you promised him your total support. Not to mention that, in addition, you were so obviously a man of substance and authority in the corridors of power. He thought that, with you behind him, it would be possible to effect the changes that he so badly wanted to bring about. Little did he know that you were nothing more than a wolf in sheep's clothing.'

'That's ridiculous,' says Cuella. 'I am the first to admit that I endeavoured to tone down some of his more outlandish proposals, but I put his peculiar ideas down to his relative youth. In time, I sincerely believed that he would come to see the value of adhering to the glorious legacy which has been passed down to us over the centuries.'

'Oh Basil, you just don't understand. You really don't get it, do you?' says de Lange. 'José wanted to make the Church more relevant to the modern world. He wanted to engage the young in the mission of the Church, just like he had done in Spain. He wanted to see more and more families flock through the doors. He wanted to tame the bankers, and push hard against incompetence and corruption in the Curia, the individual congregations and the bank itself. He wanted to end the cycle of some of the worst abuses that have plagued our organisation for generations. He wanted priests who had abused their vocation, not to be moved to new posts or hidden away on remote Caribbean islands or sent to rehabilitation centres, but to be prosecuted by the secular authorities for their crimes. In all, he wanted an open, transparent Church which would be an effective, trustworthy witness to the Glory of God. And do you know what?'

'What?' Cuella scowls. He does not like being lectured.

'At every step and at every stage, you, the Secretariat and the College of Cardinals blocked him. Every reform he suggested had to be referred to other departments or committees or commissions. He felt trapped in a never-ending cycle of inertia. He came to believe that he was becoming perceived as the public face of a corrupt, and deeply flawed, institution. And then he felt guilty, because day after day and on trip after trip, at home and abroad, he met wonderful people, striving for all they were worth to do justice to the Gospel. He despaired.'

De Lange pauses and looks at the cardinal. 'Do you know something, Basil, it would not surprise me if you had planned the whole thing all along. I often wonder if you were trying to make his life so unbearable that he would come to feel he could not carry on. Did you perhaps hope that he might take his own life? This, of course, would have left the field clear for you to take over in his place; to pursue your own agenda, because you knew that you were the obvious candidate to succeed him. I wouldn't put it past you at all. Why on earth did you, and all the rest, choose him, when it was obvious to everyone that he would want to challenge the status quo?'

Cuella has had enough. 'He was not chosen for his theological skills. He was not chosen for his managerial abilities. He was chosen to smile, deliver sermons and homilies in that rich, redolent voice. He was chosen to lay on hands and, yes, if necessary kiss babies. He was not chosen to reform the Church. It has operated very successfully for thousands of years. It does not need reform...'

'Not need reform?' de Lange is beside himself. He is aware that he is raising his voice, but the secretary of state will have to lump it, and the neighbours can go to hell if they have the misfortune to overhear. Mind you, none are in at this time of day.

'You pompous, conceited, arrogant prig. No wonder we're in such a bloody mess when we have arseholes like you leading us into the abyss. Do you realise how many lives we have ruined? Do you realise how many people we have traumatised? Do you realise how many we have abused and not asked forgiveness? How on earth are we going to stand before the Almighty at the Last Judgement and say that we were good and faithful stewards of his Creation, when we have allowed so many things that are evil and wrong to go unchallenged? You make me sick to the pit of my stomach. I think you ought to leave before I say something I might regret.'

Cuella looks at the Emeritus Bishop of Limoges. He could quite cheerfully wring the wretched man's neck, but he needs him; more so, he needs Fournier.

'I'll go, but if you ever speak to me like that again…' It is unwise to make threats but Cuella knows exactly what he will do, and he knows exactly the man who will do it. He turns and walks out of the apartment, slamming the door behind him.

II:X

Cuella strolls along the tree-lined Avenue George Mandel, towards the Place du Trocadéro, admiring the sumptuous, highly ornate, nineteenth-century town houses. It is a glorious day, much cooler than Rome, and it is impossible for his mood to remain dark in such glorious surroundings. De Lange can wait for another time. If Fournier can at least come up with some form of lead, then the trip, and its attendant humiliation at the hands of the overbearing cleric, will not have been in vain. Already he is putting the recent altercation behind him and is beginning to look forward to the pleasures that the evening has in store.

Cuella's 'hotel' will not be found in any directory written for the weary tourist seeking 'superior' accommodation for the night. Its rooms are luxurious to the point of indecency; the food is sublime; the wine list is vast; and the range of additional 'personal services' on offer is renowned, admittedly within the narrow confines of a very select and discerning elite – or at least men who like to consider themselves to be part of an elite. Each suite, for there are no rooms, comes with a king-sized bed, dressing room, huge drawing room and a sumptuous bathroom containing a walk-in power shower and a Jacuzzi, both of which have gold-plated taps. In addition, the guest has the services, available twenty-four hours a day, of at least two maids, whose only apparent goal in life is to minister to the particular needs of their esteemed client.

Cuella arrives in front of the building. The Windsor (it is reputed that the Prince of Wales stayed during a visit to Paris in the 1920s) is a very large town house, six storeys high with further floors for servants' quarters in its Mansard roof. It dates from the period of the Second Empire, when Baron Haussmann was intent on making Paris into one of the architectural jewels of Europe. Royal blue awnings cover the elaborate tall white windows on the first floor, which are protected by the obligatory wrought iron railings. The house is set back from the road by a small, but exquisitely formed, garden with high hedges blocking the view from the street. At either end of the ground floor there are two massive, black double front doors. This was not always the case, the one on the left being a recent addition. The justification for the change is to protect the privacy of the guests; the doors provide separate ingress and egress to the building, therefore avoiding the danger of residents coming into contact with somebody they might prefer not to meet in such circumstances.

Cuella approaches the door on the right which opens, as if by magic, when his feet touch the doorstep. He is motioned inside by a stunningly attractive red-headed woman who is wearing a black silk maid's uniform, the skirt being cut just above the knees to reveal long, shapely legs encased in sheer black stockings. Cuella immediately feels right at home. Crossing a chequerboard tiled hall, he is ushered into a small reception room with windows facing the front of the house. This is obviously what would normally pass for reception in an ordinary hotel. The only furniture in the room is a Louis

XIV centre table, and on it is a red, leather-bound writing book opened at a blank page. He is invited by the maid to sign the visitors' book – one signature to a page so there is no chance of seeing who else is also in residence. So far the maid has said nothing. He signs and she gestures to him to follow her.

Cuella follows her back into the black and white tiled foyer. He walks behind her up a wide ornate staircase to, what can only be described as, a minstrels' gallery overlooking the hall below. On the way, he cannot help staring at the gloriously formed legs in front of him as they mount the stairs. For much of the way they are almost at eye level. The skirt is a silky, sheer, tight-fitting satin. It fits snugly across an exquisitely shaped bottom; the material rustles seductively as she moves, and he can just make out the lines of the thong she is wearing underneath the outfit. Cuella is mesmerised. He feels a stirring in a certain portion of his anatomy, which perhaps is not totally appropriate in one of his particular calling, but what the heck – he is on 'holiday'. They walk along a plush, beautifully carpeted hallway and turn into the drawing room of his suite, which overlooks the Avenue. It is the very height of opulent luxury. Original artwork lines the walls, the subject matter ranging from the suggestive to the highly erotic. Surely that can't be an original Paul Avril? His feet sink into the carpet, and he gazes appreciatively at the leather sofas and exquisitely formed, hand-made occasional tables dotted around the room. The maid turns to face him and looks him directly in the eye. 'My name is Gabrielle,' she murmurs, 'and I am here, with my colleague Susanne, to make your stay as comfortable and as memorable as possible. We shall endeavour to meet your every requirement. You only have to ask. Your cases arrived earlier and you will find your clothes laid out in the dressing room ready for your use. The bedroom and bathroom are through the door over there.'

'Thank you, Gabrielle,' says Cuella. 'I'm sure that I shall be perfectly content here.'

'Will you be dining with us this evening? We do not have a public dining room, as most of our guests prefer to eat in the privacy of their own suite, but we have an outstanding head chef; Susanne and I would be delighted to serve you should you require. You will find today's menu on the bureau beside the window, but if you wish to dine on something that is not listed, please ask and we shall do everything we can to accommodate your request.'

'I shall dine in,' replies Cuella. 'Would eight o'clock be suitable?'

'Certainly. I can be contacted directly on the house phone system at number 23. Do ring me when you have made your choices. Susanne and I shall return at seven thirty with cocktails and canapés. Is there anything else I can do for you in the meantime?'

Her deep blue eyes seem to peer into the inner recesses of his mind and discern his most intimate desires. He is aware of the fullness of her breasts against the satin of the dress. She is offering herself. Cuella is sorely tempted to make a number of quite explicit requests, but he has been told that deferred gratification always heightens physical pleasure, so he restrains himself, and bids Gabrielle adieu until the appointed hour.

*

It is now just before ten o'clock and Cuella is in the drawing room trembling with anticipation. Earlier Gabrielle and Susanne arrived right on time at seven thirty with the drinks and canapés. Susanne is a tall, willowy blonde with shoulder-length hair and emerald green eyes. She is a slender woman, in contrast to Gabrielle's rich, fuller figure; but what she might lack in one direction is more than compensated for by wonderfully long legs, which, given that both girls' outfits are now cut several inches above the knee, are displayed in all their glory. When she puts the drinks tray down on the low-lying coffee table, Cuella is treated to the merest glimpse of taut, tanned thighs atop the black silk stockings. Susanne turns suddenly and sees Cuella staring at her legs; she smiles a beautiful, radiant, knowing smile and suddenly the whole room is transformed.

He sits on one of the leather sofas, with a brutally dry martini, while the maids lay the table. He can't take his eyes from them as they deftly and professionally arrange the cutlery, condiments, glasses and plates. At five to eight, Susanne is dispatched to the kitchen to collect the first course and dinner begins. He has passed on the soups and hors d'oeuvres, choosing instead a soufflé of *jamón ibérico* and spinach. How it arrives intact and fully inflated is a mystery he will never understand until his dying day, but it is staggeringly light and full of taste. The sole in tarragon is delicate and the *osso bucco d'agneau au cèpes* melts in the mouth. He drinks a marvellous bottle of Châteauneuf-du-Pape (loyalty forbids any alternative) from the vineyards of Henri Bonneau, and finishes the meal with a sorbet containing fresh strawberries and raspberries. It is one of the most sublime meals he has ever eaten; he feels not the slightest guilt at the price tag that accompanies it.

It is when he is sitting back in the lounge area, with a Courvoisier twenty-one-year-old cognac warming in his hand, that Gabrielle comes and sits next to him on the sofa. He is aware of the scent of her perfume, the sweep of her legs and the extent of her breasts. 'Is there anything else you would like us to do for you this evening?' she asks. 'You can ask for anything you desire. We cannot be shocked. This is your time. I don't know, and I don't want to know, what you do outside these walls, but if you are here in this place, then you will almost certainly have earned your pleasure. You only have to say.'

The whole time she is speaking Gabrielle gently strokes the inside of his thigh with her long fingers; nails painted a delicate shade of rose. He tells her. She is not the slightest put out. She smiles. 'I shall send Susanne at ten o'clock. She is expert in this field. I promise you a night that you will remember for the rest of your life.' As events transpire later that evening, it is a forecast containing a level of accuracy that would, no doubt, have delighted even the notoriously hard to please prophet Isaiah.

Just before ten o'clock Cuella hears the bedroom door, which also leads onto the corridor, open and shut. Seconds pass. The tension is almost painful. He hears the sounds of footsteps coming towards the drawing room, then the door is opened abruptly and Susanne enters. At least he thinks it is Susanne. She is dressed in an all-in-one black leather cat suit, zipped from the crotch to the throat; high stiletto-heeled boots which end just above the knee, and an ornate silver masque covering her eyes. In one hand she has a black

PVC handbag and in the other she is carrying, what appears to be, a cat o' nine tails.

'Do you not stand when your mistress comes into the room?' she hisses with compelling malevolence. Cuella stands and looks at her.

'Don't you dare look at me, you miserable lump of excreta! You bow your head before me. You are not fit to gawp at me. You are nothing. You are as much use as a fart in a thunderstorm. But I am going to train you. You will learn and you will obey. If you comply unquestioningly with my commands you may be rewarded, but if you fail, if you are a rebellious slave, then you will be punished severely. You belong to me. You are mine, totally mine. I own you. Understand?'

'I...'

Susanne raises her voice: 'You will not speak unless I tell you. You may nod if you understand. Do you understand?' Every word spoken is accompanied by a painful prod in Cuella's chest with the handle of the cat o' nine tails. Cuella nods.

'What gifts have you brought to appease your mistress?'

Cuella has been told, by others more experienced in this field, that present giving is part of the ritual and he has come prepared. He bows his head, goes over to an exquisitely carved sideboard and takes the first of three packages, all beautifully wrapped, back to Susanne. Still with head bowed, he hands her the parcel. She rips open the wrapping paper. The first gift is a pair of 100% silk Antonia thigh-high lace-top stockings. It is received in a threatening and oppressive silence.

'Is this all?'

Cuella goes back to the sideboard and returns with a small oblong box. Again the paper is ripped from the gift to reveal a bottle of Original Santal Eau de Parfum by Creed. This time a hint of a smile appears around the lips of his tormenter. 'Better, much better, but I hope there is more?'

The final parcel contains an Elsa Peretti Cabochon gold bracelet with a single inset green jade stone. This meets with approval. 'You have done quite well for a first attempt, but, should you ever return, I would expect more. I have very expensive tastes.' She turns back to face him, and the stern, almost tyrannical, countenance has returned. 'You are overdressed for a slave of mine. Strip!'

Cuella flings off his clothes and strips down to a very fetching, he thinks, pair of red silk briefs, purchased through an online store based on an industrial estate in the outskirts of London. He hardly has time to admire the view before the harridan, who is nothing like the Susanne he met only a couple of hours ago, flies across the room and begins flailing him with the whip.

'Slut, slovenly shit-faced slut,' she roars. 'Look at the way you have left your clothes. I hate untidiness. I loathe mess. Sort it out. Take them into the other room and lay them out properly.'

Cuella gathers his clothes into the semblance of an organised pile, and carries them back into the dressing room, where he lays them out with military precision on a clothes rack and an eighteenth-century dresser. The whole time Madam stands behind him, watching every move like a hawk and tapping him gently on the shoulder with the whip. He finishes.

'Better,' she says. Suddenly, without warning, Cuella

feels a rough collar fastened around his neck. Before he knows where he is, he is on a leash. He turns. A stinging blow strikes him on the back.

'I did not say turn!' she says. 'Come!' She drags Cuella by the leash back into the drawing room.

'Kneel on all fours. I am going to take my newly acquired dog for a walk.' For ten minutes she makes him crawl round the room. She ensures that he bumps into furniture. She changes direction so that the lead pulls at his neck muscles. All the time she is talking, talking, talking; she tells him that he is nothing; that his whole life is now wrapped up in her; that he has nothing to live for beyond service to Madam. By the end he is exhausted, panting like a dog, desperate for a glass of water or better still another glass of that wonderful cognac; but Madam is not to be assuaged. He is made to unpack her bag of delights which includes more whips, paddles, gags, masks, blindfolds, ties, handcuffs, and anal toys and beads. He is made to lay them out on the table meticulously – in the 'correct' position. When he fails he is beaten, but now Madam has graduated from the cat o' nine tails to a wooden paddle with metal studs. The pain is intense but it soon passes.

More tasks follow. She requires a cocktail which he must mix. Cuella is now in uncharted territory; he has never mixed a cocktail in his life. She will have a Parisian. Why hasn't he started? What does he mean he does not know what is in a Parisian?

Slap!

Even an imbecile knows that it is made up from gin, dry vermouth and crème de cassis. Go and do – now! He goes over to the drinks table, combines the constituent parts with ice, shakes it up and takes the drink back to her. She tastes and spits it right back in his face.

Slap!

Show me what you did. No, not like that: not in equal measures.

Slap!

At the third attempt he gets it right. Surely he has earned a reward now? He can't say anything but to stroke those breasts would be heaven. But no: now she wants her boots cleaned. He kneels, takes the boots off, and begins to polish them while she watches sipping her Parisian. Susanne scrutinises his work: you've missed a bit.

Slap!

The strange thing is that he wants to please her.

Slap!

He wants her to say well done. He wants her to say that he can have a treat or a reward, but she never does; she is never satisfied.

Slap!

If only he knew it, this torment is very similar to the agony Cuella puts his staff through every day in the secretariat back at the Vatican. Now she wants a foot massage. At least he gets to touch some of that soft, silky skin, but his knees are killing him, his back aches and his skin is stinging where he has been struck repeatedly. He wants it to end soon, and yet he wants it to go on forever.

'You may stop. While not all of your work has been satisfactory at least your foot massage was acceptable. You have earned your reward. Go into the bedroom and I shall follow.'

Cuella goes through into the bedroom. Susanne follows

a couple of minutes later, carrying the handbag, which he assumes has been packed in preparation for her departure.

'Turn around. Face the pillows. Kneel on all fours.'

Cuella knows better than not to comply with alacrity. He faces the wall. The leash is taken away from his neck. The red silk briefs are stripped to his knees.

'This is a special reward which I only bestow on my favourite slaves, my special ones. You have become a special one; one of the chosen; one of the elite,' she says, all the time stroking and kneading his bottom. Cuella begins to relax. But there is one last surprise in store. Out of the blue, without warning, Madam thrusts something into his backside. He is entered by a series of what feels like rather large, hard, plastic balls, and these are being thrust assertively into his rectum. Cuella gasps. He suddenly has a vision of the huge anal beads, which he laid out so precisely on the dining room table. The pain is palpable, and it is taking time to get over the shock.

'That's it, my good and faithful slave. Enjoy your reward: moan as much as you like. The walls are thick, nobody will hear your cries of pleasure. Enjoy! Enjoy! Enjoy! Does it feel good?'

Cuella wants to answer in the negative, but he does not dare. Incredibly, he does not want to displease his mistress. He loves his mistress. He would do anything for his mistress. But surely he will see her naked? Surely he cannot have gone through all this with nothing to show for it at the end?

'Yes, madam…' is all Cuella can manage before Susanne applies the *coup de grace*: she switches on a vibrating device in the balls to full speed. Cuella twitches and jumps like an electrocuted cat in a fifties cartoon. He shouts; he screams;

he pants; he groans and soon, mercifully soon, it is all over. The balls are switched off, withdrawn with excruciating slowness, and Cuella collapses onto his front on the bed, whimpering like a distressed puppy.

'*Voilà*,' says Susanne. '*C'est fini. Bonne nuit, mon cher. Dormez bien.*' And, with that, she picks up her bag and leaves the room, pleased with a job well done.

A few minutes later Gabrielle, wearing a tight-fitting blue nanny costume, with a black and white polka dot belt around the midriff, lets herself into the bedroom. Cuella is spread-eagled across the huge bed breathing deeply. He looks up at her and says plaintively, 'Nana?'

She looks down at him. 'Are you in pain?' she asks. 'Would you like Nana to take the pain away?' He nods.

Gabrielle looks at the wheals on his back, thighs and buttocks, and marvels at Susanne's incredible skill. She has such a marvellously deft touch with whips and paddles. The stripes are already beginning to fade away. Gabrielle knows from previous experience, that, by the morning, the red lines will have disappeared fully. Nevertheless, she takes some ointment from a pouch on the belt, kneels beside the prostrate man, and begins to massage the skin. Cuella sighs. With every stroke she can feel his body relaxing. Minutes pass. She turns him onto his back and is not at all surprised to see the feral lust burning in his eyes, but she can also see something else: there is cruelty, harshness and mercilessness in the small, penetrating eyes set into the vein-lined, florid, flushed cheeks. She would not like to make an enemy of him, but tonight she has work to do – extremely well-paid work.

'Do you want me to make you forget the pain and hurt?

Do you want me to help you stop thinking about the cruelty of your heartless mistress?'

He nods fervently. Gabrielle gets up from the bed, stands and slowly, seductively sheds the nanny outfit, together with the white silk lingerie underneath, until she is totally naked. At each stage of the process his breathing becomes heavier and more pronounced. He reaches for her, imploring, pleading. She taunts, teases and flaunts herself before him. Then, she gets back onto the bed, straddles him, and, for the next fifteen minutes or so Madam is forgotten as Gabrielle takes him, little by little, to a place of intense sexual gratification that he has never known previously, and will never know again.

Satiated, he collapses back on the pillow. And then the Secretary of State at the Vatican, the second most powerful man in the Catholic Church, a man who terrorises his colleagues and subordinates, does something very strange. He breaks down and cries and howls like a baby; tears stream down his face, his chest racked with almost uncontrollable sobs. And yet, were you able to ask him why, he would not be able to tell you.

II:XI

The next morning Cuella awakes refreshed and alert. He has slept deeply and well. It is as if someone has purged his mind of all the extraneous garbage that has accumulated over many decades, and now he feels tremendous – full of energy and purpose. He orders breakfast – a full English, which he feels is most appropriate given the name of the hotel, but he draws the line at including hash browns. These interlopers from the New World have absolutely no place in a traditional English breakfast. Lord Emsworth would never have allowed such an obscenity at Blandings. Somewhat surprisingly, Cuella is a great fan of Jeeves and Wooster. He has had a missal specially adapted to incorporate paperback books, so the exploits of the pair have enlivened many a drab, dull sermon, expounded by tediously painstaking clerics, in the basilicas and churches of Rome. But it is not only hash browns that fail to find favour with the secretary of state. He has never understood the British aristocracy's preoccupation with kedgeree as tolerable fare to start the new day.

Breakfast is delivered within the promised half hour, but there is no sign of Susanne or Gabrielle; instead it is served by an immaculately turned-out butler, who understands that guests are not always interested in making polite conversation first thing in the morning. To say that he is taciturn would be something of an understatement; the man somehow makes taciturnity into an art form, nevertheless he is polite and attentive even if seriously unforthcoming.

After breakfast Cuella picks up his bag and pays the bill, which is asked to be made out to *Windsor services de conseil en gestion*, for the sum of nine thousand five hundred euros inc. TVA. The cheque will be drawn against Cuella's private and very secret bank account in Zurich. He has been transferring money clandestinely, from the Holy See, for many years in readiness for just such an eventuality. Then he is picked up by his driver, and they make the short journey back to the apartment on Square Lamartine. This time Gustave opens the door. He scowls.

'Where the hell have you been?' he asks brusquely. 'We've been trying to contact you since last night. Your phone was switched off and we did not have a bloody clue as to where you were staying.'

For a man of the cloth Cuella is a consummate liar, but then, of course, he is also a diplomat. 'I stayed at a small pension just off the Rue Poussin. The room did not have a telephone, and I turned my phone off because I needed time alone to meditate and contemplate.'

Gustave looks as if he does not believe him but says nothing. 'Before you ask, we have managed to make a little progress, but I am not sure how far it will take matters forward. Franklin, Diaz and Espada all stayed in the Ibis at Charles de Gaulle. Surprisingly they used the same names as on the train tickets. Not that it will do you any good, because there is no record of any of them catching a flight from the airport the following day. I suspect that they will have taken on a third identity. What we do know is that they checked out of the hotel at about eight thirty, but after that they disappear. It is possible that we might be able to identify a couple of them on the airport CCTV, but it would take days and I would need to justify such a search to my superiors. I am not sure how I would explain to the Chief that I needed privileged access in order to search for a runaway pope and his entourage.'

'I understand,' says Cuella. 'Where do flights go at that time of day?'

Fournier stares at him. 'Where do they not go is more the question. For a start there are flights all over continental Europe and the Middle East. Intercontinental flights, as a rule of thumb, tend to go south and west in the morning and to the east at night. On that basis, I would suggest that, unless they hung around the terminals all day and flew out to the Far East in the evening, it would probably mean that they have gone to the south or the west. If you are interested, that leaves you a choice of West Africa, Central and South America, the Caribbean or North America. Quite a choice, I would say. Good luck.'

For the first time Cuella senses despair; the euphoria of the previous evening has dissipated, and he is confronted by the spectre of defeat. The task seems totally impossible. He has no idea as to what he is going to do next, but it's obvious that the mission to Paris is over. It is time to return to Rome.

'Thank you, Gustave, for all your help. When you see Maurice, please apologise for my outburst yesterday. I know he is a good man, who holds sincere beliefs, but I have been under the most enormous pressure…'

'You are a callous bastard,' snarls Fournier. 'If it promoted your interests you would have your own grandmother guillotined. You have brought this whole hideous scenario upon yourself, and God only knows how you are going to get yourself out of it.'

That's the problem, thinks Cuella. *I'm not sure God knows how to get out of this either.*

II:XII

Later in the day, Basil Cuella is back in the Citation Bravo heading south. He would like to be sitting comfortably but, after last night's exertions, this is proving impossible. Every time he tries to move he is reminded of his humiliation at the hands of the 'skilled and talented' Susanne. Earlier in his career he built something of a formidable reputation as a promising theologian, and so it is no surprise that he cannot get the maxim expounded by St Paul, in his first Epistle to the pope's namesake Timothy, out of his head. He just cannot get the words out of his head.

'*Docere autem mulieri nom permitte neque dominari in virum sed esse in silento.*'

Why on earth did he allow a woman to have authority over him? Why did he allow himself to be mortified? He is ashamed, and yet there is still a part of him that thinks it was, in just about every conceivable way possible, a cathartic experience.

On the journey to Paris he had enjoyed a couple of glasses of prosecco; now, on the return leg, he is already on his third glass of Chivas and they have all been generous doubles! Glass in hand, he looks down on the Italian Alps; some of the highest peaks still having the merest layer of snow on them, despite the incredibly hot summer. Lower down the slopes, in the valleys, the land is brown and parched; it is a metaphor for his mind: he is in a dry, arid place. There appears to be no hope. Unless he has an incredible stroke of luck, the Church is headed for catastrophe and, much more importantly, his career will be in tatters.

He jumps in his seat. What was it he just said? Perhaps it's the whisky, perhaps it's fatigue or, like St Paul on the road to Damascus, it could be a moment of divine revelation, but he's got it! He has an answer. It is not a permanent solution but it will buy a considerable amount of time while he works on a way out of this terrible impasse. *You genius*, he thinks, *it's an absolute masterstroke.* He motions the pretty young stewardess, with the generous breasts, pert bottom and long lithe legs, to refill his glass. Suddenly, life is good, very good indeed.

II:XIII

PRESS RELEASE

VIS: VATICAN INFORMATION SERVICE
12 MAY: UPDATE ON THE HEALTH OF
THE POPE

It is announced that Pope Timothy, who left the Vatican on 8 May for a period of rest and recuperation at Castel Gandolfo, has suffered a minor stroke. He is undergoing tests at the Gemelli Hospital to assess the seriousness of his condition. Further information will be released when available but it is not expected that an announcement will be made for several days.

Prayer for the Pope's Recovery

Like children draw close around our beloved Holy Father. Pray to the Blessed Virgin, Mary, Mother of God, that she may intercede with her Son to restore our beloved Pope to health, so that he may continue to teach us to journey with Jesus and love and serve the Church.

Amen.

III

PARADISUM?

III:I

Extract from the *World Wide Online Gazetteer*

Grande Batture, Commonwealth of, W.I.;

Most easterly of W.I.; fmr. French col.; a. 853 sq. km.; mtn. range N/S, highest peak Mt. Grand Sein alt. 1758 m.; land of rivers and mountains; much of interior inaccessible; diverse tropical flora and fauna; volcanic soil; 30% under cult.; agr.: bananas, formerly sugar and tobacco, now in decline; no secondary industry; tourism undevt. due to inaccess.; no major port or airport; cap. Bonaire p.2017 23,985; GDP per head $US 1853, rank 152 by World Bank.

III:II

There are few fine houses or modern buildings in Bonaire, the capital city of Grande Batture; it is much more a place of flimsy wooden buildings with corrugated iron roofs, crammed together in squalid shanty towns, having little or no access to electricity and running water. Open sewers, which flood regularly during the rainy season, run alongside potholed dirt roads. Unlike other Caribbean nations there are few colonial-style mansions and villas, as the French, who claimed Grande Batture in 1738, never really took control of the island, mainly due to its lack of a safe harbour and dearth of natural resources. The island lives up to its reputation as being one of the poorest and most inaccessible countries in the world. Life for the inhabitants really is 'nasty, brutish and short', as they attempt to eke out an existence from subsistence agriculture and small-scale fishing.

The paradox is that the people live in a veritable tropical paradise. Behind the narrow coastal plain that encircles the island, there is a massive mountain range running the length of the country, home to some of the rarest and most exotic species of flora and fauna to be found anywhere on the planet. The highest point of the island is Mt Grand Sein, a long-dormant volcano, but there are other lesser peaks which remain active, most notably Petite Soeur in the south of the country. Wild untamed rivers, cascading waterfalls and boiling hot springs abound throughout the dense jungle that covers much of the interior, most of which has never been charted or explored. It is almost certain that the lush tropical rainforests harbour some previously undiscovered plant and possibly even animal species. Around the coast there are myriads of small black, sandy beaches, while just offshore there are pristine coral reefs teeming with all manner of fish and marine life.

In normal circumstances Grande Batture would be a mecca for tourists, but two factors have inhibited the growth and development of this pernicious, but most lucrative, industry. The first is the difficulty of actually getting to the island. The airfield is, by modern standards, primitive, with an exceptionally short grass runway, which can only accommodate small twin-engine turboprop aircraft with limited seating capacity. Even if the determined tourist manages to get to Grande Batture, accommodation is a major problem as there are only two rundown and dilapidated hotels, both on the outskirts of the seedy capital. Bonaire itself is really no more than a fishing village, and so lacks the port and harbour facilities needed to welcome the vast range of massive cruise ships that clutter the Caribbean every year.

The other factor is the country's chequered political history. Grande Batture gained some independence from France in 1964, the latter being only too glad to rid itself of a non-productive, highly costly outpost of empire. There followed a mockery of a general election, which was won by the richest and most powerful man on the island: Jimarcus Deval Walcott. Within months he had suspended the National Assembly and for the next thirty-eight years, until his death in 2002, he ruled as a virtual dictator, propped up by the Diables Noirs, his own private army of thugs and heavily armed criminals. Arbitrary arrests, show trials and even summary executions were not uncommon, and the population endured four decades of appalling hardship in a society which was, to all intents and purposes, closed and shut off from the outside world. Given the violence and intimidation endemic on the island, it is perhaps not surprising that tourists chose more conducive destinations for their annual holidays. After Jimarcus's death, his son, Samuel, tried to continue the dynasty, but the people, incensed by years of repression and petrified by thoughts of more of the same, rose in rebellion. After a short but bloody civil war, the Walcott family was forced to flee to the security of its foreign homes in Montreux and Antibes. Since then the island has stagnated economically, politically and socially, any form of development stalled by a chronic lack of government funding.

In light of this economic deprivation, it could be considered astonishing that the most modern building in Bonaire is a double-fronted, two-storey bank; complete with a substantial car park (despite the fact that there are only a handful of cars on Grande Batture) and two, largely unused, ATMs outside the front door. The ground floor is just like any other commercial bank anywhere in the world. On either side of the imposing entrance there are a number of desks and comfortable chairs, where clients can discuss their financial requirements with staff. At the far end of the floor is a row of five counter windows, although there are never any more than two tellers on duty at any one time, due to the inescapable fact that The Intercontinental Commercial Bank of Grande Batture has only a small number of domestic account holders. These comprise mainly local shopkeepers, the two rundown hotels, a handful of government employees and a smattering of self-employed workers, such as taxi drivers. To the right of the counter is a broad sweeping staircase that ascends to the floor above. And this is where things change.

At the top of the stairs there is a door. It is an imposing door. It is a grey, bulletproof, steel door with a peephole at eye level. Access to the space behind can only be achieved by using the fingerprint scanner located to the right of the entrance. Not only that, but those people who wish to enter are also required to punch four numbers into an electronic keypad. To the uninitiated this might seem overkill, given the relatively small scale of the banking operation of The Intercontinental Commercial Bank of Grande Batture, but they would be wrong because on the other side of the door there is one of the most sophisticated, technologically advanced banking operations in the Caribbean. In a dimly lit open-plan area there are several workstations, which contain banks of digital display systems and desktop monitors. At the far end of the room, one wall is loaded with eight flat screen televisions connected to twenty-four-hour news and business channels. Luxuriant blue carpet on the floor deadens the sound. The four traders who work in the room disregard the unruly practices of trading floors across the globe, and talk in hushed whispers, both to each other and on the phones to their counterparts in foreign climes.

In the back office, with picture windows looking out over the main room, Luigi Pedrosa, the controller of this impressive organisation, is a man supremely content with his lot in life. He views his empire with undisguised pleasure. It cost an absolute fortune, and took many months, to gather the equipment together and transfer it to the island, piece by piece, on two specially converted Beech 90 Cargo Liners – one of the few planes that could cope with the ridiculously short runway at the airfield. But the installation is complete and has been a model of smooth running in its first year of operation. A graduate of the Harvard Business School, although originally from Trapani in Sicily, he was made an offer he could not refuse by some prominent businessmen in Palermo, and has not regretted, for a single moment, his decision to relocate to the other side of the world. Nor have his partners: Enzo from Adrano, Leonardo from Milazzo and the brothers Fabiano and Tommaso from Catania. It is a good life.

As he skims through a spreadsheet of the previous day's transactions, he notices a particularly large deposit of twenty-three million dollars. It is impossible to tell where the money originated, but the account, *Philanthropos Tropos*, has been growing steadily for a couple of years, though usually by modest amounts. Pedrosa can only imagine that this has been done to avoid government tracking programmes aimed at curtailing money laundering, or the possible involvement of terrorist groups. He is fascinated by the name of the organisation, given that none of his other 'clients' are in the business of philanthropic benefaction. The most recent deposit is intriguing in its size, but it is by no means his largest account so he turns his attention to other matters.

Two days later Pedrosa is a little surprised when he is told that someone from *Philanthropos Tropos* wishes to see him. When the necessary security formalities have been checked and are seen to be in order, a short fat man, wearing the most garish floral shirt and plain Bermuda shorts, is shown into his office. He introduces himself as Enrico Marquez, says he will be the official representative of *Philanthropos*, and requests that all future dealings with *Philanthropos* should be channelled through him. He is currently residing on a secure compound, in the south of the island, in the company of Snr Joachim Taveras, who is the head of the organisation. Pedrosa wonders what the men have to hide, because the security features surrounding the compound are the talk of the island; it is like an impregnable fortress, but he says nothing and awaits developments.

It is obvious from the outset that the man is highly experienced in matters financial. Better still he speaks Italian, and so communication between them is straightforward. However, given his somewhat idiosyncratic accent, Pedrosa suspects that he is most certainly not a native speaker; the bank manager guesses that he is probably Irish. Marquez tells Pedrosa how *Philanthropos Tropos* will operate in the future. Pedrosa is well versed in maintaining a veneer of inscrutability when dealing with clients but even he, with all his experience, is amazed by the scope of what is envisaged. He has never heard anything like it in his life; well, at least not in the somewhat murky world of offshore banking, but 'the client is king', and so he agrees to facilitate his instructions and the meeting comes to an end. When Flanagan has gone Pedrosa sits back in his chair, lights a foul-smelling cheroot and reflects on the unpredictability of his chosen profession.

III:III

(SEVEN MONTHS LATER)

The plane trees outside the offices of the BBC Natural History Unit in Whiteladies Road, Bristol, are bare, with only a few russet brown leaves frantically clinging onto the naked branches, swaying in an icy cold northerly breeze. Set in a part of the city dominated by Victorian villas and verdant avenues, the unit has been in residence since 1957 and has, over the years, developed a formidable international reputation for wildlife programmes of the highest quality. It is normally a place of tranquillity and reflection; somewhere to consider the next major project to be undertaken, in order to bring the wonders of the natural world directly into the living rooms of the licence-fee-paying public. It is a place of meetings: planning meetings, pre-production meetings, budgetary meetings, sales and marketing meetings, post-production meetings – in fact any sort of meeting one cares to imagine. But today, although meetings are taking place all over the building for all sorts of different reasons, the work of this august body of scientists, presenters, producers, directors and managers is not the main topic of conversation. Scandal is in the air!

The silver-haired doyen of the organisation sits quietly in a well-appointed conference room overlooking the plane trees of Whiteladies Road. In one way or another he has been a part of the unit since its move to the West Country, but, in all his dealings with the NHU, he has never faced such a delicate situation. While he no longer has a formal role within the institution, having long since passed the age of retirement, he has, nevertheless, been called upon to use his formidable diplomatic skills in order to ensure that the unit does not tear itself to pieces in the full glare of media publicity.

Three nights previously a reception had been held, at The Royal Crescent Hotel in Bath, to celebrate the Natural History Unit's many successes at the highly prestigious 'Wildlife on Film' awards, held in Barcelona the previous month. The function had been attended by a whole host of 'A' list celebrities, from soap opera stars who feign an interest in wildlife, to slimy politicians and ageing rock stars. Also in attendance was the newly appointed Director General of the BBC, and his much younger, devastatingly attractive wife. Dressed in a long, navy, chiffon Jovani evening gown, with a split almost to the top of the thigh and décolleté which exposed a generous amount of expansive cleavage, Samantha Stone was the very centre of attention. The canapés circulated, the champagne flowed and the air was full of witty, humorous stories and anecdotes of jolly good times spent in the wild, both on and off screen.

Julian Briggs-Hamilton was in his element. The new rising star of the Unit, who had just completed the critically acclaimed *Life in the Mound,* and who was also a protégé of the silver-haired doyen, was enjoying himself enormously. Gosh, this was so much more fun than ramming a pin-sized camera into a mound of unsuspecting termites on the road from Entebbe airport to Kampala in Uganda. However, due possibly to long periods of enforced abstinence from alcohol, and indeed sex, while filming in the rolling hills of central Africa, it was soon apparent to friends, enemies and colleagues alike that several glasses of champagne were beginning to exert a profound influence on him. Of this fact, Julian Briggs-Hamilton was blissfully unaware; a state of mind that was to continue long after the reception had ended and the damage had been done. It is his indiscretions at the party that has led to him being summoned to the meeting in the NHU's sterile conference room.

The doyen wonders how best to approach the forthcoming interview with his friend and colleague of many years standing. There is absolutely no doubt that Briggs-Hamilton is a gifted film-maker who demonstrates a real empathy with, and understanding of, the natural world. He has a massive intellect and, when sober, an engaging personality, both of which shine through on the small screen. Sadly, the days of his sobriety are few and far between, except when he is on location and then his abstinence from all forms of intoxicating beverage is total. This would no doubt have endeared him to Asbjøn Kloster, who founded the first Norwegian temperance society in the mid-nineteenth century.

The doyen is well aware of the views of the director general concerning Briggs-Hamilton's behaviour at the party, and recalls the rather painful meeting with him, in the company of the current head of the NHU, in the immediate aftermath of the debacle at the reception. The DG is perhaps not the most 'liberal' individual ever to hold the post, and, in a previous incarnation, would almost certainly have demanded 'satisfaction' for the abuse and humiliation heaped upon his young and enchanting wife. Frankly, if it were left to him, Briggs-Hamilton would have been shown the door and told that his services were no longer required at the BBC; however, he appreciates the fact that this might leave the Corporation open to litigation, through the insidious and sinister employment tribunals (which were allowed to flourish under the previous government!), so he has agreed to leave it up to the head of department and the doyen to come up with a sensible solution. They are to keep him fully informed. The doyen has taken a couple of days to consider the options available and thinks that he may have arrived at a workable outcome which should mollify the DG, as well as preventing the loss to the NHU of a gifted presenter; but he is not sure that it is going to be an easy sell as far as Briggs-Hamilton is concerned.

The door to the conference room bursts open and the man himself bounds into the room. He is in his late thirties, dressed in a Harris Tweed three-piece suit, plus fours and Glencarse boots. His mane of curly brown hair is, at best, unkempt, and his bushy beard has probably not been trimmed in weeks. Horn-rimmed glasses perch unconvincingly on the end of a sharp, pointed nose and his eyes blink incessantly, rather like a Sudanese monkey on a legal high. It is this slightly old-fashioned, unconventional appearance that endears him to millions of viewers across the world, who regard him as the quintessential eccentric Englishman.

'Whatto, me old mocker,' he says cheerily. 'How's it all hanging?'

The doyen is not impressed. 'Do you have to talk like a second-rate actor from a fifties B grade movie?' he asks.

Briggs-Hamilton is not at all put out by this rather curt and abrasive salutation. He beams with delight and throws himself into a seat on the opposite side of the pine conference table. Outside an ambulance or police car flies by, sirens screeching. Is it a prescient omen of things to come? If so, Briggs-Hamilton is bathed in blissful ignorance. 'To what do I owe the pleasure of this summons into the hallowed presence of the greatest wildlife presenter of the twenty-first century?'

'I would have thought that it would be patently obvious, even to you,' replies the doyen acerbically.

Briggs-Hamilton looks absolutely mystified. 'Reveal all, O truly enlightened one,' intones the rising star, after a brief pause to consider where he might have fallen short.

'It's about your appalling behaviour at the reception the other night.'

'Wonderful bash, thankfully at the licence fee payers' expense, but can't say that I can remember a great deal about how it all ended. Did I make a speech?'

'You most certainly did, and it ended with the hotel security dragging you, almost senseless, out of the room; a young lady in floods of tears and the director general baying for your blood. It took Sandra and me over half an hour to calm him down. What on earth did you think you were doing?'

'I can't remember a thing about it.'

'So, you can't remember uttering the words, "My God, look at the magnificent arse on that", or saying that you hadn't seen such superb, firm tits on an animal since you were close up and personal with a highly playful young orangutan in the rainforests of Borneo? You can't remember asking her what the hell (you added several expletives which I shall not repeat) she was doing with a geriatric old fart who probably couldn't get it up anymore? You can't remember telling her that if she wanted a real man, with a rock-hard nine inches of thrusting manhood, he was standing right in front of her? You can't remember kneeling in front of the poor woman, protesting your undying love and adoration, for her while rubbing your grubby paws up and down the inside of the slit in her skirt? You can't remember the DG threatening to take you outside and thrash you to within an inch of your miserable, worthless life?'

'Can't say that I do, old chap,' says Briggs-Hamilton jovially. 'It sounds like a good time was had by all! Gosh, that rock hard bit was jolly good; toothsome-looking wench, old Samantha!'

'That's not quite the way the DG saw it. Your behaviour was totally inexcusable, abysmal and atrocious.'

'Well you know what they say: "Boys will be boys"!'

'Boys holding their P45 in the queue at Jobcentre Plus, you mean?'

Briggs-Hamilton blanches. 'Now steady on, old man, it was only a bit of harmless fun.'

'To you, and the other semi-moronic cretins of the laddish generation, it might be, but to those of us raised with certain standards of behaviour, especially in relation to how men treat women, it was nothing short of an absolute disgrace.'

'So I'm in real trouble?'

'That can truly be said to be the understatement of the century.'

'Would an apology help?'

The doyen looks sadly at his protégé. 'I very much doubt it,' he says. He thinks for a couple of seconds. 'Tell me – do you know how Mussolini died, and what then happened to his body?'

'Sorry, old man, I was in the Science band at school. Last thing I really remember about History was something to do with a battle down Hastings way. Couldn't even tell you the *dramatis personæ*.'

The doyen gets up from his chair and begins to pace up and down, his hands on the lapels of his sports jacket and begins to lecture. 'Towards the end of the war, Mussolini was captured by the partisans and executed along with his mistress, Clara Petacci.' He warms to his task. 'Their bodies were taken to a Milanese petrol station where they were kicked and spat upon by a rampaging mob, and then hung upside down, along with a few more of Mussolini's cronies. As they swung to and fro in the breeze more shots were fired into them. It was even reported, though never proved, that Mussolini's penis and testicles were cut off and thrust into his mouth. The police had to use considerable violence to disperse the protestors.'

'And you're saying that this is what the old DG wants to do to me?'

'Only after he has had you keelhauled and quite possibly hung, drawn and quartered,' replies the doyen. 'Now when the Gunpowder plotters were…'

Briggs-Hamilton has had quite enough history lessons for one day. 'So what the hell am I going to do?' For the first time he appears to recognise the gravity of his situation and his anxiety is palpable. This is the opening for which the doyen has been waiting. He returns to the conference table and sits down.

'I think the only solution is for the BBC to suspend you for three months. There is a precedent for such a course of action, when that ghastly talk show presenter – can't for the life of me remember the man's name – overstepped the mark with a prank phone call. I suggest that you agree to the punishment and offer complete contrition and remorse.'

'But...'

'At the end of the three months you will be restored to your former position, and will be in a position to continue with your glittering career.'

'But...'

'No doubt you are wondering what you will do with your three-month vacation. I take it that, as usual, you have squandered the money from the last project and are now totally skint.'

'Yes.'

'I thought so. It comes as no surprise.' The doyen pauses for effect, and then changes tack: 'Tell me, what you know about the island of Grande Batture?'

'Pardon?'

'The island of Grande Batture: what do you know about it?'

'Island in the Caribbean... virtually inaccessible... used to be part of France. Why?'

'Hardly encyclopaedic knowledge, is it? But you get three out of three for starters. If you agree to my proposal, however, I suggest that by the spring you will be one of the world's leading authorities on the island.'

'Meaning?'

'Let me put my proposal, for your short-term future, in some form of context. A couple of years ago I saw the writing on the wall. I saw the cuts to the BBC budget coming, although I must admit that I never appreciated the scope of the savage barbarity that was to be unleashed on the organisation by the current government. Anyway, as you know, I started my own production company…'

'*Monitum Finalem?*', interjects the ever-helpful Julian.

The doyen frowns, not best pleased to have his erudite exposition interrupted. 'Yes, and for my sins I sold my soul to the fiends of Firmament Television. To be fair, they do have access to some massively impressive technology and so, while I have always been a little uncomfortable in making a pact with the devil incarnate, it appeared to be the only way that I could continue to make the programmes I have always wanted to make. There really was no other option.' He pauses. 'Anyway, I have always been fascinated by Grande Batture…'

'Why?'

'I'm coming to that, but the good news is that Firmament has agreed to fund a definitive work on the landscape and wildlife of Grande Batture. I am delighted because it is something I have always wanted to do, ever since I visited the country for the first time over fifty years ago. You will obviously know why the island is unique, and has fascinated botanists and zoologists for most of the last century?'

'Something about a shipwreck, which introduced loads of different species onto the island about a hundred years ago.'

'It actually took place in 1840,' says the doyen. 'James Nathanial Adams, a fundamentalist Baptist from Anniston in Alabama, and thirty of his followers, were washed up on Grande Batture, together with a vast range of botanical specimens and animals, which had been gathered together from all over North America and the wider world. A few years before, another preacher, William Miller, had predicted that the world would end sometime between March 1843 and March 1844. Adams was a Posttribulationist who believed that, before the second coming of Christ could occur, there would be famine, war, hardship and suffering across the world. This was something Adams was determined to avoid; and so he and his followers set sail from Pensacola in Florida, on *The Trumpet Shall Sound*, in an attempt to find an uninhabited island in the Caribbean, where they would be safe from the worst excesses of the Tribulation, and would be in a position to preserve as much of God's glorious Creation as possible. They saw themselves as sort of modern-day Noahs.'

'But they came a cropper.'

'Indeed they did. None of them, as far as we can tell, had any form of maritime experience, and it was more by good luck than judgement that they made it as far as Grande Batture. For several weeks they had zigzagged across the Caribbean, even managing to negotiate a course through the treacherous Martinique Passage, but then, several days later, disaster struck when the ship hit a reef off the island, and was stranded high and dry, damaged irreparably.

'The Caribs on the island were magnificent. They rescued the passengers and what passed for a crew, and took them into their own homes, tending to their injuries where necessary. Risking life and limb they cleared everything from *The Trumpet Shall Sound* – all the plants and the whole host of animals that the Tribulationists had decided that God wanted them to preserve. Over time the Caribs built houses for their visitors, and did everything they could to make their recently arrived guests as comfortable as possible. Given that Grande Batture was, and still is, way off the major shipping routes, it soon became apparent to all and sundry that this might well not be a temporary arrangement.'

'And, of course, the world did not end in 1844,' observes Briggs-Hamilton helpfully – for the first time demonstrating impeccable historical knowledge.

'No. We will never know whether the castaways realised that the "prophesy" had not been fulfilled. What is clear, however, is that, as time passed, the American interlopers became more and more dominant and aggressive. You must remember that slavery was still, by and large, the order of the day in the southern states and, of course, the white men had guns. They began to behave like many of the plantation owners they knew back home: they treated the "natives" as slaves, controlling every aspect of their lives, sometimes with extreme cruelty. Beatings, rapes and executions became commonplace. The Caribs who, unusually for the Caribbean, had never been subject to slavery, were made to work from dawn until dusk, six days a week, sometimes in the most appalling conditions, while all the time the "gospel" of Christ was being drummed into them constantly. Finally it became all too much for the indigenous population. They rebelled and, despite taking heavy casualties, overthrew the invaders slaughtering every single one of them – men, women and children – using primitive knives and machetes. One of the rivers on the island is still called the Red River, because it ran red with the blood of the victims for days after the massacres.

'The interesting thing is that the locals have never

forgotten their "Great Tribulation", and so, unsurprisingly, Grande Batture is the only island in the Caribbean where Christianity has failed to make any form of impression. Catholic missionaries from the Society of Mary attempted three times to convert the Caribs in the 1880s, but none of the parties ever returned; they just disappeared and were never seen again. Since their disappearance, probably as much due to its inaccessibility as anything else, the people of the island have been left to their own devices. France claimed Grande Batture back in the eighteenth century and has never fully relinquished the claim, although a considerable measure of self-governing independence was granted to the islanders in the sixties. Nor has the countryside been ruined by hoards of tourists, from those hideous cruise ships and package holiday flights, so all this time the island has continued to evolve as a tropical paradise, with the species introduced by the 1840 intruders thriving in and integrating into the existing ecosystem – which, my boy, is where you come in!'

The doyen beams genially at Briggs-Hamilton. He has so enjoyed displaying his erudition, even if it is for an audience of only one. B-H is well ahead of his master. 'I take it you want me to go to Grande Batture and conduct some sort of preliminary assessment.'

'Correct. Sadly, I no longer have the physical capacity to do such things myself, but in you I have the most wonderful substitute. Your abysmal behaviour the other night has been something of a blessing in disguise, and seems to provide a highly satisfactory solution to all our problems: I get high quality research for my latest project; the DG thinks he has got your head on a platter; you get to keep your job and do not face a period of unpaid gardening leave, and I'll probably cut you in for some of the royalties to the best-selling book which will undoubtedly follow the award-winning series. *Oblata arripe! Rapiamus, amici, occasionem de die!*

Briggs-Hamilton has no choice. He could raise objections, but it cannot be denied that the proposed solution would almost certainly have had even the mighty King Solomon reaching for the Bollinger. He is about to spend three months in humid, tropical heat; pounded by rainstorms and possibly hurricanes; in the company of people who have not always demonstrated a good track record in returning visitors to the bosoms of their families, but there really is no alternative. He looks at the doyen and nods, and is rewarded with an enormous smile, a hearty handshake and several vigorous pounds on the back.

'Good man! Good man!' says the doyen genially. 'You know it makes sense!'

III:IV

Government House on the island of Grande Batture could be said to have much in common with the extension to the National Gallery in London which, decades ago, was lambasted by the Prince of Wales as a 'monstrous carbuncle'. It sits uneasily halfway up a hill, behind the slums and squalor of Bonaire, a lasting testament to the delusional fantasies of the power-crazed President Walcott. Educated at an expensive and exclusive international school in Switzerland, he had spent many happy summer holidays cruising along the Rhine and, perhaps in homage to his misspent and dissolute youth, he ordered the construction of a carbon copy of the Schloss Drachenberg, between Königswinter and Bad Honnef, to act as the new presidential palace. Its pseudo-gothic turrets, sharply angled roofs and huge clock tower dominate the landscape, and are a constant reminder to the impoverished population of the hideous consequences of insane political megalomania.

In a beautifully appointed office high in one of the towers, replete with luxurious Axminster carpet, reproduction Louis Quinze furniture and ersatz mediaeval wall tapestries, a dapper little man, with a greying goatee beard and wearing a cream safari suit, sits behind a massive mahogany desk with an inane smile on his face. His Excellency the Right Honourable Dexter Barrington Taylor, current President of the Republic of Grande Batture, as the psalmist would no doubt have said, hates the grotesque building with a 'perfect hatred'. It is a symbol of everything that was wrong with the country for so long, but, as he sits in his air-conditioned office with magnificent views of the cerulean sea in the distance, he is a very happy camper indeed. In his hands he holds the latest edition of *Avanse*, Grande Batture's only daily newspaper, and it makes very good reading indeed, especially if, like Taylor, you are facing the prospect of an election in less than a month. The leading article is highly complimentary. He has already read it several times but his eyes are drawn back to the best bits.

> Readers will know that this newspaper has not always been an avid supporter of the President, (Too bloody true, thinks Taylor) but now credit must be given where it is due. The recent developments on the island, especially the enhancement of the runway and facilities at the airport, promise to thrust Grande Batture into the twenty-first century. The construction of the new school, with its emphasis on business and technology, will give our children educational opportunities that their parents could only have dreamed about. The recruitment of international doctors and nurses, to lead and train our medical staff in the hospital, will result in increased life expectancy and improved health of our people. And, we are told, there is more to come.
>
> Some cynics have said: 'Where's the money coming from? Why is all this only now happening? Has it got anything to do with next month's election? Will there be a price to pay later?' President Taylor assures us that these advances are a direct result of his managing

to negotiate international grants and donations that will have no impact on the Exchequer, that there will be no sudden rise in taxation, and that our children will not be saddled with generations of debt. If this is the case, and at present there is no reason to doubt him, then this newspaper is delighted to endorse his campaign for re-election, and to urge all right-minded people on Grande Batture to ensure that he is given another five-year term in order to fulfil his dream.

VOTE FOR TAYLOR!

'Vote for Taylor!' What a transformation. This time last year *Avanse* was one hundred percent behind his opponent, the odious Brahami; but now the election is a shoe-in; he cannot possibly lose! Taylor gets out of his armchair, under the gently whirring fan, and surveys the view from his study window. He thinks back to the visit from the short fat man in the hideous tropical shirt, which was gaping open to reveal a generous paunch and huge, gold, tacky medallion dangling on his hairy chest. He remembers the conversation vividly. At first the president thought he was the subject of some hideous practical joke, but as the meeting progressed, he realised that far from being the jester in the pack, the hideous specimen in front of him was actually his saviour. In all his years in the grimy field of politics he had never heard anything like it at all; it seemed too good to be true. There must be a catch but no, the man appeared to be totally genuine. When he finally left, Taylor sat back in his chair, popped a cooling mint humbug into his mouth, and reflected on the total unpredictability of his chosen profession.

III:V

It is quite conceivable that the Smugglers Hotel, just outside Bonaire, was once an extremely pleasant place to spend a few tranquil, tropical days; the views are certainly spectacular. Violently green rainforests cascade from the hills all around the single-storey, whitewashed hotel, meeting the black volcanic sand of the beach almost at the water's edge. The sea is a brilliant aquamarine and one can just make out, a couple of hundred yards offshore, the outline of unspoiled coral reefs with brilliant white foamy waves breaking over them, sending surges of water soaring high into the air. Dotted along the beach are a series of brightly painted octagonal timber-frame chalets, which give the residents stunning views of the ocean, although these are somewhat misleadingly named 'villas' in the hotel's promotional literature.

It is in one of these beach huts that Briggs-Hamilton awakes, somewhat grudgingly, barely ready to meet the demands of a new day. The effects of a considerable number of 'Captain Fleury's Blood' cocktails consumed the previous evening, mainly to erase all traces of an almost inedible Creole chicken dished up in the restaurant, weigh heavily upon him. His mouth is parched; his head thumps almost in time to the rhythm of a Caribbean calypso, and his eyes feel as though they are impaled on a number of blunt knitting needles. But he is not alone. His misery is witnessed by several *Hemidactylus mabouias* who cling precariously to the walls, occasionally dropping small pellets of faeces, which narrowly miss the multitude of cockroaches that roam freely across the hardpan floor. The sound of the surf pounding on the offshore reef should soothe him into some form of blissful consciousness, after all he is in paradise, but it does not; he has come to hate this accursed place. He hates the hotel. He hates the 'villa'. He hates the fact that he has not had a decent shower in weeks; the plumbing is mediaeval in its sophistication. He hates the food. He hates the fact that he has already been robbed twice, once at the point of a gun. He hates the high winds and driving rain, which pound him incessantly each afternoon when he is working on location in the field. He has, however, been extremely fortunate not to have been exposed to a violent tropical storm or hurricane, although it has to be said that these are relatively uncommon at this time of year.

But there is one thing he does not hate, and that is the island itself. James Nathanial Adams and his misguided followers have left a botanical legacy that stretches the bounds of credibility. When they sailed on *The Trumpet Shall Sound* they had obviously collected specimens from across the known world. Briggs-Hamilton has already discovered an opossum (*Didelphis virginiana*) and a colony of marsh rice rats (*Oryzomys palustris*), both of which are indigenous to the Yellowhammer State of Alabama, rather than the tropical islands of the Caribbean. He also suspects that he has seen a swamp mud snake (*Farancia abacura ssp.*), from the same state, in a small slough not far from the hotel but he cannot be sure. Whenever he thinks he has made a significant discovery, if a very inconsistent communication system allows, he shares his findings with the doyen and his team back in Bristol. The old man is beside himself. Briggs-Hamilton's stock is firmly in the ascendant.

Grande Batture is also awash with rare orchids and ferns, nearly seventy species of the former and over one hundred and fifty of the latter; but what has blown Briggs-Hamilton away the most is the discovery of a vast range of brightly coloured butterflies, with weird and wonderful names such as the fiery skipper and the Caribbean buckeye. The pursuit and identification of these glorious insects has become a passion that he shares with the owner of the Smugglers Hotel. Brandon Jamieson is a laconic Aussie, thousands of miles away from home, who looks more like Ernest Miller Hemingway than Hemingway himself. He is a bull elephant of a man in his late fifties, heavily suntanned, with a long silver beard and deep blue, almost hypnotic, eyes. He usually dresses in a khaki shirt, unbuttoned to below his barrel-like hairy chest, khaki shorts and open-toed sandals. Whenever he leaves the confines of the hotel buildings, Jamieson always wears an Australian army issue Boonie bush hat. It's a legacy from his father, who wore it every day during his two periods of service in Vietnam and, Brandon argues, it camouflages him superbly when he is engaged in his all-consuming obsession of butterfly observation. Jamieson claims to have photographed every species on the island, and the vast number of butterfly photos on the walls of the Jean Fleury bar, in the main body of the hotel, tends to bear witness to his claim.

Briggs-Hamilton moans softly, stiffens the sinews, summons up the blood to get out of bed, and heads for what passes as the bathroom. He stands under a tepid, dripping shower for as long as the water lasts, and dries himself with a threadbare towel that has long since seen better days. The renowned TV presenter dresses slowly and painfully, puts on his sunglasses and goes outside. It is a gloriously sunny day, with the temperature in the mid-thirties centigrade, but this is probably the last thing that Briggs-Hamilton needs right at this minute. The prospect of breakfast is too appalling to contemplate, however, he is convinced that he is in serious need of a coffee.

The dining area at the Smugglers Hotel is open to the elements and covered by a large thatched roof. Jamieson is sitting at one of the tables drinking a latte, from a smoked-glass Arcoroc coffee mug, staring out to sea having already breakfasted, as is evidenced by a large plate, swimming in grease, next to his hairy right arm. He motions Briggs-Hamilton to join him and Julian slumps into a wicker chair opposite *Le Patron*. Brandon takes one look at the wreck of humanity in front of him and immediately exudes sympathy.

'Jeez, mate,' he says, 'you look bloody awful. How many did you have last night?'

'Dunno, lost count.' Even the simple act of talking is torture. Briggs-Hamilton is in the act of deciding that not a single drop of alcohol will pass his lips ever again.

'Never fear, Brando's here,' says his host genially. 'What you need is one of Brando's guaranteed pick-me-up and hangover cures. Never fails. Shall we head for the bar?'

Briggs-Hamilton is in no position to argue, and he stumbles after Jamieson into the main part of the hotel. The thatched and timbered Jean Fleury bar is cool and, better still, dark. The air is redolent with the smells of stale beer and cigarette smoke. Two filthy fans rotate slowly in the beams of the roof. Grimy rattan chairs have been placed upside down on top of the tables, probably to facilitate easy cleaning of the floor, but it is doubtful whether the bar's surfaces have seen a cloth or mop anytime within the last decade. Briggs-Hamilton sits on a bar stool and Jamieson takes his place behind the counter.

'First things first,' says Brando. 'Which of these bastards did for you last night?' He points to the range of bottles behind the bar. Briggs-Hamilton points wearily in the general direction of the Goslings Black Seal Bermuda Rum.

'I take it that you had more than a couple.'

Julian nods. 'I think I lost count after the first few,' he croaks.

'Men have won the Victoria Cross for less,' says Jamieson, in genuine awe of his customer's act of misguided heroism. 'But Brando's cures have never failed. I guarantee that within the hour you'll be wolfing down your brekkie like a ravenous dingo with a newly killed jumbuck.'

The picture conjured up in Briggs-Hamilton's mind is not all that appealing, but Jamieson is not to be discouraged. He takes the bottle of rum from the shelf and slams it down on the bar. The noise reverberates in Julian's head like a thunderclap. Next the hotel owner rummages in a drawer beneath the aged cash register. He finally finds what he is looking for, and puts a pot of black-headed pins on the counter next to the bottle.

'Stage One,' he says. 'I want you to stick as many of these pins as you can into the cork of the bottle.' Julian looks at him blankly.

'Stick as many pins as you can into the cork of the bottle,' Brando repeats patiently.

'Why?'

'Don't argue and do what I say. They swear by it in Haiti. It's some form of voodoo thing that punishes the spirits that caused the pain and distress. While you're doing that I'll mix up the restorative libation which will transform you back into your cheerful, happy self.'

Briggs-Hamilton begins sticking pins into the cork, at first with some hesitancy and then with increasing ferocity: he hates the bottle; he loathes the bottle; the bottle is wicked, the bottle deserves to be punished! As he unleashes his fury on the totally innocent container, Brando gets a large straight glass, into which he breaks an egg without disturbing the yolk. He adds a generous dash of Worcestershire sauce, salt and pepper, a liberal splash of hot chilli sauce and stirs it gently, before placing it in front of the patient.

'There you are, mate,' he says enthusiastically, 'a genuine Prairie Oyster, guaranteed to cure all your ills within thirty minutes or your money back.'

There is no way out. Briggs-Hamilton will have to drink the noxious potion. It looks revolting. He takes the glass in his left hand and raises it to his lips. He shuts his eyes and downs the contents in one go. The chilli sauce sears his mouth. The egg feels like slime. The Worcestershire sauce, normally so delightful in a Bloody Mary, is acidic and bitter. He slams the glass down on the bar and looks triumphantly at the hotel proprietor. Within seconds he feels nauseous. He begins to sweat like a marathon runner approaching the twenty-mile mark. He turns white. Suddenly the naturalist rushes from the room and emits, what Brando would no doubt call, an ear-splittingly loud technicolour yawn, into the brilliantly colourful rhododendron bushes just next to the door leading to the Jean Fleury bar.

'Beauty,' says Brando. 'Bloody works every bloody time!'

*

Half an hour later Briggs-Hamilton is sitting at a table in the dining area, pale faced but beginning to feel more like his normal self. He has been ordered to drink a couple of litres of tepid Evian water and is waiting for breakfast, which Brando is preparing himself. The chef arrives bearing the fruits of his labours on a huge oblong plate; it is piled high with food. Briggs-Hamilton blanches as he inspects the contents: two eggs resting leisurely atop a generously sized sirloin steak; bacon, sausages, mushrooms and a grilled tomato floating on a sea of grease and oil. But having said that, even in his wretched state Briggs-Hamilton cannot help admitting that it smells absolutely wonderful. Much to his surprise, he attacks the platter with considerable gusto and within fifteen minutes it is empty.

'Reckon you should go easy today, mate,' says Brandon. 'You've been working your knackers off ever since you got here. You're not a bludger, chuck a sickie, no one will ever know.'

'You're right,' admits Briggs-Hamilton, although he has no real idea as to what is meant by the term 'bludger'. 'Might just take a drive down to the south of the island. I haven't really investigated that area at all. Anything of interest down there?'

'Pretty good if you're interested in my field,' says Brandon. 'If you're down by Scorpion Bay it might pay you to go up into the hills behind the beach. A few years back we had a couple of wowser entomologists from the States. They swore blind that they had seen a blue morpho in a clearing in the forest. I don't believe it for a minute. I've never seen one in the twenty-five years I've lived on the island. As far as I know the nearest known habitats are in Columbia.'

'They're big buggers though,' says Briggs-Hamilton. 'I suppose that it's possible that one could have been carried on the wind, but it would be pretty unlikely I suppose, given that the prevailing air currents come from the other direction. By the way, what's a wowser when it's at home?'

'People who avoid alcohol. Bastards never bought a drink the whole time they were here, and they were bloody vegan to boot. God Almighty, they were a real pair of dags.'

Briggs-Hamilton decides not to pursue the subject of dags; he gets the general idea and takes his leave of the proprietor, before further vitriolic abuse can be heaped on other unfortunate guests who have had the dubious pleasure of staying at the establishment. He goes back to the 'chalet' and picks up his latest toy: a Sony A7 high speed camera which, according to the advertising material that accompanies the technological masterpiece, allows him to take 'rapid automatically focused pictures in silent mode'. He heads to the car park to pick up the battered Land Rover Discovery he has rented, at an exorbitant rate, for the duration of his time on the island. Unusually, today it starts first time.

At the gates of the hotel Briggs-Hamilton pauses; Smugglers is several miles north of Bonaire on the western side of the island. He can turn right and travel through the capital, or he can turn left and take the coastal road that goes right around Grande Batture. The drive through Bonaire is shorter, but the traffic in the narrow, twisting, dirty, crowded streets packed with delinquent pedestrians, insane cyclists and moth-eaten, bleating goats can be a nightmare. It is further to use the coast road, but it is a pleasant drive and he can stop along the way to stretch his legs if he so desires. And anyway, Grande Batture is hardly a huge island: roughly forty miles long and twenty-five at its widest, shaped roughly like a slightly uneven number eight. He makes the decision and turns left.

A couple of miles down the dusty road he reduces speed as he passes the elementary school. Children are hurling themselves around the playground, in front of rickety buildings which have long since seen better days. Panes of glass are missing from the louvered windows, and the corrugated iron roofs are coated with thick, red rust. However, next door a new building is taking shape. Workmen, stripped to the waist and sweating in the thirty-five-degree heat, are constructing a new school, and a very impressive building it will be when completed. Made of, what appears to be, solid concrete, it is raised on pilings a couple of metres above the ground, and all the windows are protected by hurricane shutters. Two satellite dishes, perched on the roof, gaze at the heavens alongside a host of air-conditioning outlets. It is all most impressive, but Briggs-Hamilton, who has been appalled by the poverty endemic on Grande Batture, wonders where on earth the money has come from.

He drives on towards the north of the island. On his right, the rainforest sweeps down from the slopes of Mt Grand Sein, a towering dormant volcano, and comes right to the edge of the road. It is dense, lush and a rich, pulsating green, occasionally illuminated by the dazzling red of heliconia and poinsettia plants; it is easy to see how people could get lost in the jungle, even if they were only a few metres from the road. To the left the terrain is somewhat more open, with occasional tantalising views of the ocean beyond the tall, swaying coconut palms. The road is not metalled and is pitted with potholes, but it is virtually empty, even though it is the main access route to the airport.

The airport itself is on a narrow strip of coastal plain, right at the most northerly tip of the island. When Briggs-Hamilton arrived on Grande Batture a couple of months previously, in an aged, somewhat dilapidated Dash Eight, there was extensive building work going on, with a new runway and terminal building under construction. As he drives past the security fence surrounding the airport, he notices that the work looks to have been completed. Opposite the new, brilliant white passenger terminal, there is a huge billboard advertising plans for the erection of forty luxury apartments as well as an airport hotel, the picture showing sumptuous new condominiums surrounded by rainforest, replete with swimming pools, tennis courts and an eighteen-hole golf course. Next to the sign is another. It shows a devastatingly attractive air stewardess carrying a tray containing some sort of fruity tropical beverages, announcing a new weekly service to New York on Batture Air's new Airbus A319. Again Briggs-Hamilton wonders where the money is coming from.

He drives southwards along the coastal road, leaving the towering presence of Grand Sein behind him. It is replaced in the distance by a smaller, but still active, volcano named Petite Soeur. The landscape remains magnificent, and, over the growling noise of the ancient Land Rover's engine, he can hear the sounds of parrots and parakeets squawking and screeching in the undergrowth. Towards the south of the island the road veers several hundred metres inland, and is covered on both sides by dense vegetation. However, occasionally on the seaward side, Briggs-Hamilton can just make out the sight of more construction, only this time it looks like builders are erecting a series of opulent mansions, each with their own long stretch of private beach and extensive tropical gardens.

The ordeals of the early morning are put behind him. He never thought when he got up that, by just before lunchtime he would be feeling on top of the world. It's a lovely day. It's good to be alive. One hand on the steering wheel, his left arm resting on the opened window, Julian Briggs-Hamilton, who believes that he possesses a fine baritone voice, breaks into song:

> *The flowers that bloom in the spring,*
> *Tra La,*
> *Breathe promise of merry sunshine –*
> *As we merrily dance and we sing,*
> *Tra La,*
> *We welcome the hope that they bring,*
> *Tra La,*
> *Of a summer of roses and wine,*
> *Of a summer of roses…*

'Bloody hell!' he shouts as, having turned a blind corner at speed, he is forced to slam on the brakes. The Land Rover comes to rest just inches short of an unforgiving chain link fence, which has been built right across the road. 'What bloody lunatic…?'

He backs up, parks on the verge, and gets out of the car to take a look at the obstacle. The fence stretches into the jungle on either side of the road. A sign on the structure proudly states that it has been made to the highest specifications required by the US Chain Link Fence Manufacturers Institute, based in Columbia, Maryland, by the Security Fence Company of Red Lion, Pennsylvania. It is certainly an impressive piece of work, but it is immediately obvious that Briggs-Hamilton's circumnavigation of the island is at an end.

He goes back to the car, takes a swig of water from one of the bottles left over from breakfast, and surveys the landscape in front of him. He knows that he is alone, but has a very real impression that there are hundreds of eyes staring at him through the dense foliage. It has suddenly become eerily quiet. It is all quite unnerving. He looks around. On the other side of the road, he can just make out a narrow path going up an incline into the rainforest. Oh well, he might as well take a look; after all Brando did recommend going into the hills and, by his own reckoning, Briggs-Hamilton must be close to the southernmost part of the island.

He goes round the bonnet to the passenger side of the motor and opens the door. A ragged, old school satchel lies on the seat. It contains the camera, binoculars, another full bottle of water, a machete and thirty-five small, circular, white metal discs. These discs are an essential part of his survival kit. Whenever he goes into the bush he drops a disc every ten paces or so, in order to create a trail of markers, which will enable him to retrace his steps if he has the misfortune to lose his way. It is a sensible precaution, given the density of the undergrowth within the confines of the rainforest.

Briggs-Hamilton crosses the road and starts up the narrow, muddy trail between the trees; many are entwined with lianas thrusting up towards the forest canopy. Branches brush his face, and he is obliged to use the machete several times to clear the way forward. The track rises steeply in places causing his feet to slip, and, the further he goes into the jungle, the smell of decomposition and decay becomes almost overpowering. After fifteen minutes he has only dropped ten of the white discs on the ground, which means that he has probably not gone much more than a hundred yards. Julian pauses to catch his breath, slapping at a couple of over-confident mosquitoes that are intent on using his forearm for a little light luncheon. He sets off again and is surprised when, only a couple of minutes later, the wooded areas come to an end.

He finds himself in a small clearing, three sides of which are bounded by rainforest. To his left the trees have been cleared, which means that he has a clear view of a small bay containing wonderfully blue sea, shimmering in the bright sunlight. The floor of the glade is awash with wildflowers: brilliant blue cornflowers, white and orange African daisies and colourful yellow snapdragons. It is also clear that Brando is absolutely right when he says that this part of the island is a veritable paradise for lepidopterists. Within a couple of minutes Briggs-Hamilton has identified a host of different skippers, hairstreaks, whites and sulphurs that are darting across the meadow, flashing in and out of the forest. In the centre of the clearing, a pile of rubble and decaying timber suggests that, at one time, there has been a house on the site, but that the inhabitants have long since departed and nature is gradually reclaiming the land.

Briggs-Hamilton works his way around the three sides of the glade hemmed in by rainforest, as he cannot bring himself to trample on the wild flowers. This, he thinks, would be akin to trampling on an antique Persian Tabriz rug in a pair of muddy, dung-infested Doc Marten boots. He takes a photo every couple of yards so that the researchers back in Bristol will be able to identify the range of flora on display; it is not really his field and he wants to give them as much information as possible. This will help them decide whether it is worth sending a camera crew when filming gets underway. Finally he comes to the more open fourth side of the space, and looks down at the small cove with its unbelievably clear, translucent water.

At the head of the bay, part of the land has been cleared and a house has been erected. It reminds Briggs-Hamilton of a New Guinea *long haus*, in that it is a long rectangular shape and is raised on wooden stilts. The walls appear to have been made from interwoven palm leaves and these are covered with a thatched roof. The middle section of the building is open to the elements, and contains a variety of light brown wicker chairs and small tables; the floor being covered with highly colourful rugs and carpets. On either side of the open living area there are two enclosed spaces, which, Briggs-Hamilton assumes, are probably used for sleeping and cooking. The slightly incongruous sight of two air conditioners, poking out from the walls on the left hand side of the house, suggests that he might be right. Steps lead down from the living area to a large expanse of wooden decking, on which are laid a couple of sun loungers and a large circular table with six chairs. There is nobody about, but the evidence of paperback books next to the loungers, as well as coffee cups on the table, indicate that it has been inhabited recently. He notices that the wire fence, which inhibited his tour of the island, now forms an impenetrable barrier around the house, while tracks leading away from the decking imply that there might be other dwellings close by.

Briggs-Hamilton turns away, taking some random photos of the clearing before making his way back to the car. He wonders how he can find out who used to live in the ruin in the clearing, and ponders on the possible identity of the occupants of the *long haus*. Money is obviously no object to them, especially since they are apparently pre-occupied with security – the fence would not have been cheap. He turns the key in the ignition and heads back to Smugglers; determined not to repeat the misdemeanours of the previous evening, both in terms of alcoholic consumption and the ingestion of another Creole chicken; a nice cheddar cheese sandwich, with a bit of Branston Pickle, would be a wonderful way to end the day but, as Alice once said, 'There's no use trying, one can't believe impossible things.'

Later that evening, he is propped up on a cockeyed wooden bar stool in the Jean Fleury, nursing a Kalik Gold, and is showing an interested Brando pictures of his afternoon's endeavours. 'Have no idea how you found it,' the Aussie says, looking at shots of the clearing. 'I must have been down there hundreds of times, but I never knew it existed. No idea who would have lived there either and I've been here for donkey's years.'

'Do you know who lives in the house by the cove?' asks Briggs-Hamilton.

'Bit of a mystery man really. He arrived around May/ June last year and moved straight into the house, which somebody, God only knows who, had been building for about six months. Keeps himself to himself, but I do know he's got a pair of ace-looking sheilas in residence, as well as a couple of offsiders who run errands for him. Odd though – ever since he arrived things seem to have been happening.'

'What do you mean?'

'Well, take the new airport runway and terminal. There was no thought of that this time last year. Same for the school and the lairy holiday mansions development you passed today. Every one of those projects has started in the last twelve months, which sort of coincides with when he arrived here. Some people say he's a criminal on the run and that he has bribed government officials to protect him. Rumour is that President Dexter Barrington Taylor, our glorious leader, would do anything for the bastard, but the truth is that nobody knows who the hell he is. He just stays in his house, miles away from anybody else, with his bimbos and hangers-on, surrounded by that ridiculous fence and about twenty guards. He never leaves, is never seen in public. It's a mystery, but... Strewth! Hooley bleeding Dooley!'

'What?'

'Stone the crows – I don't believe it!'

'What?' asks Briggs-Hamilton, desperately trying to get to grips with a linguistic construct different from anything he has encountered in his life up until now.

'Fair suck of the sav – it can't be!'

'What on earth are you talking about?' says the naturalist; surely modern Australians no longer speak like this. Given the way the conversation is unfolding, it would come as no surprise to him if Chips Rafferty were to appear suddenly at the bar and order an ice cold sherbet; but nevertheless Briggs-Hamilton is intrigued by his agitated host as he stares at the screen on the camera in total disbelief.

'Look!' Brando thrusts the camera under the naturalist's eyes.

'What?' All Briggs-Hamilton can see is a photo of the long side of the clearing. It's just trees and dense foliage, there's nothing to see.

'Look there,' intones Brando. 'Look at that branch. Can't you see it?'

'See what?' Julian stares at the branch. Suddenly he sees it, but he is not sure what it is he is actually seeing; it looks like a green-feathered bird, about the size of a thrush, with a pure white beak and some red markings on its head. Its almost perfect camouflage makes it blend right in with the opulent greenery of the rainforest.

'What the bloody hell is it?' he asks. 'I've no idea what it is at all; never seen one like it before.'

Brandon goes over to a battered bookshelf that is attached unsteadily to one wall of the bar. He grabs a moth-eaten, mildew-soaked and regally red leather-bound tome with gold-edged leaves, and opens it. '*Birds of the Caribbean*,' he says. 'It's the definitive work on all birds living, threatened and extinct in the region. If I'm right, you may have unwittingly stumbled on a bird that was first described back in the eighteenth century, but which most modern ornithologists are convinced never existed at all.'

He pauses. 'Look,' he says, 'here: it's a bloody Guadeloupe parakeet.'

He hands Briggs-Hamilton the open book. Julian reads a short description of the bird, looks at the ancient coloured illustration by Labat, looks back at the camera screen and then repeats the process. It is staggering. The two images are almost totally identical. Julian appears to have photographed an extinct and, what many experts considered to be, mythical, parakeet.

'Mate, you gotta go back,' says Brando. 'My God, if it's what we think it is, then you have made the West Indian equivalent of the ornithological discovery of the bloody century. I'll come with you tomorrow. We'll make up a bird blind and see if we can catch the bastard again. My God, this calls for a celebration.'

With that he goes over to the bar and pours two generous measures of Goslings Black Seal Bermuda Rum. Julian Briggs-Hamilton, the discoverer of the Guadeloupe parakeet, moans and resigns himself to another of Brando's magical hangover remedies in the morning.

III:VI

Before dawn the following day, Briggs-Hamilton is back in the clearing snugly ensconced in a compact, spring-loaded, beautifully camouflaged bird hide, on the opposite side of the glade from where the parakeet appeared the day before. He and Brandon have decided that, at the outset, it is best not to try to get too close to their prey, on the grounds that they do not want to scare the bird into leaving the scene. The hide is not large, about twenty square feet, but it is sufficient for Julian to position his camera by the rectangular window, and to store enough food and water to last well through the day, and possibly on into the evening. Brando leaves mid-morning, convinced that this manoeuvre will fool the bird into thinking that there is no one in the hide; Briggs-Hamilton is more circumspect, but there is certainly more room without the presence of the large, undeodorised Australian. It is also more tranquil, and the presenter of natural history programmes is relaxed, doing what he loves most: waiting for the star of the show to make an appearance.

However, the star appears reluctant to materialise. The day passes interminably, getting hotter and hotter with each passing hour. As is his custom, Briggs-Hamilton refuses to consume alcohol when on duty, but water is vital in the close, humid atmosphere; consequently he works his way through several half-litre bottles of Evian. This, of course, can have only one possible outcome; as a result, by the middle of the afternoon, the need to heed the call of nature is overpowering – Julian is forced to break cover and head for the nearest shrubbery. This happens to be on the side of the clearing overlooking the bay and so, from a position of some security, Briggs-Hamilton is able to get a closer look at the enigmatic house and its environs. There is still nobody about but, on the table, the coffee cups of yesterday have been replaced by plates and wine glasses. Blessedly 'relieved', he returns to the hide to await developments; still nothing happens and, at dusk, concerned that he might not be able to find his way back to the road in the twilight, he leaves the clearing, having first secured the hide to ensure that it does not blow away in the night.

The following day is almost an exact carbon copy of the day before, except that Brandon stays on for an extra couple of hours. The lack of ventilation in the tent means that the air in the confined space becomes a trifle fusty; thus it is an enormous relief to Briggs-Hamilton when Brando finally leaves, to take care of 'the lunchtime rush' back at the hotel. Julian does not argue, although he has never actually seen more than half a dozen people in the bar or restaurant at any one time. The afternoon drags by. He relieves himself by the same bush and sees that the house is still deserted; surely they can't be nocturnal? By day's end, he has decided that he will give it a final try tomorrow. If he has no success then, when the Firmament team arrives, he will get one of the junior researchers to spend time in the glade just in case the Guadeloupe parakeet reappears. Little does he know that he will never return to the island, and that the programme, so coveted by the doyen, will never be made.

Day three of the vigil starts again before dawn and, as he walks around to the hide, he notices that a small blue and white fishing boat is moored next to the decking in front of the house. This may provide some form of explanation as to why the compound has been deserted for the last couple of days; perhaps the residents are keen fishermen – Briggs-Hamilton is aware that some of the best blue and white marlin fishing can be found in the waters off Grande Batture, so that may well be the explanation.

As before the day passes slowly; the soporific heat grows in intensity as the sun rises towards its zenith; even the butterflies are finding the temperature too much to bear, and are conspicuous by their absence. Briggs-Hamilton begins to become drowsy – it would be all too easy to drop off to sleep. Suddenly his somnolent state is disturbed by the sound of voices, female voices. Intrigued, he leaves the safety of the hide and peers through the vegetation in the direction of the house. The loungers are occupied by two lithe, bronzed young women – one blonde, one brunette – lying face down and topless, wearing only the tiniest of tie-sided bikini briefs. At the table a tall man wearing yellow and red board shorts, his long brown hair held in place by a brightly coloured bandana, is peering intently at a laptop. With him is a short fat man, wearing the most hideous floral shirt, plain Bermuda shorts and open-toed sandals. It is rather like looking at 'Robinson Crusoe meets Oliver Hardy' thinks Briggs-Hamilton. They are deep in discussion, and totally oblivious of the exquisitely formed human flesh on display only a few yards away. Julian has no such inhibitions; he is not a prude – if it is on display he has every right to feast his eyes. Of course, it could be argued that the girls in question are under the impression that they are enjoying a certain amount of privacy, and are completely unaware that Briggs-Hamilton is doing a more than passable impression of an extremely randy Hades eyeing up the unfortunate, soon-to-be-undone, Persephone. Forgetting the purpose of the natural history exercise, the lecher rushes back to the hide, picks up the camera and positions himself in the shrubbery, where he can get the best possible photographic results. The Sony's high speed, silent shutter action is ideal for taking rapid multiple shots of unsuspecting birds without disturbing them – so it is absolutely perfect for the task in hand. For fifteen minutes Briggs-Hamilton is in total heaven, all thoughts of the Guadeloupe parakeet dismissed – which is a pity because the bird in question is actually perched on exactly the same branch as it had been only a couple of days before. If the animal could talk it would be screaming, 'Oi! You! Over here! I've been in bloody wardrobe and make-up for the last two bloody days getting ready for the bloody photo shoot.' Sadly, it is common knowledge that our feathered friends cannot talk, and so a chance to make ornithological history is missed when the disgruntled creature flies away.

Down on the decking, Hardy is folding away his laptop and is about to take his leave. Then Crusoe does a most peculiar thing: he stands, places his hands on the fat man's head, and appears to say a few words; it is almost as if he is giving him his blessing. The man in the hideous shirt ambles away, his sandals flip-flopping on the wooden surface of the decking, and the tall man turns to face the women lying on the loungers. The blonde raises her head, giving Briggs-Hamilton, in the process, the most exquisite glimpse of a full, firm breast. She motions Crusoe over to her, reaches down beside the lounger, picks up a bottle of suntan cream, and makes it clear that she is in need of assistance. The tall man flicks open the top of the container and squirts a generous amount of white liquid onto his hands. First he massages it into her ankles and calves, progresses on up to her thighs and then on to her back. He moves slowly and rhythmically, with all the thoroughness and dedication that would have been required from a Nubian slave massaging aromatic oils into the body of the Queen of Sheba. The girl's skin glistens in the sunshine as Crusoe's hands move over the firm, tanned flesh.

As he takes his photographs, Briggs-Hamilton is fascinated. Were he in the fortunate position of the Robinson Crusoe lookalike, he would undoubtedly find the whole experience highly erotic, but the man appears to be oblivious to the sexual nature of his task; it is almost as if he is a servant ministering to his mistress. Briggs-Hamilton is also aware that there is something about him that is familiar, but he cannot tell what it is; and this is not helped by the fact that, for most of the time, Crusoe's back is turned towards him, so the naturalist cannot really see his face. The man finishes rubbing the lotion into the blonde woman and repeats the same slow, long, lingering process with the brunette; then wipes his hands on a towel and begins to walk towards the house. Just before he gets to the steps he stops and turns round; perhaps one of the girls has called him? He looks back towards the loungers; it is only now that Briggs-Hamilton has a clear look at his face. His jaw drops in amazement. He recognises the man.

Surely, it can't be, it really can't be, but it is, it really is, even with that ridiculously theatrical beard, it really is him: Briggs-Hamilton is looking at the pope! He sends the camera into overdrive, desperate to get a close-up of the man's visage before he goes back into the dwelling. Julian is in luck. In the instant before he mounts the stairs, the runaway pope looks directly up at the spot where Briggs-Hamilton is hiding, and the naturalist is able to zoom in to get a close-up. It is only later, when Briggs-Hamilton reviews the photographs, that he notices the look of pure pain and anguish on the pope's face; it is almost as if he knows that he is going to be exposed, and that his time in paradise may well be coming to an end.

Briggs-Hamilton heads back to the clearing, packs away the hide, and goes back down to the car; his departure being watched by a very disgruntled Guadeloupe parakeet, high up in one of the trees. On the way back to Smugglers, he asks himself what the hell the leader of the Catholic church is doing on a remote Caribbean island, in the company of two nubile females and a man with the dress sense of a stereotypical American tourist on a cheap budget holiday to Acapulco – you could not possibly make it up. He thinks he has vague memories of reports of the pope being taken ill, but isn't this carrying convalescence a bit too far? Of one thing, though, he is convinced: marketed to the right people (not very nice people, admittedly), the material is worth an absolute fortune, especially those shots where *Il Papa* is 'pressing the flesh' of his delectable acolytes. Briggs-Hamilton could become a wealthy man almost overnight. He might even have enough capital to follow in the footsteps of his mentor, and set up a production company through which he could make his own programmes. He pictures being able to tell the director general, not to mention his bitch of a wife, into which orifices they could ram their precious Natural History Unit. Oh, happy days; he smiles contentedly. As far as Briggs-Hamilton is concerned 'the flowers have bloomed', springtime is blossoming and the sun is most certainly shining.

His meditations continue on the drive north back in the direction of the hotel. Julian soon comes to the conclusion that he cannot just send the photos electronically to his many friends in the gutter press; it would be far too insecure, and, to be perfectly frank, he would not trust them as far as he could throw them – they really are thoroughly unpleasant, unprincipled people. No, the solution must be to deliver them in person, in order to be able to drive the best possible deal face to face. Approaching the airport, he makes a spur-of-the-moment decision, and turns into the car park by the terminal building. He goes up to the Batture Air ticket office; enquires about the flights to New York; is told that the next departure is tomorrow at 1135 and, yes, there are still a number of seats available in Business class and, yes, they can arrange an onward connection to London Heathrow. He purchases the tickets, momentarily appalled at the price but, what the heck; with what he's got in the camera, he will soon be a well-heeled, wealthy man about town. He continues his drive back to the ghastly hotel a very happy camper indeed.

The following morning, having taken his leave of a mystified Brando, he sits by a window in Batture Air's Grand Class, and watches as the twin peaks of Grand Sein and Petite Soeur recede into the distance. He sips at his champagne and dares to dream of the brave new world which he is about to inhabit.

III : VII

Sitting in a plush grey armchair in the United Airlines Club lounge at Newark Liberty Airport in New York, Monsignor Angelo Tardelli, formerly Private Secretary to Pope Timothy, is a man at peace with the world. Relieved of his onerous duties when the pope had his 'stroke', he has had the massive good fortune to be reallocated to the post of Secretary to the Pontifical Council for Inter-religious Dialogue. It is an absolutely stress-free job, in massive contrast to the daily grind that working for the pope entailed. All he has to do is to: pen inspiring press releases targeted towards adherents of other faiths at certain times of the year, for example to Muslims setting off on the Hajj; run a small administrative office in the Vatican; and attend conferences and symposiums across the world, aimed at promoting inter-faith understanding and co-operation. He is on his way back to Rome after attending a Christian-Hindu 'interface' seminar based at the luxurious New York Palace Hotel, which has proved to be one of the most bizarre experiences of his life. Funded by a wealthy Indian businessman, who has retired to live a life of contemplation on an ashram in Uttar Pradesh, no expense has been spared in order to engage the participants in spiritually meaningful and engaging dialogue. Tardelli has no idea why the meeting was held in such opulence, especially in New York, but he has had a splendid time; the only downside being constant exposure to vegetarian cuisine, which has had a deleterious impact on the workings of his digestive system. However, business class flights were included in the invitation to participate, so Tardelli settles back into the comfortable armchair in the Club lounge, sips a Jack Daniels and awaits the call for UA40 to Rome. Around him, in the cathedral-like hush of the lounge, with bespoke-suited businessmen gazing intently at their laptops and tablets, it is hard to imagine that Tardelli is, in fact, a high-ranking member of the Vatican Secretariat. He is dressed casually in fawn chinos and a striped red and blue shirt. Angelo has found, from bitter experience, that clerical attire is not always conducive to a peaceful, untroubled flight. People always seem to want to confess, or have deep religious conversations, when sitting next to a priest within the limited confines of a tube hurtling through space at over 500 miles an hour. Perhaps it's because they are closer to God, and so are reminded of their mortality, but Tardelli is determined not to endure twelve hours of purgatory on his way back to the Holy See.

His quiet contemplation is disturbed by the arrival of an unkempt, bearded man in a tweed jacket. 'Is anyone sitting here?' the dishevelled apparition asks, motioning to an unoccupied chair across the table. Tardelli shakes his head and the man sits down.

'Going far?' asks Briggs-Hamilton.

'Rome,' says Tardelli.

'One of my favourite cities,' states the naturalist emphatically. He slaps a battered old briefcase on the floor by the seat, and puts a camera case on the table.

'Could you do me a favour and keep an eye on my stuff while I pop over there and grab a G&T?' he asks cheerily.

Tardelli nods his head; the last thing he wants right now is to get involved in a tête-à-tête with this unwelcome interloper.

Briggs-Hamilton returns clutching a tumbler filled to the brim with effervescent liquid as well as a plate of canapés. He takes a long swig of the drink, burps discreetly, and begins to attack the morsels of food on the gold-rimmed plate. The fastidious monseigneur is appalled by the man's lack of table manners; he eats with his mouth open, and makes smacking noises as he bolts through the food at a frenetic pace. Tardelli begins to think that the next hour and a half, before his flight is called, could well seem interminable, but worse is to come: Briggs-Hamilton gets his iPhone from his jacket pocket, presses a contact and begins a conversation, chunks of smoked salmon still visible in his mouth. Tardelli feels physically sick.

'Hi Guy, it's Julian, Julian Briggs-Hamilton,' begins Briggs-Hamilton. 'Long time no see… I'm in New York waiting for a plane… be back tomorrow morning. Look Guy, I need your advice. Can't tell you where I've been, but while I was away got the most amazing photos that I think a lot of people will want to see… no, not of a bleeding orangutan, you bloody fool, something much more interesting… something that could easily appear on front pages of sordid, grubby papers like yours… going to make a fortune… no, sorry can't tell you what it's all about, but when the photos are published they are going to cause some people major embarrassment, the repercussions will be huge… question is, how do I maximise the wonga my work deserves… OK, call it "Religious Leader in Compromising Position"…'

Suddenly, Tardelli is all ears. What on earth is this loathsome man doing? What has he been up to? Where has he been? What religion? What person? He begins to pay particular attention to the snippets of conversation that he can make out. It is obvious that Guy is advising Briggs-Hamilton on the pros and cons of the various options open to him; using an agency to promote his pictures will get maximum, rapid exposure worldwide, but the highest amount he can expect will be roughly 70% of the proceeds. If, on the other hand, he goes straight to a specific newspaper, preferably tabloid, he can get a major upfront payment and subsequent royalties, but only if the photos are explosive and generate global interest.

'Explosive,' says Briggs-Hamilton. 'Is the pope Catholic?... Yup, you can take that as a hint! But no more now – airport lounges have ears.' He looks pointedly at Tardelli. 'I'll fill you in when I see you.'

Tardelli jumps. As a man of the cloth he is obviously meant to believe in miracles, but the coincidence is just too impossible to believe. Surely, this wretch of a human being cannot possibly have discovered the whereabouts of the missing pope? He turns his attention back to Briggs-Hamilton, who is finishing the conversation. 'I'm on UA29 to Heathrow. I think it arrives about half past seven tomorrow morning... Terminal Four, OK... Who did you say you are going to get to meet me?... Global Press International, who the hell are they?... Really?... OK. Catch up with you tomorrow. Bye.'

Briggs-Hamilton stumbles off to the bar area to refill his glass, leaving his camera on the table. It is in playback mode and a picture is displayed on the screen. Although it is on the other side of the wooden surface, Tardelli can just make out that it is of a beach scene, with some form of primitive-looking house in the background. There are a couple of people in the foreground; looks like two women and a bearded man, but he cannot be certain. Two women and a tall bearded man? Surely not. But it could well fit in with the gist of the telephone conversation he has just heard. Tardelli begins to feel a wave of nauseous excitement in the pit of his stomach. When Briggs-Hamilton returns Tardelli seizes the opportunity; he has to find out where the man has been.

'Heading home?' he asks.

'Too bloody true. Been away from civilisation for far too long,' mumbles a bleary-eyed Briggs-Hamilton.

'I would have thought that New York, for the most part, was reasonably civilised,' replies Tardelli.

'Haven't been in New York,' slurs the increasingly drunk naturalist.

'So you're in transit?'

Even though he is somewhat the worse for wear, Briggs-Hamilton is suddenly on the alert. His previously monosyllabic partner is now beginning to sound more like the notorious Grand Inquisitor Tomás de Torquemada, enquiring into the nature of a victim's religious predilections. He is immediately suspicious.

'What's it to you?' he replies brusquely.

'Nothing at all, nothing at all, just making conversation to pass the time.'

Briggs-Hamilton retreats into sullen silence, and stares fixedly out of the window at the departing and arriving planes, as if he is gazing upon one of the Seven Wonders of the Ancient World. Tardelli comes to the conclusion that the man is not going to give anything away, in particular his original point of departure. The silence becomes oppressive. Tardelli looks at his watch. UA40, bound for Rome, will be departing in about an hour. He quickly calculates the time in Rome. It is now just after four in the afternoon in New York; that means it will be nine at night in Rome, or possibly ten – he can never keep up with the machinations of daylight saving. No matter; perhaps he should contact Cuella and apprise him of his suspicions. If he does make the call he certainly cannot do it in front of his suspect, so he gathers up his belongings and takes his leave of Briggs-Hamilton, who pointedly ignores him. Tardelli goes to the other end of the business class lounge, but stands where he can continue to keep an eye on his erstwhile companion, gets his iPhone, draws out Cuella from his list of contacts and presses the icon.

*

Four thousand miles away in the Eternal City, Cuella is at dinner in a sumptuous dining room in the Palazzo Medievale. He is entertaining a couple of visiting cardinals from South America, and this has given him the opportunity to push the culinary boat far into the middle of the ocean. The veal *scaloppini* with morel mushrooms is excellent, and the Montestefano 2004 is the most perfect accompaniment. When he feels his phone vibrate in his pocket he is not best pleased. He insists that dinner is the one time of day his staff may not contact him. He considers ignoring it altogether and blasting the miscreant the following morning, but, on impulse, he checks to see who has the temerity to contact him at this most sacred time. It's that idiot Tardelli; what in the name of all that is holy does he want at this time of day?

Cuella excuses himself to his dinner guests, and goes into a small antechamber off the dining room.

'What the blazes do you want?' he growls.

'I think I've found him... well, not actually found him... but I think I might know someone who knows where he is... it's a miracle... I can't believe it... God is great... He works in a most mysterious way... but I really do think I've found him... or someone who does...'

'Stop babbling and tell me what the bloody hell you're talking about,' whispers Cuella, anxious not to allow his use of immodest language to reach the ears of the cardinals in the other room. Tardelli brings him up to date with his encounter with Briggs-Hamilton.

'What flight did you say he was on?' he asks at the end of Tardelli's confused discourse.

'UA29 arriving at Terminal Four at about seven thirty in the morning.'

'Did you catch his name?'

'It was a long name. I think it had three words.'

'Very helpful,' mocks Cuella.

Tardelli considers: 'His first name was Julian, but I just can't remember the other two.'

'And he's being met by?' Tardelli pauses. For a terrifying couple of moments he can't remember; what on earth did the man say?

'Come on, man, think,' roars Cuella, oblivious to the effect his bellow has on the occupants of the other room.

'... Global... Global Press International,' replies a highly relieved Tardelli. 'Global Press International... I'm sure that's it... yes that's it alright.'

'Say nothing to anyone about this, especially when you

get back to this cesspit of rumour and intrigue,' says Cuella, and then he does something particularly unusual. 'Well done, Angelo, you have done well.' He ends the call.

Four thousand miles away in the United Airlines Club lounge, a bemused and relieved Tardelli stares at the phone in amazement, and then he does something particularly unusual: displaying a new-found confidence, he goes over to the bar and pours himself another huge Jack Daniels. It is a reward richly deserved!

III:VIII

Produrre il Papa

It is over a year since our beloved Pope Timothy suffered a stroke and was moved to Castel Gandolfo to recuperate. Since then we have had only occasional updates from the authorities as to his progress towards recovery. There have been no images of him in either pictorial or video form. Rumours abound that he is dead or that he is close to death; some 'informed sources' have even claimed that he has completely disappeared, although this has been denied by the Vatican Secretariat.

It is time that those in authority within the Holy See are open and transparent with us, the people. We need to know how he is. We have a right to know his condition and the prognosis for his future. This paper is of the view that, for the good of all loving Catholics and for the millions of devoted followers across the world to the One True Faith, the Vatican must PRODURRE IL PAPA!

In normal circumstances, Cuella would have been appalled by the tone of the comment column in the leading Catholic newspaper in Italy, but as he sips his morning coffee, he is sanguine about the situation. Based on his conversation with Tardelli the previous evening, plans have been put in place to meet a man called Julian at Heathrow. While he does not know the specific details, he is convinced that, within the next couple of days, he will learn of the whereabouts of the miscreant and his associates. Then the people can have their pope back, but perhaps not quite in the way they might have hoped. A smile breaks out across his face – but it is one that not even a mother would love.

III:IX

Reginald Alexander Potts (Radley College and Oriel College, Oxford) is a man at peace with the world. He loves his job. It is not exactly the sort of profession originally envisaged for him by his father when the child was born twenty-seven years before in the leafy stockbroker belt of the Home Counties, but Potty, as he is affectionately called by all who know him, could not care less. An undistinguished intellectual career at school would normally have disbarred him from thoughts of academe, especially at a leading university, but Potty had one enormous advantage. He was the outstanding oarsman of his generation at Radley, and, in his final year, had stroked the school's eight to a stunning victory in the Princess Elizabeth Challenge Cup at the Henley Royal Regatta. As a result, despite his obvious intellectual shortcomings (one tutor later describing him as being capable of communicating only through the medium of monosyllabic grunts), he found that university admissions officers fell over themselves to offer him a place within their establishment. Oriel College at Oxford was an obvious choice, given the dominance the institution had demonstrated in the sport of rowing for generations. Within a remarkably short space of time he was a permanent feature of the Oxford eight, again in the stroke seat, and was part of two victorious crews in the annual Boat Race with Cambridge on the River Thames. Given Potty's pre-eminence among his peers in the noble pursuit of paddling, one might have assumed that he would become President of the University Boat Club; but his total inability to string more than a couple of simple sentences together rendered any meaningful dealings with the media, and teammates alike, totally inconceivable. However, he did have his uses as a 'poster boy' for the Oxford crew. At well over six feet tall, with an impressive physique, flaxen shoulder-length hair and boyish good looks, he was a 'natural' – the camera loved him.

But today Potty is a happy man as he drives a Mercedes Benz S class saloon towards the short-stay car park at London Heathrow Terminal Four. It is not his car, for he is merely employed by Heathrow VIP Intercontinental Transfers to ferry the great and the good, or at least those who think that they are great and good, between the airport and their destination within the immediate environs of the metropolis. However, the menial nature of his chosen vocation does not concern Potty in the slightest. It is still only just before seven in the morning, but he has already had a two-hour training session on the Tideway, with his coach Buster Alfredson, in preparation for The Diamond Challenge Sculls at Henley, which is now only a couple of months away. The day job is a means to an end: it feeds his passion and gives him time and space to pursue the love of his life. Potty is already looking forward to an afternoon in the gym, followed by another workout on the river in the early evening. All he has to do first is to pick up a chap by the name of Briggs-Hamilton, on UA29 from Newark, and take him across the city to the offices of Global Press International in Docklands – piece of cake. On the top-stitched, beautifully upholstered seat next to him, he has the distinctive red and white Global Press International sign board, with Briggs-

Hamilton's name printed on both sides. His peaked chauffeur cap sits proudly on top of the board.

Potty drives the car into the short-stay car park and goes down to the second floor. Passengers from UA29 will not be emerging into the arrivals hall for nearly an hour, but he prides himself on his punctuality and, as it has been known for transatlantic arrivals to be early, especially if they have the benefit of a trailing wind, he is determined to be on time. He strolls into the terminal, pops over to Costa Coffee for an espresso and wanders over to the arrivals gate. Potty is a bit of a softy; he loves watching the happiness generated by the reunions taking place in front of him: children fling themselves into the arms of fathers returning from business trips; lovers embrace and kiss lingeringly; and elderly parents, probably from the look of them returning from Caribbean cruises, are welcomed by middle-aged 'children'. He sips his coffee, greeting board under his arm, and awaits developments. Suddenly he becomes aware that there are a couple of rather large men standing very close by. He moves slightly to one side in order to give them more room, but they move as well and give every impression of being glued to him. His every motion is matched by theirs. To say the least it is somewhat disturbing. Things become even more disconcerting when one of them whispers softly into his right ear:

'You are waiting for Julian?' Potty has a quick check of his board.

'Yes, why?'

'UA29 from Newark?'

'Why?'

'Answer the question.' The voice is loaded with threat, menace and is, quite obviously, not English.

'Yes.'

'Come with us.'

'If you don't mind I'd really rather not. I might miss my client.'

The men are now almost welded to him and, much to his surprise, Potty feels something, rather like a small electric razor, thrust into the base of his back. Reginald Alexander Potts is a large man and he is also a brave man. He turns to face his verbal assailants, and is confronted by the sight of two huge individuals towering above his own, not inconsiderable, six-foot-three-inch frame. The one closest to him is holding the weapon under a gabardine raincoat, and bears more than a passing resemblance to an unfriendly mountain gorilla who is having a particularly trying day.

'You come with us now.'

'Don't be ridiculous,' responds Potty testily. 'If you don't piss off, I'll call the police.'

'I ain't gonna ask you again,' says the gorilla reasonably.

'Sod off,' replies Potty, with a great deal more conviction than he actually feels.

There is a soft fizzing sound; Potty experiences a second of blinding pain in the base of his back, then he blacks out completely and collapses onto the floor, much to the horror of those around him.

'Don't worry,' the gorilla reassures the bystanders. 'He often has these attacks. We know what to do. He'll be OK.' With that they haul the unfortunate Potty out of the arrivals hall, taking the greeting board and cap with them, and thrust him into a waiting BMW, which drives off in the direction of the Southern Perimeter Road. The leading thug puts on the cap, picks up the board, and takes his place near the doors leading from the arrivals hall.

An hour later, after an interminable wait at Immigration and a lengthy argument with a belligerent customs officer, who requires detailed answers as to the provenance of Julian's Sony camera, a tired, dishevelled, angry, annoyed Briggs-Hamilton is met by the 'representative' sent from Global Press International. The world famous naturalist is whisked away to the 'meeting' which will change, and subsequently end, his life. He goes to sleep in the back of the car oblivious to his fate. The Mercedes heads not for Docklands, but rather a small, secluded village on the outskirts of Cambridge, where Briggs-Hamilton will be encouraged to share, with persistent and often brutal interrogators, his knowledge of the whereabouts of the missing pope.

Potty, on the other hand, is more fortunate. He is found twelve hours later, battered and bruised, but alive, on an isolated country lane just off the B3055, not far from Brockenhurst Manor Golf Club in the New Forest. The poor man is totally mystified and bemused as to what has just happened to him. He has no recollection of the events which led up to his collapse in the terminal, and is unable to assist the police with their enquiries into the disappearance of Julian Briggs-Hamilton, who it transpires never turned up at the offices of Global Press International. They suspect that Potty has had some role in the abduction, but there is absolutely no evidence linking him to what is looking increasingly like a crime. Two days later, upon his return to Heathrow VIP Intercontinental Transfers, his employment is terminated with immediate effect.

III:X

You're watching BBC News 24 with me, Simon Brown, and Anita Harrington. Before the headlines at 1130 we have an item of breaking news from our Look East studio. Police in Cambridge, looking for the missing BBC presenter and naturalist Julian Briggs-Hamilton, have discovered the body of a man near the town of St Ives, some thirteen miles from the university city. It was found by a couple, walking their dog on Hemingford Meadow, at approximately six thirty this morning. No further details have been released, but sources locally have suggested that it is indeed the body of Mr Briggs-Hamilton, who has not been seen since arriving at Heathrow last Thursday on a flight from Newark, New York. He had been on temporary leave of absence from the BBC and was thought to have been working on a forthcoming project, somewhere in the Caribbean. As I say, no details have been released but we'll keep you updated if and when further information becomes available.

IV

PARADISUM PERDIDT

IV:I

Even by the miserably low standards of twenty-first-century politicians, the Right Honourable James Alexander Porteous, Minister of Education for the nation of Grande Batture, is a most unprepossessing example of his profession – if indeed it can lay claim to being called a profession. Dressed in a bespoke Savile Row worsted three-piece suit, university college tie and black patent leather shoes, James is not exactly attired for the climate of a blazingly hot tropical paradise; he appears, sartorially at least, to be the proverbial fish out of water. He peers myopically out at the world through thick-rimmed prescription sunglasses that, no doubt, would have found some measure of favour with the notorious Tonton Macoute on Haiti. Behind his back, though never to his face, his cabinet colleagues refer to him as *The Cocoya*, in reference to a West African spirit who devours children and then turns them into drastically different shapes. Many feel that his radically conservative education policies have much the same effect on the unfortunate children of Grande Batture.

Perhaps one should not be all that harsh on James because, it could be argued, for most of his life he, as the historian G R Elton once said in reference to the Crown of England, had been the plaything of forces he could not control. While still an infant in arms, his father had fled the warmth of Grande Batture after a particularly bruising, and near lethal, confrontation with President Jimarcus Deval Walcott. The family was uprooted to the bleak, cold, austere climate of Aberdeenshire in Scotland, where his father had found work as a mechanical engineer servicing the nation's growing oil exploration industry. It was a harsh environment for the child especially when, seduced by all things Scottish, his obviously Carib father: changed the family's name to Porteous; renounced his former citizenship and took up golf in the summer and curling in the winter. He had even started wearing a kilt on high days and holidays. Unfortunately this had the effect of making him the subject of ridicule in the small village in Aberdeenshire where they lived. His father remained completely unaware of the sniggers behind his back, but his son, a sensitive lad, was hideously embarrassed by the grotesque transformation. Thus, James became an isolated child with few friends, spending most of his time alone in a drafty, freezing bedroom reading voraciously, devouring at least two books a week. At the age of eleven it was no surprise, to his parents or his teachers, that he won a scholarship to a minor public school in the north of England.

James was sent away to board at the school, only returning home at half-term and for longer holidays. It was a miserable and distressing experience. He was bullied incessantly and responded by adopting an arrogant, superior attitude that only made his plight worse. The problem was that he was significantly brighter than his peers; he knew it and they knew it, so the wanton boys responded in the only way they knew how: they terrorised him. Six long, dreadful years passed, although as he grew older the bullying subsided, only to be replaced by a form of social exclusion, which, in many ways, was worse than the physical violence. The staff expressed concern, but it was hard to be totally sympathetic when it was obvious that the boy brought a measure of the distress on himself, largely through the total contempt with which he treated his classmates and his superiors. All parties were relieved when his time at the school came to an end, and the news finally broke that he had been awarded a place at Lady Margaret Hall in Oxford.

Life at Oxford was a revelation. Liberated from boorish schoolmasters and even more boorish peers, not to mention liberated from ghastly cross-country runs across the icy Cumbrian fells, he finally found people who were his intellectual equal. The fact that many of them were also socially inept and immature was an added advantage – he 'fitted in' beautifully. James threw himself into a number of societies and groups ranging from science to international relations. He always attended Oxford Union debates and was even considered briefly, by many of his contemporaries, as a serious contender for the post as President of the Union. He found that he had a talent for writing, and became a regular contributor to *Cherwell*, *Isis Magazine* and even *The Owl Journal*. All in all it was a full and challenging three years, probably the happiest time of his life, but he did not leave with the expected First in English. Much to the surprise of all his tutors, he left with a mere 2:1 Honours degree.

Obtaining employment presented no problems. His love of writing and interest in both local and international politics, combined with the connections he had made at Oxford, guaranteed that he would have no trouble securing a position as a journalist, and so it proved to be. Cutting his teeth on a couple of regional newspapers, it was not long before he landed a job as a political correspondent, and later leader writer, for *The Telegraph*; but rapid promotion masked an unpalatable secret: the editors of the two regional papers who had supported his applications for advancement had only done so because they were desperate to be rid of him. To quote, what is known in some circles as, 'management speak': 'Porteous is not a team player'. His arrogance and superiority, especially when dealing with what he regarded as junior menial staff, meant that James was almost universally detested by his 'country' colleagues. His condescending, supercilious attitude continued at *The Telegraph*, where he was aloof, almost to the point of being haughty; his beady, flickering eyes blinking out from behind the thick-framed spectacles, which were constantly balanced on the end of his hawk-like nose. This obvious contempt and disdain for those around him did not go down well, especially among those who regarded themselves as the elite of the profession. It was only a matter of time. Friendly advice to change his attitude went unheeded. Formal warnings were ignored. The 'axe' when it came was brutal. He was given thirty minutes to clear his desk, humiliatingly in front of a largely silent newsroom, and was then frogmarched to the front entrance of the building by a concierge, who made no attempt to hide his pleasure at the widely desired turn of events.

It came as no surprise, given the incestuous nature of the journalistic grapevine, that securing further employment, within the heady realms of the Fourth Estate, proved to be somewhat problematic. Porteous was a proud man, and his unceremonious eviction from *The Telegraph* had left him battered, bruised and, to all intents and purposes, beyond the pale as far as serious prospective employers were concerned. For several months he existed in a social and occupational limbo, brooding on the past and worrying about the future. His salvation, when it arrived, came from a most unlikely and unexpected source. President Dexter Barrington Taylor, on the first ever State Visit to the United Kingdom by a leader of Grande Batture, held a cocktail reception at the Embassy, to which the great and the good of Grande Batturian society resident in London were invited. Such worthies were about as thick on the ground as ticks on a dog in the 'Best in Show' at Crufts, so it was not unexpected when Porteous received an invitation to the ambassadorial beanfeast. During the banal pleasantries, with a morsel of bacon-wrapped jalapeno pepper in one hand and a Painkiller cocktail in the other, Taylor asked him if he had ever thought of returning to the land of his birth; there would be a host of opportunities open for a man with his undoubted talents. James had not previously considered this as an option, but, as the evening wore on, the potential for such a life-changing move appeared more and more attractive. He could be what he had always wanted: a big fish in a little pond; a man of substance and authority. After a few Painkillers, even offering to serve as Grande Batture's ambassador in North Korea would have appeared inviting; so, by the end of the evening, he had made up his mind: like General Douglas MacArthur before him, he would return!

Now, only two years later, his life has been transformed. He has been elected to the country's parliament, and is a senior member of the cabinet with particular responsibility for education. Not only that, he has also been tipped as a future president when the present incumbent steps down after his next term in office. Given that President Taylor is a red-hot favourite to win the forthcoming election, Porteous's future looks very bright indeed. But if things do not work out as envisaged, there is always his rapidly growing Swiss bank account to fall back on; it has grown exponentially since he took over at the ministry. The new school building programme, funded by the strange recluse living down in the south of the island, has offered many profitable opportunities to siphon not inconsiderable amounts of money offshore. The recluse is otherwise known to the inhabitants of Grande Batture as 'The Man', but he has not been seen in public since the day his privately chartered jet touched down at the airport, and he was whisked away to the high security compound where he currently resides. All communications with him are done through a most peculiar little fat man who has absolutely no taste in tropical shirts. It is for Enrico Marquez that Porteous awaits in his somewhat primitive office in the terraced bungalow which passes for the Ministry of Education. The new school, which Briggs-Hamilton passed on the way to the airport, is soon to be finished, and Porteous needs to pass messages to 'The Man' through his intermediary.

Marquez arrives promptly at the arranged time of three o'clock. His shirt today is particularly hideous, combining colours of lime green, red, blue and bright yellow, arranged in an ornate kaleidoscopic pattern, not dissimilar to the worst excesses of the psychedelic art movement of the sixties. His short, fat, hairy legs poke out of khaki shorts, and terminate with brown leather sandals encasing thick, stubby toes. But his brown eyes are wary; from experience, Porteous knows that this man is highly intelligent and has the shrewdness and guile of a cobra evaluating its prey. Pleasantries are exchanged, and the minister gets down to business.

'As you know, Señor Marquez, the school is nearly complete and should be handed over to us in two weeks' time. We are all so very grateful for your employer's generosity and his sincere desire to improve the lives of the people here on Grande Batture. The president has asked me if you would allow us to name the school in honour of him. From our entry records, we see that his name is Hugo Joachim Taveras, and we would be honoured if you could ask him whether we could call it The Hugo Taveras Academy.'

Marquez's face remains impassive. Porteous wonders if the fat man is a card player because, if he is, Enrico would make a formidable opponent.

'I shall discuss your kind offer with Snr Taveras, but I suspect that, in all probability, he will decline. He does not court publicity and seeks no recognition for his philanthropy. He will no doubt suggest that the institution is named after your esteemed president, who has done so much to move Grande Batture into the twenty-first century.'

Porteous has already anticipated this response and is not displeased with the answer; the naming of the school after Dexter Taylor will increase his own personal standing with the president. He moves on.

'I do understand your position, but I would be grateful if you could still ask Snr Taveras. I shall not approach the president until I have heard from you.'

'By all means. I shall convey his answer by this time tomorrow.'

'Thank you. On another matter, we would obviously be greatly honoured if Snr Taveras could attend the formal opening – which we have pencilled in for the 28th of this month.'

'Again, I shall ask upon my return to the compound and get back to you with the answer.'

'Many thanks.' The conversation is so sickeningly polite that it would not be out of place in any of the novels by the Brontë sisters. Porteous plays his trump card.

'Could you also pass these onto Snr Taveras?' He passes a sheaf of papers across to Marquez. 'The children have written individual letters to him, some with pictures, entreating Snr Taveras to attend the ceremony. They have been working on a song in his honour to perform at the opening, and would be bitterly disappointed if he did not attend.'

For the first time Marquez appears to be taken by surprise. He clutches the letters uncomfortably but agrees to give them to his boss. After a couple of sentences of small talk about the potential ferocity of an imminent thunderstorm, he takes his leave. Porteous waits until he hears the sound of Marquez's car fade into the distance, then picks up the phone. He dials a private number at Government House. It is answered on the third ring.

'Well?' asks President Dexter Barrington Taylor.

'He's just gone,' says Porteous. 'I think Taveras will turn down the offer to name the school after him. So, dear president, your name will live on in the community for as long as the school stands…'

'And the other: will he attend the ceremony?'

'It's a little too early to say, but I can't see how he can turn a deaf ear to the entreaties of little children; some of the letters are really quite charming. Marquez is getting back to me tomorrow, so we shall know by mid-afternoon. What I don't understand is why you are so keen for him to attend.'

'Need to know, Alexander, need to know and, quite

frankly, at this stage you do not need to know.' And with that the President of Grande Batture terminates the conversation. He smiles briefly and picks up the phone again. He rings a direct line, deep inside a mediaeval palace, five thousand miles away in the Eternal City. The phone is answered on the first ring.

'Well?' says a deep, dominant and, in some ways, malevolent voice.

'I think I can safely say that we shall be able to deliver the commodity as we agreed in our previous conversation,' replies Taylor.

'Excellent. Upon completion of the transaction you will find, as our transatlantic brethren might say, that the cheque is in the post. Good day.'

Secretary of State Cuella sits back in his opulent chair, in his opulent private apartment, takes a contented puff on his Julius Caesar Churchill cigar, and smiles the smile of a man fully convinced of victory. '"Will you walk into my parlour?" said the spider to the fly,' he whispers. 'Your days, my friend, are numbered.'

IV:II

Blanca Concepcion Fernandez Diaz, previously known as Sister Carmen of the Order of Elena the Servant, has something of a reputation as a typically feisty, hot-blooded, Andalusian woman. She would find it difficult to accept the recommendation of James the Just when he exhorted the early Church to be 'quick to hear, slow to speak and slow to anger'. Carmen has had a great deal to say about the crass stupidity of the pope attending the opening ceremony for the new school. Nearly all the inmates of the 'Sanctuary' agree with her, but the most important member of the group does not agree, and stubbornly refuses to listen to reason. Peter Jackson has said that he wants nothing to do with it and will not attend, nor will Callum Flanagan, but the girls are not prepared to allow the 'Boss' to be left to fend for himself so, with great reluctance, they have agreed to accompany the pope.

So now she finds herself in the back of an aged and battered Cherokee jeep, next to Elvira, following a pick-up truck bearing the pope to the launch of the Dexter Barrington Taylor Academy. Cheering crowds line both sides of the dusty street. It is a blindingly hot day and she is seething. Carmen, however, is oblivious to the noise of the multitude, or the sweet, almost overpowering, bouquet of the golden frangipani trees that line the road. Surely it will all end in disaster. The whole point of the construction of the compound, on a remote Caribbean island, was that He would be able to disappear completely. Now He is standing on the bed of the truck, in full public view, acknowledging the ovation of the crowd, which is lined up three or four deep as they get closer to the school. Some are even throwing flowers and garlands at him.

The cavalcade pulls up at the front entrance of the seashell white academy gleaming in the bright sunlight. The smell of frangipani is immediately replaced by the heady stench of fresh paint. Porteous is there to greet them and escort the party into the relative cool of the entrance foyer. There they are met by President Taylor, pleasantries are exchanged and the party is led into a large, airy assembly hall, filled to overflowing with children in smart blue uniforms, teachers sweating in their gowns and academic regalia, and parents dressed to the nines in their Sunday best. As the pope and the president are led to the stage (the girls have to stand at the back of the hall as no provision has been made for them) there is a burst of applause, which reaches a crescendo as the honoured guests mount the dais.

The ceremony is endless. The headmaster, an elderly French expatriate with a disconcertingly high squeaky voice, sweating profusely under the weight of his woollen hood and black and green silk gown, begins by introducing the 'Distinguished Guests'. His prodigiously long white hair has a disconcerting habit of flopping across his face, and he pushes it back nervously whenever it offends the laws of gravity. The public address system has obviously not been tuned finely, and it is sometimes impossible to hear what he is saying above the monotonous hum of the air conditioning in the background. The first of the eminent panel to speak is Porteous. Having honed his oratorical skills within the confines of the Oxford Union, he is clearly an accomplished speaker, but the content of his peroration, with its oblique references to classical antiquity, is lost on the children and parents and probably most of the staff as well. Finally he closes and sits down to relieved and polite applause. There follows an interminable series of songs, dances and historical tableaux performed by what begins to feel like every child in the school. The headmaster then introduces the president who, given the proximity of the forthcoming election, treats his captive audience to a thorough exposition of his achievements in office and his plans for the future. To give him credit, he warmly, and apparently genuinely, acknowledges the contribution made by Snr Taveras to the school's foundation. However, given what follows after the ceremony, it has to be said that his comments are disingenuous to say the least. At long, long last he turns to a small green and yellow curtain at the back of the stage, pulls back the material and reveals a plaque commemorating the official opening of The Dexter Barrington Taylor Academy; with that the formalities are completed.

The Guests of Honour are ushered into a room behind the stage at the front of the hall. However, Carmen and Elvira are not 'Honoured Guests', so they are obliged to wait in the hall until the dignitaries have been wined and dined. In the meantime they find themselves surrounded and engulfed by the departing families, staff and less important guests. Even if they wanted to join the festivities, it would be impossible to go against this tide of sweating, chattering humanity; but there are people who appear determined to try. The girls watch a group of five men, two of them by their sheer size and dark suits almost certainly bodyguards, who are jostling their way towards the room containing the pope. There is something familiar about one member of the party. Carmen is certain that she has seen the little man in the impeccably cut three-piece suit before, but she can't think where. The heavyweight minders take no prisoners as they push people out of the way, until the entourage is finally at the entrance to the antechamber. They do not bother to knock but just push their way into the room, slamming the door behind them. Time passes. Carmen stares at the closed door, frantically trying to place where she has seen the small man before. Then, suddenly, everything clicks into place: it is Obest Geisinger from the Swiss Guards. She's only ever seen him at a distance but she is sure it is him. Carmen grabs Elvira by the arm and whispers in her ear. Elvira's head jerks round to look at her and then, as one, they begin to push their way towards the antechamber. It seems to take an eternity; people are not willing to move, and the girls lack the weight and physical presence of the bodyguards that had escorted Geisinger across the crowded hall.

When they finally get to the entrance, they are disconcerted to find that the door will not open. The handle will depress but there is obviously something blocking it on the other side. They try pushing at the frame but to no avail. They knock – no answer. The girls retreat into the hall to consider their options. While they are wondering whether it would be worth going outside to see if there is a window or external way in to the room, the door suddenly swings open. The five men and Timothy walk out into the virtually empty auditorium. The interlopers completely surround the pope, who looks rather like an early christian martyr on his way to 'entertain' plebeians in the Coliseum. He sees the girls, makes some eye contact and, with a slight shake of the head, makes it clear that he does not want them to get involved. After all, two suntanned, attractive young women in tight-fitting denim shorts and cotton T-shirts could not possibly be further removed from the pasty, dowdy, plain females who tend to inhabit the convents and religious communities of Rome. But, of course, Carmen comes from Andalusia; she tends to speak her mind – a character trait that her superiors in the Order had not always appreciated or admired. When she had become a nun she had embraced the notion of poverty, accepted the privations of chastity, but had always had a serious issue with the whole concept of obedience. The siren from Sevilla is across the floor of the hall in a flash and confronting Obest Geisinger. Beyond the obvious advantage of surprise, she has one other trump card up her sleeve: her height of five feet eight inches makes her a good three inches taller than the hapless Swiss officer. Carmen does not feel that the situation requires opening small talk; she gets straight down to business.

'What the fucking hell do you think you're doing?' she shouts. This is not necessarily the sort of language that would be normally associated with a former nun from the Order of Elena the Servant, but time away from the confines of the cloisters has broadened her vocabulary somewhat. Perhaps it is the influence of a rather extensive collection of videos and DVDs she found at the compound on her arrival, featuring stand-up comedians such as Richard Pryor and Billy Connolly, which has helped to bring about the remarkable extension of her vocabulary. Anyway, it has the desired effect: Geisinger reacts as if he has just been slapped across the face with a dead and smelly porcupinefish; however, his powers of recovery, as one might expect from the Commandant of the Swiss Guards, are exceptional.

'And who, young lady – although after that outburst I am tempted to use the word advisedly – are you?' he asks.

'I am Blanca Diaz and I am a friend of Snr Taveras. Where are you taking him?'

Before Geisinger can reply one of the other men interjects: 'Well, well, well,' says Monsignor Tardelli, taking off his sunglasses. 'New hair colour and style, Sister Carmen, very fetching, it suits you and, if I may say, a stunning improvement in wardrobe and make-up.' He casts an appreciative look over her suntanned legs. 'I am reminded of that delightful Spanish phrase, *La mona aunque se vista de seda, mona se queda*. It's really rather apt in the circumstances.'

Carmen stares at him in disbelief. The bronzed man in the tropical white suit is a far cry from the austere, nervous, nerdy priest she had known in the papal apartments. She had just not recognised him at all.

Tardelli turns back to Geisinger. 'The phrase, KG, roughly translated, means: although a monkey dresses in silk it is still a monkey. Herr Geisinger, I have the pleasure to introduce sisters Carmen and Elvira, who used to reside in the convent of the Order of Elena the Servant in our own beloved Vatican City, and who were meant to look after domestic arrangements for the pope. I'm not sure that the current arrangement featured in the original job description. Anyway, they appear to have had, what our American friends would call, a 'makeover'. I am sure that the mother superior will be more than prepared to welcome them back with open arms. We do have plenty of space on the plane to expedite a quite extraordinary rendition.'

Carmen looks at him in disgust and then turns to face President Taylor, who is standing on the fringes of the group. 'You had something to do with all this, didn't you?' she says bitterly. 'I don't know why or how you did it, but you've betrayed the very man who has done so much good for this god-forsaken, fleapit of a country. You have stabbed him in the back. *Hijo de puta!* Judas!' She spits in his face.

Taylor is seemingly unfazed by this outburst of anger and hostility. 'No, my dear,' he says evenly, 'I am not a Judas. Think of me more as a modern-day Pontius Pilate. I want nothing more to do with this man. He has served his purpose and now it is time to move on. Have a good flight!'

The president walks away. Geisinger gestures to the minders, and the girls are thrust into place on either side of the pope who, by now, is as white as a sheet. The group are muscled through a side entrance to the building, and herded into a waiting minibus bearing the school's name and logo. Somehow the phrase, '*Honesty, Industry and Integrity*' seems faintly incongruous in the circumstances. The van is driven at high speed through the main gates, past scattered remnants of the crowd that has still not completely dispersed. Among their number is Jackson who, while totally disapproving of the insane exercise, has found it impossible to stay away and not witness events at first hand. He is appalled but, in all truth, not terribly surprised to see the disastrous proceedings unfold as his friends are driven off in the direction of the airport, surrounded by characters whom Central Casting might well deem suitable to play the part of villains in the next Bond movie. A large, black and rather grubby hand taps him on the shoulder.

'I am somewhat surprised that you weren't included on the guest list,' says a deep, resonant, distinctly stereotypically Caribbean voice. 'I thought you were well in with those people.'

Jackson turns. He recognises the man as the proprietor of the only supermarket on the island, from which the group have been obliged to purchase all their essential provisions.

'I don't know what you mean,' he says.

'I thought you were one of them,' replies the man pointing towards the van, which is now speeding into the distance in a cloud of dust and dirt.

'Good God no!' exclaims Jackson, all thoughts of succumbing to the sin of blasphemy lost in the terror of revelation generated by the moment. 'I have had virtually nothing to do with them at all. I was no more than a general dogsbody and errand boy.'

The tall slender man, wearing a filthy blue and orange New York Knicks T-shirt, looks perplexed. 'That's strange,' he says, pointing after the van. 'It looks like they are heading for the airport. Surely, if they were heading back to the Sanctuary they would have been taking the road south.'

Jackson is intrigued. 'Sanctuary?' he asks.

'Why surely,' says the man, sounding more like Paul Robeson than Paul Robeson himself. 'Look at it this way. Foreigners arrive from nowhere, out of the blue you might say. They lock themselves away in the remotest part of the island. The ring road is blocked in both directions not far from their compound, and the fences built around it are totally impenetrable. Guards patrol the perimeter twenty-four hours a day. They must be hiding from something. They could be international criminals for all we know. I reckon people have been looking for them and now they've been discovered. Pity, because they were very good for business.'

The supermarket owner is disconcertingly close to the truth. Peter takes his leave somewhat abruptly, and heads back to his ancient, somewhat infirm and rusting Citroën Five, intending to follow the party to the airport. It seems futile but in the circumstances there is nothing else he can do. He arrives at the airstrip's perimeter fence just in time to see the ensemble being escorted onto a small executive jet. The pope seems resigned to his fate; his head hangs down and his gait is laboured. Carmen, on the other hand, is fighting all the way, but her diminutive size renders the struggle futile against the combined efforts of the black-suited thugs. The doors of the jet are hurriedly closed, and within seconds the engines are powering up and the Gulf Stream is taxiing out onto the runway. The kidnapping has been incredibly well planned. As the plane blasts down the tarmac and screeches into a cloudless sky, he returns to his car, bereft and alone. It is also true to say he is exceedingly frightened; surely it can only be a matter of time before they return for him. Before he can reach the car, he finds his way blocked by a stunningly attractive young woman wearing a highly colourful floral dress. She is distraught and has obviously been crying.

'Why?' she says, to nobody in particular. 'Why are they deserting us? Ever since they arrived, the island has changed. Until they came, living here was like existing in hell. We had nothing. Now we have: the new school, the hospital, the airport. There are jobs for the people and things are so much better. So why would they go? Why would they leave? I just don't understand.' She looks at Peter imploringly. 'Why have your friends deserted us?'

Peter looks at her, emotions in turmoil. 'How the hell should I know?' he responds. 'I don't know what you're thinking but I have no knowledge of these people. They mean nothing to me.' And with that he stalks back to his swelteringly hot vehicle. Slumped across the steering wheel he takes a deep breath, and wonders what in God's name to do next. It's all a terrible, terrible mess, and he has no idea how he and Flanagan are going to get out of the situation.

On the spur of the moment, he decides to go into the airport building to see if he can find out the destination of the executive jet. He parks the battered car in the pristine new short-stay car park, and goes into the air-conditioned luxury of the terminal. His cheap rubber-soled shoes squeak noisily on the grey, marble-effect concourse as he makes his way to the information desk. The place is virtually deserted mainly due to the fact that the entire airport caters for only three to four flights a day, and the last has already departed. The flight information boards are advising only about planes that will leave in the morning.

The information desk is staffed by a man in his early twenties, who is reading a well-thumbed travel magazine. There is obviously not a lot else to keep him occupied at this time of day. He is somewhat inappropriately dressed, given the nature of the climate, in a three-piece suit, starched white shirt and bright plain yellow tie.

'How can I help you, sir?' he enquires politely. It must be something of a welcome diversion to have a client with whom to engage.

'The flight that just left, the small jet – do you know where it was heading?' asks Jackson.

The man does a double take. 'I'm sorry, sir, can you be more specific?'

'The Gulf Stream – what was its destination?'

There is a long, lingering pause; the official is obviously formulating an appropriate response. It takes rather a long time. He appears embarrassed.

'I'm sorry, sir, but I am afraid that information is highly confidential. Even if you were to have a connection with some of the passengers on board, I would have to refer you to the Office of the President. Do you have a connection with the flight, sir, which would enable me to expedite a positive resolution to the question you have posed?'

Leaving aside the overly ornate flowery language, which might well imply an education obtained, at considerable expense, in an international context rather than in one of the hideously deprived schools of the 'old' Grande Batture, Jackson is stumped. He has nowhere to go.

'No,' he says. 'I was just intrigued. I have no meaningful connection with the people on the plane. I do not know them.' He turns and walks out of the terminal.

Once outside the building, Peter weeps.

IV:III

L ater that evening, back at the Sanctuary, which is now a manifestly inappropriate nomenclature, Jackson and Flanagan meet to consider their options. It is obvious that Grande Batture is no longer the safe haven it once appeared. Their hideout has been discovered, and it is inconceivable to think that there won't be further incursions by the Vatican authorities into their lives. Flanagan assures Jackson that money is not a problem; he still has access to accounts held by *Philanthropos Tropos* which, despite all the spending on the 'worthy causes', has several million dollars in available funds. The problem is where to go from here. Their forged travel documents proved their value during the escape from Rome, but the pair has no way of knowing if they retain the same level of authenticity that served them so well in the past.

They agree on three things. First, they are not safe in Grande Batture: the Vatican cabal obviously knows where they are, and may well attempt to effect an appropriate solution to their continued existence – possibly through an enforced return to Rome or, equally likely, permanent termination. In the circumstances it would be insane to remain on the island. The second decision is more immediate. Flanagan will go to the bank in the morning to meet Luigi Pedrosa, and will endeavour to facilitate the release of sufficient money to ease their departure from Grande Batture. Finally, though less specifically, they agree that a move to an LEDC is going to be more advisable than an attempt to enter the United States or Europe; fewer questions are likely to be asked, especially if one has the means to grease palms or offer brown envelopes.

In a previous incarnation they would have ended the meeting in prayer; but tonight they content themselves with the best part of two bottles of Jamaican rum, with the result that they sleep the sleep of the innocently intoxicated – deep, pleasing and untroubled. Sadly, after tonight, they will never sleep again.

*

The following morning, very much hungover and feeling the worse for wear, Flanagan is ushered into Luigi Pedrosa's plush office at the bank. Despite the state-of-the-art air conditioning, the air is malodorous with the stench of stale cigar smoke. For the first time in their relationship, Pedrosa appears to be half-hearted in his greeting. Flanagan turns down the offer of coffee even though, given his semi-inebriated condition, it might be in his best interests to accept, and the two men get down to business. The disgraced cleric says that he wishes to release funds from the *Philanthropos* account in cash, in order to meet some unspecified obligations arising from the construction of the new school. Pedrosa looks uneasy.

'I'm afraid that will not be possible at this time,' he says.

'Not possible?' Flanagan responds in disbelief.

'I fear not.'

'Why on earth not?' says Flanagan, alarm bells screaming in his befuddled brain. 'By my reckoning there's still over three million dollars left in the account.'

'Three million, four hundred and twenty thousand, eight hundred and seventy three dollars and forty-seven cents to be precise,' replies the meticulously correct Pedrosa.

'I'm sorry, I don't understand.'

'Your account has been frozen.'

Flanagan experiences a moment of blind panic. His heart rate rises. His hands become clammy. His left eyelid begins to twitch – always a sign that he is under pressure. He strives to maintain control. 'Who has blocked the account?' he asks.

'Well, I fear that it is more than a mere block.'

'What the bloody hell does that mean?'

'The fact is that the government has sequestered all monies in the *Philanthropos* account. As an honest and legitimate banker,' (Pedrosa is not above being somewhat economical with the truth) 'I abhor the authorities interfering in my clients' affairs, but there is absolutely nothing I can do. My hands are tied.' He shrugs his shoulders apologetically.

Flanagan is stunned. It simply can't be possible. He and Jackson have just about enough cash in hand to survive for a couple of months, but only if they are careful. After all, the cost of living on the island is relatively cheap, but there is no way they have sufficient funds to get off the damned rock, let alone set up a new life in some other part of the world. They are trapped. It is hopeless.

Flanagan then does something that takes both him and Pedrosa totally by surprise: he bursts into tears. His body shakes violently and he sobs uncontrollably and inconsolably, as the desperate nature of his predicament becomes brutally apparent. Pedrosa, sitting on the other side of the large oak desk, is totally nonplussed, not at all sure how to proceed. Just for something to do, he presses a button on the intercom, asks for coffee, sits back in his chair, lights a small vile-smelling cheroot and waits for the storm to subside. It takes fully ten minutes before Flanagan is in some semblance of control. He slurps noisily at his coffee, and then begins to gabble, at times almost incoherently.

'It was a crazy idea from the start,' he moans. 'We should have known we would never get away with it, but the bloody man was so persuasive…'

'Taveras?' asks Pedrosa.

'If that's what you want to call him,' says Flanagan.

'What do you call him?'

'Don't you know?'

'No, I have absolutely no idea.'

'I thought you might have guessed, after all you are Italian.'

'I suppose it never crossed my mind to question his identity. In my profession it is usually better not to ask too many questions,' muses Pedrosa.

'We call him José – José Ignacio,' says Flanagan.

'So he's actually Spanish?' asks the banker. Flanagan nods. There is a long silence while Pedrosa tries to make sense of the information, then the light dawns on the banker; it is a moment of pure revelation and Pedrosa's mouth drops in surprise.

'You mean?… No!… Surely not… But he's… he's had a…' The words evaporate into the air conditioning. There is silence; the silence that comes with perfect understanding.

In the half hour that follows Flanagan reveals all; frankly he has nothing left to lose. The last two remaining members of the Sanctuary have nowhere to go once the money runs out. Flanagan finds the process cathartic, almost confessional, but this time Pedrosa is the confessor and Flanagan is the penitent. It is an interesting reversal of roles!

The bank manager finds himself in an interesting position. His 'clients', without their leader to guide them, appear to be something of a liability but, as a Sicilian, and so by definition a devout Catholic, he has an instinctive sympathy for men of the cloth, especially those who have fallen on hard times. *But*, he thinks, *there must be an angle, some way to derive pecuniary and political advantage from the situation.* Nothing springs to mind immediately, but he is convinced that there must be an opportunity or two lurking in the wings. For now, he decides that doing nothing really is the only sensible option. He goes over to Flanagan, who has graduated from coffee to Courvoisier, and puts a consoling arm around the man's shoulders.

'I am so very sorry,' he says soothingly. 'At the moment I cannot see a way out of your predicament, but I have friends, good friends, influential friends who might be able to come up with a solution which, at the very least, might be able to delay the inevitable. Go back to the compound, keep your head down, and give me forty-eight hours to see what I can come up with.'

Flanagan looks at him much in the way a Springer Spaniel might regard an indulgent owner approaching him with a morsel of tender fillet steak. He is grateful; ever so grateful; desperately grateful – and begins to hope that there might be some way out of this terrible, terrible impasse. Flanagan takes his leave from his new benign benefactor, and sets off for the compound with a spring in his step and a sprinkling of optimism dribbling through his veins.

Alone in the office Pedrosa looks at the time on his Patek Philippe masterpiece. At this time of year Italy is five hours ahead of Grande Batture, so the object of his call should be well and truly awake by now. He taps out a series of numbers on his Vertu Signature phone, waits for it to ring nineteen times and then hangs up. He dials for a second time and lets it ring eight times before terminating the connection. Then he dials again and this time disconnects after seven rings. His Provenzano codename has been activated. He rings once more and the call is answered immediately. The voice at the other end of the line is obviously that of an old man, but, even at a distance of around 7000 kilometres, there is no mistaking the authority behind the quavering delivery.

'*Buon giorno*, my dear Luigi, this is an unexpected pleasure. It has been far too long since we talked. What can a frail, impotent old man in faraway Leonforte possibly do for such a globally renowned financier?'

Pedrosa allows himself a brief smile. Only one of the man's three qualifications is at all accurate: true he is seventy-four years old, but he also has a string of nubile, much younger, mistresses, and practises Krav Maga (the Israeli martial art designed to enhance a street-fighting mentality) for two hours every morning. The man is old, but he is most certainly not impotent or frail. He is also the leader of one of the most feared Mafia clans in Italy, with connections to crime syndicates across the world. It would be a foolish man who underestimated Don Calogero.

'Don Calogero, what a delight it is to hear your voice,' he begins. 'And how is Donna Antonia?'

'Well, she is very well, for her age,' the old man replies. 'She will be so pleased to learn that you have phoned.'

There is a pause, and then Pedrosa begins: 'Don Calogero, I'm not too sure where to begin, but I have one hell of a story to tell you…'

*

As the phone call to Don Calogero gets underway, Flanagan is driving back to the compound, smiling and whistling a happy tune, but blissfully unaware that he is being tailed by a car containing two dark-suited, mean-looking, swarthy Italians. In only a few short hours' time, they will ensure that Flanagan and Jackson never leave the 'safety' of the Sanctuary.

V

ARBITRIUM

V:I

Abbess Francesca Adriana Escatores swears loudly, eloquently and blasphemously when the phone in her office rings shrilly, breaking the torpid tranquillity of a blazingly hot Italian afternoon. To put it mildly, the Mother Superior of the Order of Elena the Servant, the convent of which is located just outside the hallowed environs of the Vatican City, is irked beyond measure. This is meant to be her time, her private time, a time when she gives strict instructions not to be interrupted or disturbed. It really is too much; can nobody obey simple orders?

It is often said that a woman is never more beautiful than when she's angry, however, this is not the case with Abbess Francesca. She might be shrouded from head to foot in the black habit of her vocation, but any independent observer would readily agree that she is a devastatingly good-looking woman all the time. True, her face is the only part of her anatomy on 'public display', but it is a glorious face – one might say a 'heavenly' face. Her skin is flawless and lightly tanned, with deep brown penetrating eyes hinting at the possibility of some form of North African antecedence. This is a distinct possibility because, when only an infant in arms, she was taken in as a foundling by the Escatores family, one of the more belligerent clans within the Sicilian Cosa Nostra, and so her actual parentage is a matter of some speculation.

Ironically the Escatores family, while notorious for exterminating all who opposed them with a brutality that would have made even Caligula blanch, were also deeply religious, and saw it as their Christian duty to take care of the vulnerable and needy. Thus the enchantingly beautiful child grew up deep in the mountains of Sicily, surrounded by love and affection, while the family went about their day-to-day business of ensuring that those outside their immediate circle, who had the temerity to challenge their pre-eminence, remained poor, needy and oppressed.

When the girl turned sixteen a family conference was held to decide her future path in life. Despite her staggering beauty, or perhaps because of it, it was decreed by her adoptee grandfather, Don Calogero Salvatore Escatores, that she should pursue a vocation within one of the religious orders; God in his goodness had given the child to them, now it was time to give her back to God. She would devote her life to prayer, interceding with the Blessed Virgin for the family's redemption and ultimate salvation, although what was left unsaid was that this might prove a somewhat daunting and possibly impossible task. There were no dissenting voices to this pronouncement; Francesca was not consulted, her opinion was of no consequence because, within the Family, nobody opposed the Don – his word was law.

Fortunately the girl, throughout her formative years, had demonstrated great intellectual ability and an outward piety which, while somewhat theatrical, was seemingly genuine. She had also developed an iron will and acute political acumen, almost certainly as a result of growing up in a family where the works of Machiavelli could easily have been prescribed bedtime reading. Thus a combination of her personal qualities, not to mention the staggering levels of mediocrity found within the upper echelons of most holy orders, meant that by the time she was thirty she was already a mother superior, admittedly with one of the more minor religious communities.

Now the bloody phone is ringing and she is not best pleased. Wednesday and Saturday afternoons are sacrosanct, a time when she can commune with her father confessor and escape the stresses and rigours of religious life. She grasps the jangling impediment to her afternoon's serenity and lifts the ancient Bakelite receiver to her ear.

'Yes?' she shouts angrily.

If Don Calogero Escatores is surprised by the brusque nature of her salutation, he does not show it. '*Ciao, mia bella bocca di Leone. Come stai oggi?*'

There is only one person in the world that would liken her to a beautiful snapdragon. Francesca immediately softens and, in an instant, she is translated back to the sunshine-filled days of her childhood when, hand in hand, she and *Nonno* would explore the gardens of the house near Leonforte in Sicily, and take delight in the multi-coloured snapdragons reaching up to the heavens on the ancient, burnt orange, shaded walls.

'*Nonno*, oh, *Nonno*, it is so good to hear your voice,' she says. 'I was only thinking about you and *Nonna* this morning. How are you both?'

'As well as can be expected at our time of life, I suppose,' says the old man. 'I would have thought that in your vocation telling the truth was of paramount importance but, thank you, I shall treasure your obviously sincere felicitations. By the way, you'll be pleased to know that the snapdragons are truly magnificent this year.'

Aware that the Don is not a man prone to making courtesy calls, the Mother Superior of the Order of Elena the Servant decides it is time to get down to business. 'How can I be of assistance, Grandfather?' she asks.

'I understand that you have very recently welcomed back into the superfluity two recalcitrant and errant sisters who have been on an exotic, and possibly erotic, sabbatical from the sanctuary of your venerable precincts?'

It is posed as a question but, in all reality, it is said as a statement of fact. Francesca is shocked. Only an extremely small group of her immediate acolytes are aware that Carmen and Elvira are back in the convent, and held in solitary confinement in an isolated, disused part of the building. She maintains a discreet silence while she gathers her thoughts together. The old man continues, totally ignoring the lack of an immediate response to his question:

'And were you also aware that the young ladies were returned, to the bosom of the Holy See, in the company of an extremely important, but probably somewhat fragile, package?'

No, the mother superior is not at all aware. Nobody has mentioned anything about an accompanying 'extremely important but somewhat fragile package'. All she has been told is to keep the girls apart and isolated. In no circumstances is she, or any other member of the convent, to talk to them, and nobody on the outside, even her father confessor, is to be made aware of their presence. Given the specific nature of her instructions (and she has been assured that they come from the 'very top'), this places her in a very difficult position with her much beloved grandfather.

'Francesca?'

There is still silence as the mother superior grapples with her conscience. She knows what her grandfather has been, what he is and what, she suspects, he will always be; after all he is not nicknamed 'the grim reaper' for nothing. She has always been aware of the bloody nature of the family business, but this is the man who took her in and gave her a life of which she could never have dreamed.

'Francesca, are you still there?'

There is just no time for considered reflection; anyway 'blood is thicker than water', even if the alternative is 'holy water'.

Francesca makes up her mind. '*Nonno*, you are absolutely right about the ladies in question but I have no idea what you mean by fragile package.'

'So they didn't tell you who also returned with the girls?'

'No.'

'Not surprising, I suppose, given the circumstances,' the old man muses. The tone of the voice changes; it is soothing, reassuring and downright manipulative. 'Francesca, my angel, I want you to do something for me.'

What is to follow is not a request: it is an order. As a woman, Francesca has never had to swear an oath of allegiance or loyalty to the Family, but total, unquestioning, utter obedience to the 'Cause' is very much engrained in the DNA of every member of the clan.

'Yes, *Nonno*, what do you want me to do?'

'Question the women, separately or together, it's up to you. I want you to ask them one simple question...'

'Yes, *Nonno*?'

'Ask them if they know the location of the "secret

package" that travelled back with them from the Caribbean.'

'Caribbean?' Francesca is not really surprised; the girls did look remarkably healthy and tanned upon their return. She can well imagine that the colour will rapidly be leaving their cheeks, given the dark, dank cells in which they are being incarcerated.

'Yes, Francesca, the Caribbean, incredible as it may seem. Always wanted to go to the Caribbean but never got round to it,' the Don says wistfully. 'Closest I got was your Uncle Eduardo's condo in Key Biscayne.' There is a pause but then the Don continues: 'I suppose it's a bit late now.'

The mafia boss gets back to the business in hand. 'I want you to question them closely. Use subtle persuasion, or blackmail or even brute force if necessary – I know you're remarkably good at that – but do anything you think is necessary to get the information. I must know where the package is currently located.'

'*Nonno?*'

'Yes, my child.'

'What is the fragile package?'

'It is probably best for you that you don't know. It is possible that you may find out inadvertently, which could cause you some consternation, but, as long as you use the exact phrase I have used, you will almost certainly find that they know what you mean. Will you do it…?' there is another long pause, '… just for me?'

The answer is a foregone conclusion. The woman owes him an enormous debt of gratitude and thus loyalty. 'Yes, *Nonno*, just for you.'

'When exactly?'

'After Compline tonight when the sisters are asleep. My position gives me the freedom to go wherever and whenever I want.'

'Good. I shall expect to hear from you tomorrow. *Addio fiore.*'

'Goodbye, *Nonno*. Give my love to *Nonna*.'

Francesca replaces the receiver in the cradle of the ancient telephone. She wonders if any of her forebears had such a weird and amazing conversation on the self same phone. It has been a most peculiar and unusual fifteen minutes. In one sense she feels immense pride that her beloved grandfather has placed such trust in her, but, God forbid (she crosses herself), if things were to go wrong it could easily lead to the most horrendous complications and consequences.

Francesca walks around her wood-panelled office, acutely aware of the peering eyes of her predecessors looking down at her from ill-conceived and ill-executed paintings hanging on the walls. She is surrounded by centuries of dowdy, unattractive, though probably highly worthy women who, no doubt, would have seriously disapproved of her unforgiveable breach of religious discipline. She takes in the threadbare carpets and old-fashioned, chipped and stained office furniture, and tries to breathe normally in the hot stuffy atmosphere. It is not easy. It crosses her mind that, now she has reached the pinnacle of her chosen profession, this may well be all that she has to look forward to for the rest of her life; and, it has to be said given the longevity of many sisters and nuns, it could be an exceptionally long life. The prospect is too ghastly to contemplate.

There is a buzz on the intercom on her desk which links Francesca to her private secretary; Father Giovanni has arrived to lead her in her twice-weekly Spiritual Exercises. She brightens immediately, a broad smile breaking out across her face – life could be worse!

*

There is a discreet knock on the door. It opens, and her confessor and mentor enters the room. She wonders if Titian were still slapping paint on the old canvas whether he might consider using Father Giovanni as a life model for Adonis. He is drop-dead gorgeous: brown curly hair, finely chiselled nose, perfect natural lips, strong chin, intense brown eyes and a well-muscled, vigorous body. He has also been remarkably well 'endowed' by his Creator which, in the context of the nature of his 'calling', Francesca finds a trifle baffling – it seems such a waste. The priest locks the door; it is vitally important that their 'exercises' are not interrupted. Francesca feels a surge of anticipation as he turns to face her.

'Are you prepared, my child?' he asks.

Oh yes, Francesca is totally prepared, and very aware of the latest purchase from Victoria's Secret hugging every contour of her exquisitely shaped body under the unwieldy weight of the drab, black habit which constitutes her daily work attire.

'Yes, Father. I am,' she replies obediently and somewhat breathlessly.

'Then come...'

She crosses the room, kneels in front of the cleric, and begins to undo some of the thirty-three buttons on his soutane, concentrating on those located in the general region of his bulging groin. As she does so, Francesca looks up at Giovanni with those hauntingly beautiful, Moorish eyes and whispers:

'Forgive me Father, for I am about to sin...'

The priest's breathing becomes increasingly laboured; he shuts his eyes and tries desperately to dismiss all thoughts of Vesuvius.

*

By nine o'clock in the evening the mother superior is back in her stuffy antiquated office. Compline is over; the sisters of the Order of Elena the Servant have begun the 'Great Silence' and have gone to their cells to retire for the night. The 'peace that passes all understanding' has settled on the convent after another blisteringly hot, yet unusually eventful, day. The cool of the evening has not yet penetrated the building's thick walls; Francesca's office is thick with dank, fetid heat. She is still feeling somewhat weak at the knees after the strenuous exertions of the afternoon; indeed they were very strenuous: three 'exercises' completed in just under two hours – something of a record!

It was during the final 'exercise', when Father Giovanni was labouring with high physical intensity but only limited finesse, that the true nature of the 'fragile package' suddenly dawned on the recumbent abbess. The priest's final forays were nearly always protracted affairs, and so this gave Francesca plenty of time to think, as he lumbered towards the ultimate satiation of his carnal appetite. If truth be told, she had never been fully convinced by the story promulgated from the Curia of the pope's illness, and she had wondered occasionally about the coincidence of the timing, between the disappearance of the girls and the pontiff's retreat from public view. Now it all appeared to fit neatly together, no matter how unbelievable it might seem.

During the afternoon and evening, Francesca has been trying to work out how to approach the women. It promises to be a very difficult, not to say delicate, conversation. They will almost certainly be on the defensive, and may well feel it their duty to protect their spiritual leader. In addition, Francesca has no idea whether they will have been on intimate terms with him, in which case they are likely to embrace a vow of silence. Good Lord, what a thought: the two of them and the pope entwined in ecstasy – it doesn't bear thinking about! Mind you, she thinks, he was a very good-looking man; a very, very attractive man indeed. She allows her mind to wander, imagining herself in the same situation – what a delicious thought! Suddenly, she is startled out of her erotic reverie by an enormously loud pounding on the door, and, without waiting to be asked, an amazon of a woman ushers two frightened, defeated and devastated girls into the office.

Every convent or monastery needs an 'enforcer' to maintain standards and discipline. The Convent of Elena the Servant is no exception to this rule, but the behemoth that accompanies Carmen and Elvira seems to take intimidation to a new level. Sister Anna Marie is over two metres tall and has a massive physique, which would not be out of place within the confines of a super heavyweight weightlifting contest. Her face is pock marked and flabby, with massive, sagging cheeks and wildly staring eyes. When she talks one can clearly see that she does not have all her teeth; the few that remain are brown and stained. In many respects she resembles a rather unattractive Atlantic wolffish, a species not widely known for its good looks or engaging personality. One would not be wholly surprised if, it were to be discovered that, her diet consisted largely of anabolic steroids, washed down with liberal helpings of whey protein shakes. It is obvious, by the way she hurls the girls in the general direction of two rickety chairs, that she is both eminently well qualified for, and thoroughly enjoys, her work. Furthermore, it is clear that she has performed her task with a high degree of competence, as the women are obviously traumatised, and so, as there is no discernable reason for her continued presence in the office, she is dismissed by Francesca. The scowl on Anna Marie's face suggests that she is unimpressed by this release from her duties, but she complies with as much grace as possible in the circumstances, although she does slam the door very firmly shut on her way out.

Francesca turns her attention to Carmen and Elvira. Don Calogero had suggested the potential for the use of physical force, but it is immediately apparent that this option will not be necessary. They are in a pitiful state. In only a few days, the healthy tan of the Caribbean has been replaced by the dull pallor of the prison cell. Their hair is matted and dirty and their eyes are red from continuous weeping. They are quite clearly beaten. The abbess decides that her planned 'softly, softly' approach is the most likely to bear fruit.

'What I am about to say will remain secret between us,' she begins. 'Do you understand?' The girls nod their heads.

'I understand that when you returned from your ludicrous escapade, you were not alone. You were in the company of, what best can be described as, a highly important but somewhat fragile package. Am I correct?' The pair, eyes down, stare at their hands on their laps. Francesca tries again.

'Am I correct?' There is still no response.

'I admire your loyalty to your partners in crime and I am sure that, before you were returned to me, you were threatened with the direst consequences if you revealed the truth, but unless we locate this fragile package there is a real possibility that it might be destroyed…'

Francesca does not get a chance to finish the sentence; two heads shoot up at once. The girls stare at her, and the mother superior sees very real fear in their eyes.

She continues: 'Unless we can identify the location of the package, it is quite conceivable that it will disappear and never be seen again. I have some friends who are willing to help ensure that that eventuality never happens. But it is essential that they know the location of the item in question. God forbid it may already be too late. You must help. You really must help. Have you any idea where it might be? Did anyone on the trip back give any idea as to, what might be termed, 'a forwarding address'?'

The mother superior can see the girls frantically weighing up their options. Can they trust her, or is this yet another ghastly trick? Francesca reads their minds.

'You just have to trust me. Difficult it may be, but I don't see that you have any choice. Time is of the essence. All I want to do is to get the package back to its rightful owners.'

It is Elvira who breaks the silence. 'The only thing I heard was the man from the Swiss Guard…' Somehow Francesca manages to retain her composure; the Swiss Guard were involved in the kidnapping of the pope? Surely not; it is too incredible for words. '… talking about Messina…'

'No,' says Carmen. 'It was not Messina, it sounded more like Misurina. I think he said something about mountains and a lake, but I can't be sure. It's all I can remember.'

The two women look blank. Francesca discerns that they are desperate to help, but it would appear that the brief interrogation has revealed the sum total of their knowledge: they know virtually nothing of any substance. She might as well send them back to their cells, but... but... there is one question she just has to ask before she can let them go.

'When you were with the pope – oh yes, I do understand who the fragile package is – did you ever...?'

Both girls immediately discern her meaning. 'No,' says Elvira quickly, '*that* was not ever a part of our relationship with Him.'

'So you are both still...?'

'Yes.'

'May I be very personal and ask: *would* you have, had he asked you?'

There is no response from the pair, but Francesca, as a woman of the world, can see in one of the girl's eyes that the answer, almost certainly, would have been – yes!

The mother superior then reverts to type. Again, she swears them to secrecy, and orders them to devote the rest of their lives in obedient service to God within the confines of the convent. The girls agree readily. This comes as no surprise because, for the last few days, they have both thought, quite realistically, that their days on Earth were numbered.

Francesca summons the gorgon, and Anna Marie frogmarches the women back to their rooms. As it is early,

Francesca decides to report her findings to Don Calogero immediately. She lifts the handset on the antique brown telephone, but even as she is dialling the number she is thinking that it all seems so little to go on.

V:II

High above the Dolomite mountains in the north of Italy, between Misurina Lake and Monte Cristallo, a golden eagle is circling, searching for its prey. Way below, the terrain is harsh and unforgiving, reminiscent of a sterile, barren luna landscape. Jagged outcrops of grey *Dolomia Principale*, from which the mountains derive their name, tower above isolated valleys and ravines which, one would have thought, are incapable of sustaining life; but the bird knows better, for beneath the desolation of the rocky peaks the tree line begins. Thousands of acres of pine, larch and beech are host to colonies of marmots, hares, polecats and other woodland animals. If an unsuspecting rodent strays from the protection afforded by the green canopy to bask on the baking hot sedimentary rocks, the eagle will swoop, and the unfortunate sun worshipper will, almost certainly, find himself the *plat du jour* for rapacious chicks in some distant eyrie.

But it is questionable whether even the eagle's penetrating eyesight would be able to make out the hermitage of the Order of San Giacomo Distruttore Del Mori, set into the side of a grim, forbidding, bleak, barren valley. If the hermits crave seclusion from public view, then they have chosen their location well. From the air it is virtually invisible; their cells are carved like caves into the grey dolomite of the steep hillside, and there are no discernable outbuildings of any description. The valley floor is littered with a confusion of boulders and debris dating back to the formation of the landscape millions of years ago, when the sea receded from the mountains. It would be hard to imagine a more remote, isolated and highly appropriate spot to pursue an austere mendicant vocation.

The Order was founded in 1986, shortly after attacks by Arab terrorists on Rome and Vienna airports. It is a highly secretive sect, founded with the purpose of confronting, what they perceive to be, the twin scourges of Arab nationalism and Islamic fundamentalism. Its patron saint, St James, Slayer of the Moors, is reputed to have taken part in the Battle of Clavijo in Spain in 844AD, when, mounted on a white horse, he set about butchering as much of the opposing Moorish army as he could. St James is probably a mythical figure, as it is extremely unlikely that the alleged battle ever took place; but this is a matter of sublime indifference to the uncompromising hermits of the Order of St James, for whom the symbolism is far more powerful than the need for historical accuracy. They believe they are involved in a *bellum sacrum*, and that as *Milites Christi* they have a divinely inspired mission: to eradicate the Saracens and Moors from the face of the Earth. Given that there are only fifteen of them, this might seem something of an uphill struggle, but it would be unwise to underestimate their fanaticism and devotion to the 'Cause'. Smaller cadres of men and women have turned the world upside down in the past. Indeed, the group has the advantage of friends in high places. While not formally approving of the militaristic nature of their enterprise, certain powerful clerics are not above calling on the Order's 'specialist expertise' when circumstances dictate.

An unusual element of the group's activities is their practice of engaging in the Korean martial art of Tang Soo Do, which they believe releases their *Gi* or energy force. For twenty-two hours a day they remain confined to their cells, theoretically engaged in prayer, meditation and contemplation – although as each cell has high speed internet access and the latest mobile phone technology, the actual amount of time devoted to spiritual exercises could be open to question. But for two hours every morning the hermits are released from their isolation, when they undertake a rigorous programme of stances, techniques, patterns, sparring and free fighting, through which they hope to enhance their self-awareness and empathy with the world around them. These exercises also have the advantage of making the group a formidable fighting force; however, it is a fundamental tenet of the Order's credo that their skills should only be used in self-defence – except, of course when confronting Saracens or Moors!

The rest of the time the hermits are segregated from one another. Meals are brought to their cell, by the 'duty' chef for the week, and pushed through a flap in the bottom of the door. Silence is maintained at all times; even the computers, tablets and mobiles come with their own headphones, to ensure that the peace and serenity of the hermitage is maintained. It is a simple life. From time to time one or more of the brothers may disappear for a few days, but there is never any question of the others seeking to find out where they have been and what they have done.

Today, instead of the usual fifteen inhabitants, there are sixteen men in residence, but the sixteenth is never seen. To all intents and purposes the pope is a prisoner, and has been for several weeks, having been transferred to this inaccessible, bleak location upon his return to Italy. His cell is locked twenty-four hours a day, and he does not take part in the daily Tang Soo Do exercises, not that the absentee minds this at all. The period of incarceration has given the pope time to think, to meditate and to find some solace in the unblemished purity of his religion. His only concern is for Jackson, Flanagan and the two sisters. He is burdened with guilt that his selfishness placed them in such an invidious position, but there is nothing he can do about the situation. He is powerless. All he can do is pray.

It is interesting to note that the pope never prays for his own release. This is not just because he believes that he deserves to be punished for his recent transgressions, but also because there is a very real part of him that would be quite content to remain in his cell at the hermitage for the rest of his life. After all he has been through, the contemplative life would appear to have a lot to offer; however, there are two caveats to this. He craves exercise; he would love to be able to get out into the fresh alpine air and walk in the mountains. The second is the rather 'peculiar' nature of his hosts. They really are a trifle weird and he is not fully convinced by the juxtaposition of Eastern Mysticism and Catholic Orthodoxy. Timothy is also concerned that their *raison d'être*, namely the destruction of Islam, does not sit all that comfortably within the context of a forward-looking Catholic church, especially in a tolerant, global, multi-cultural society.

Unbeknown to the pontiff, his period of new-found tranquillity is about to come to an abrupt end. Above the valley, on top of a desolate ridge in the shadow of Monte Cristallo, three men, dressed from head to toe in black, gaze down on the magnificently camouflaged hermitage. It has taken them two hours of hard walking and climbing over mountainous terrain, from their chalet in the hills above Lake Misurina, to get to this spot but they do not complain. They have been charged with a mission of the utmost secrecy and importance – and they won't let Don Calogero down. Anyway, they are well used to trekking over unforgiving landscapes, and are as sure footed as a Girgentana goat in the foothills of the Hyblaean Mountains in their beloved Sicily.

Discovering the pope's whereabouts has not been easy. Locating Misurina itself was reasonably straightforward; after all, it is a relatively well-known, if small, tourist destination, nestling in the shadows of the Cadini di Misurina, next to a crystal clear lake which bears the same name as the town. The western shores are lined with small hotels and *pensiones*, which are a haven for summer trekkers, mountain climbers and winter skiers. In the surrounding hills, there are a considerable number of chalets, smallholdings and isolated farms, in which it would be simplicity itself to ferret away a person who one did not wish to be discovered. Don Calogero is decisive. He sends a team of six of his finest operatives – three men and three women – and commands them to use any means necessary to discover whether the pope is indeed in the area surrounding the town. They have no idea why the Don is so interested in locating their quarry, but it is not their role to question. Their role is to carry out his orders to the letter.

Initially this proves to be a fruitless task. Using a small chalet on the outskirts of Misurina as a base, the team spend a fortnight searching an area within a radius of ten kilometres from the resort, but all to no avail. It really is like trying to find a needle in a haystack. The pope could be anywhere in the district or nowhere at all. The lack of success is extremely frustrating, but a breakthrough finally comes as a result of a chance discussion with a waiter in the restaurant of the Hotel Quinz Locanda Al Lago. The team are seated on the terrace on a glorious, early summer's evening; the lake is so calm that the reflections of the nearby mountains are mirrored almost perfectly in the water. They are surrounded by tanned, fit young people in their thirties, ostentatiously sporting their affluence and status, dressed in Armani and Lauren and McCartney and Dolce and Gabbana, their aviator sunglasses roosting in expensively styled 'iconic' heads of hair. They are loud, very loud, and speak as if they want to be heard beyond the confines of their table; they want it to be known and appreciated, in particular by the lumpenproletariat in the immediate vicinity, that they are to be admired and envied. In all reality, they are ghastly!

Despite the disappointments generated by endless days of unsuccessful searching, the Sicilians are thoroughly enjoying an excellent *antipasto tipico* washed down with a more than acceptable *Schioppettino*, before moving on to the main courses, when a ray of hope descends. One of the team engages the waiter in conversation; pointing in the direction of Monte Cristallo she asks if anyone lives in such a forbidding and hostile environment. The waiter replies that the area is totally deserted, although rumour has it that there is a bunch of *strane persone religiose* who live, in some form of remote community, up in the mountains near Monte Cristallo. He is not sure exactly where. By now the group are very much clutching at straws, but they decide to contact the Don anyway, to let him know that they might possibly have a lead worth investigating, but that if it is a dead end, it may also be the end of the road in Misurina.

That evening Antonio, the team leader, makes a call to Leonforte. He explains the situation to the Don, who is both intrigued and excited by the prospect of possible progress. Given the difficult nature of the terrain between the town and the potential location of the religious community, Don Calogero instructs them to charter a helicopter to see if they can make anything out from the air, but he limits the time allowed to three days; after all, he's not made of money! It is not until the third day that Antonio finally spots something unexpected on the ground below. He is staggered to see a group of semi-naked men practising, what looks suspiciously like, martial arts exercises, although when they hear the sound of the helicopter they disappear like thieves in the night.

On his return to the chalet, Antonio consults the rest of the group and they decide that, even though it is going to be devilishly difficult to get to the site, it is probably worth closer inspection. It seems such an obvious place to hide someone as well known as the pope; an isolated religious order would be most logical in just about every respect, but it takes the team several days of detailed planning to work out how to access the spot. There are chairlifts which will take them close to the western end of Monte Cristallo, but one can hardly 'kidnap' someone as famous as the pontiff, and then move him to the waiting getaway car on public transport. Anyway, the operation, if a rescue has to be effected, will have to take place at night when the lifts are not operating. Finally, they manage to find a series of interconnecting hiking paths which will take them from just outside Misurina to within striking distance of the valley, although the last few hundred metres will be arduous, especially if the weather closes in and the way is shrouded in mist and fog. They do a couple of trial runs along the narrow, in places treacherous, trails, and then spend two days monitoring events in the valley from their elevated vantage point. It soon becomes obvious that one of the residents never leaves his chamber, not even for the martial arts exercises each morning. His is the most easterly cell on the compound. This has the advantage that it is easier to access than the other, more centrally located, cells. It is a long shot; the inhabitant could easily be a member of the sect who has fallen from favour with his colleagues, and is being punished by being isolated from the rest of the community; but an attempted intervention is a risk they just have to take. They have come too far to back down; the Don would never forgive them were they to fail, and that is something that they just cannot countenance.

Their plan, when formulated, is simple. They have noticed that the hermits tend to retire early; the electric generator, from which the hermitage gets its power, is turned off meticulously every evening at precisely eight o'clock. After this there is no sign of life in the compound. They decide that they will leave it for an hour or so, go down to the end cell, pick the lock (Antonio is a master at the craft), ensure that their quarry is actually the pope, and then, if it is, spirit him away into the night. One of the team, Bruno, will remain behind in the cell and replace the pope as prisoner. It is important that the disappearance of the pontiff is not noticed for as long as possible. As none of the other friars actually enter the chamber where he is held, it should be relatively easy to maintain the deception, at least for a few days. Bruno is being very handsomely rewarded for his period of voluntary incarceration, and so is quite sanguine about a spell of splendid isolation. Antonio and his accomplice will escort the pope back across country to a car, which will wait for them five kilometres south of Misurina, and then they will drive to Belluno Airport, about an hour and half to the south, where the Don has chartered a small executive jet to fly them back to Sicily. It is a good plan.

Two nights later it is put into operation. Antonio, Bruno and Giuseppe set off back up into the mountains, relieved that the weather forecast has predicted a clear moonlit night – it will make the whole process so much easier. By now they are all well used to the gruelling climb, and have also identified the pinch points on the tracks where they will have to exercise special care. Making good time, the group arrives above the hermitage just before dusk, and the trio hunker down to wait for darkness to fall. As the sun sets slowly in the west, the grey sedimentary slopes turn glorious shades of pink and red, vividly contrasting with the apple greens and stunning golds of the forests below. It is a truly beautiful sight, but they have other matters to exercise their minds; communing with the glories of the natural environment is pretty low down on their list of priorities right at this minute.

Just after nine, the group head off down the slopes and, after ten minutes of delicate scrambling down the unstable scree, they are outside the cell. Antonio picks the lock effortlessly and the team enters the room. The pope is so immersed in his contemplation of a particularly convoluted passage in *De ente et essentia* that he does not hear them arrive, and when confronted, at first is somewhat sceptical that the thugs standing before him have been sent by a *grande amico* to effect his rescue. It is only when Antonio makes it abundantly clear that they will use force to achieve their goal if necessary, that the pope finally agrees to change clothes with Bruno – a cassock is hardly appropriate garb for the challenging trek to the car. Within five minutes the transfiguration is complete, and the pope is clambering up the side of the mountain, demonstrating remarkable agility for a man who has endured several weeks of enforced indolence.

Back in the pontiff's former prison, Bruno is unpacking a small rucksack. It contains some 'essential reading' that he intends to get through during his period of confinement. It is open to question whether Thomas Aquinas would approve of Panarello's *Centro Cohpi de Spazzola Prima di Andare a Dormire* or Cano's searingly erotic *Trilogia* but, as they might say in Italian, it is a matter of *cavalli per I corsi*. By the time the pope and his rescuers arrive at Belluno Airport to get the jet to Sicily, Bruno is well into his third seduction. It's a tough job…

V:III

A small, four-seat SportJet 2 sweeps low over the Malta Channel and heads north- west towards a disused airfield, not far from the town of Trapani on the island of Sicily. Bo-Rizzo (or Chinisia as it has also been called) was home to sections of the United States Air Force and, for a time, 255 Squadron of the RAF, during the Second World War, but fell into disuse in the seventies when the Regia Aeronautica finally pulled out. Today all that remains is a section of the runway which, despite neglect, is still in reasonably good condition, and a few derelict buildings; it is a perfect place for a discreet entry into Sicily.

Making landfall between Torretta Granitola and Triscina, the plane flies low over isolated farms and vineyards, avoiding the few remote villages and hamlets which dot the landscape. It hugs the ground in the moonlight, attempting to hide itself in ground clutter, thus reducing the chances of radar detection. Mind you, given that it is in the early hours of the morning, and the nearest airport is closed at night, the chances of being discovered are highly improbable. In the plush, surprisingly spacious, cabin the pope sits ashen faced with three of his 'rescuers'. He does not enjoy flying at the best of times and he finds the plane's wild gyrations, as it seeks to evade discovery, more than a little frightening. It is devoutly to be hoped that, up in the ethereal realms, St Christopher is on duty and hard at work on his behalf. He keeps his eyes firmly closed and recites all the prayers for travellers he has ever come across; surely the ordeal must end soon!

After what seems an eternity, the plane finally makes a rather bumpy landing on the dimly lit airstrip, four flares defining the boundaries of the runway, and taxies across to the deserted buildings, where a car is waiting to take the pope to Calogero's stronghold near Leonforte. It is a BMW X5 armoured security vehicle which, in the Don's line of business, is a necessity rather than a luxury; he has no intention of enabling his many enemies to copycat the assassination of Giovanni Falcone in 1983. Even though the route is longer, they take the main SS115 southerly coastal road as it passes through less populated centres. At the ancient city of Agrigento they turn onto the SS640, and head up into the island's interior, before joining the A19 and then finally turning left onto the SS121 just before Enna. It is still dark and so the pope cannot really make out much of the scenery; consequently he dozes fitfully for much of the time. The journey takes over three hours as the driver, not wanting to attract undue attention from the Polizia Stradale, is meticulous in keeping within the speed limits; but the luxurious nature of the car's interior means that the lengthy trip is not exactly onerous.

It is just after dawn when the group finally arrive at Don Calogero's bastion. They pull up in front of ornate wrought iron gates, set into a grey stone boundary wall which must be at least four metres high. It stretches in either direction as far as the eye can see; is topped with vicious-looking razor wire, and littered with CCTV cameras. The Don appears to take security very seriously. Within seconds of their arrival the gates swing open automatically; it is obvious that they have been expected.

The BMW drives up a long avenue of cypress trees, behind which are acres and acres of olive groves and fruit orchards. Being Spanish, the pope instantly recognises the distinctively spiky-shaped olive trees, but he is less sure about what else is being cultivated. Bizarrely some of the fruit on the trees appears to be wrapped in white paper bags. Even in his exhausted and apprehensive state, the pope is intrigued.

'What fruit is that?' he asks.

Antonio stares at him as if his prisoner has asked a ridiculously stupid question. 'Peach,' he mutters. Antonio is a man of few words.

'Why is the fruit wrapped up?'

Up until this point Antonio has maintained an uncommunicative silence but now he becomes positively loquacious. 'It's a form of pest control,' he says. 'It also extends the growing season. We sell when other growers have stopped producing.' He slumps back in his seat, apparently worn out by the effort of stringing more than a couple of sentences together.

Any attempt at further conversation is terminated by their arrival in front of a massive three-storey house located behind a huge granite-paved courtyard. The top two floors are dominated by eight large, perfectly symmetrical, casement windows, protected by green louvre shutters; they look out on the town of Leonforte in the distance, which looks as if it is clinging on to the top of a mountain. At ground level, on either side of a central portico, floor-to-ceiling French windows open onto the courtyard; it is full of rustic, wooden garden furniture, and a profusion of terracotta flowerpots bursting with brightly coloured blooms. To the right of the main building, there is a single-storey extension with a wide-sweeping verandah leading onto a large terrace, in the middle of which is a generously sized kidney-shaped swimming pool. The lavishness and extent of the building both suggest that crime does indeed pay, and pay handsomely.

The pope follows Antonio across the terrace, past the swimming pool, which is surrounded by beds of red, gold, pink and cream snapdragons, and on through an opening in the garden wall. He passes a series of barns and outbuildings which, he assumes, is where the work of the adjoining farm is probably done. There is also a well-appointed stable yard with boxes for about a dozen horses, although only half of them seem to be occupied. Finally, they arrive at a large warehouse piled high with boxes and packing cases marked 'Villarmosa Estate Premium Extra Virgin Olive Oil', the labels of which are all in English. One assumes that these will be shipped out to the Sicilian diaspora: from Brooklyn and the Bronx in New York to Brunswick and Bulleen in Melbourne. The varieties seem endless. There are crates containing truffle-infused olive oil, balsamic-infused olive oil and even caramelised onion olive oil; there appears to be no end to the indignities inflicted on the poor, humble, much-put-upon olive.

Timothy is ushered into a dimly lit, spacious office, simply furnished with dark, old-fashioned wooden furniture. A single bulb hangs from the ceiling; it is coated in dust. Behind an imposing mahogany desk, that has obviously seen better days, there are rows and rows of dirty bookshelves containing ancient-looking ledgers and account books; but nowhere in the room is there any evidence of the impact of modern technology, not even a telephone. It is deserted. Antonio motions his guest to stand to one side, rolls back an ancient, tattered, shabby carpet, and punches a sequence of numbers into his iPhone. Nothing happens for several seconds but then, virtually silently, a section of the floor in the middle of the office, about two metres square, rises up majestically until it is waist high. It is yet another surprise, in a day of surprises, for the increasingly bewildered pontiff. But there is more to come. An elderly, male voice penetrates the silence: 'Do come down, Your Holiness. Please take great care on the steps, they can be quite treacherous.'

The pope treads somewhat gingerly down a flight of narrow stone steps and, as he does so, the trap door closes noiselessly above him. What he discovers at the foot of the stairs is quite astounding. He finds himself in a brightly lit cellar of cavernous proportions. To his left is a fully fitted, modern kitchen, littered with an incredible array of electrical gadgets and appliances. There is also a sleeping area containing a king-sized four-poster bed. It is made up with crisp, white, linen sheets, royal blue duvet cover and a multi-coloured throw, which is meticulously positioned at the bottom of the bed. Beyond this, there is an open door, through which the pope can see a gleaming white bathroom which, he assumes, is as beautifully equipped as the kitchen and sleeping area. The walls are covered with a series of colourful posters, dating from different periods of time, all advertising various products associated with Villarmosa Olive Oil; but what attracts his attention the most is the sight of an elderly man, sitting in a luxuriously upholstered armchair, who is staring intently at him.

Don Calogero is a man of considerable presence. His silver hair and deeply lined, nut brown face bear testament to his advanced years, but the eyes, the disconcertingly blue eyes, are vital, alive and clearly show that he has not lost any of his mental faculties. He is dressed in a rather traditional English manner: exquisitely cut Jaeger blazer, a Ted Baker light blue shirt, cream Paul Smith slacks, Barker McClean men's brogues and a deep red silk cravat; but, while his smile of welcome is broad, exhibiting dazzling white teeth, the eyes tell a different story. The pope, a shrewd judge of character borne of many bitter experiences, immediately discerns that there is very little compassion, empathy or warmth in this man; he is dangerous, highly dangerous. The Don introduces himself.

'Welcome to my home, Your Holiness. My name is Don Calogero Escatores but I suspect that Antonio has told you that already.' He pauses for a second. 'I do hope that you did not find the journey too demanding. It must have been extremely tiring and taxing, not to mention being, quite possibly, rather confusing. I shall explain everything in due course, but first, will you join me in a glass of our own *piersica*, produced right here on the estate? I know it is rather early but I find that a single glass first thing in the morning helps me face the rigours of the new day. Oh, and I do apologise most sincerely for the somewhat unusual location of our meeting, but I am reliably informed that the local police will be paying us a visit sometime in the next few hours, and I am keen for them to discover that I am "not at home". No doubt they will report the results of their search to the Guardia di Finanza, so one can never be too careful.' He clicks his fingers and a black-suited flunky appears, as if from nowhere, with two glasses of lightly coloured brown liquid on a silver salver. The Don motions to the pope to be seated in a second armchair directly opposite his own.

'*Saluti*,' says the viper raising his glass, and takes a delicate nip of the aromatic liquor. Given that he is totally under the control of the Mafia boss, and therefore has no option but to comply, the pope raises his glass in return and takes a small sip. It is a good thing that he does not take a mouthful; even though he has been raised on the powerful anis of Andalusia, he still finds the *piersica* incredibly potent stuff; it is all he can do not to cough or splutter.

'Forty-five percent, if you are wondering,' says his outwardly courteous host. 'It is something to be treated with respect, but should be appreciated and enjoyed.'

The pope has to agree; strong it may be, but the liquor has a remarkable smoothness and a gloriously light, silky aftertaste. He says nothing and settles back to see what happens next. Now that he knows the identity of his '*grande amico*', he is more than a little uneasy; such people are not to be taken lightly – they have a formidable reputation for the most unspeakable brutality. Timothy does not have long to wait: the Don is a man of business and a man of action; he did not get where he is today through prevarication or obfuscation. Yet Calogero seems to have a need to place what he is about to say in some form of wider context.

'I have always tried to be a good Catholic, Father,' he says, 'but in my line of work, as you can appreciate, it has not always been easy.' He waits for the pope to say something but there is no reply; the priest is well attuned to the value of silence in the confessional. The old man shrugs and continues, staring into the distance; he is somehow in a world of his own.

'It may come as something of a surprise to you but, whatever you think of me and people like me, I have always had a deep desire to improve the lives of the ordinary people. In "business",' the Don smiles, 'I come across men who are only interested in their own personal enrichment and advancement, nearly always at the expense of others. My passions, on the other hand, are to protect my family and the people close to me, as well as those who, through no fault of their own, are in no position to defend themselves.' He pauses again, but there is still no response from the pope. He continues:

'Let me explain. My belief in the need for philanthropy, and in the merit that comes from good works, was instilled in me by my grandfather, Don Eugenio, who was first moved by the plight of those who suffered terribly as a result of the earthquake in Palermo in 1908. In the immediate aftermath of the disaster he instructed his men to rescue survivors from the rubble, and then distribute food and water to those from whom everything had been taken. Later he funded, discreetly of course, the rebuilding of several schools and an orphanage, as well as the reconstruction of two churches. He had to be circumspect because, had his actions been known more widely, then his generosity might have been seen by his enemies as a sign of weakness. Since then, every time there has been a catastrophe on the island, my family has often been at the forefront, always anonymously, of providing assistance to the distressed. We really do open our hands wide to our brothers and sisters and the needy and poor in our land…'

The pope is startled by the Don's choice of words; never in his wildest dreams did he expect to hear a notoriously vicious Cosa Nostra boss paraphrase, almost directly, from the Catechism of the Catholic Church. It is quite a revelation, and a very surprising one at that, but Calogero is not finished.

'I suspect that I know what you're thinking,' he says. 'That the generosity of spirit, the concern for the common good, is funded from the proceeds of crime: prostitution, people trafficking, drug sales, gun running, financial crime, cyber crime and, yes, even murder. So I suppose the fifty million lire question is: can good come from what you and those like you would describe as evil? I have come to believe that it can. You, no doubt, would disagree totally.'

The pope does disagree, he fundamentally disagrees, but how should he respond? He is in no position to engage in theological semantics and risk alienating his captor. He decides on a measured response.

'I have to admit to being a little taken aback by some of the things you have described to me,' he says. 'I never knew that the "Families" were engaged in activities aimed at the promotion of the "Public Good"…'

'Not all,' mutters Don Calogero, 'only ours!'

'That may be so,' replies the pope evenly, 'but it all rather appears as a contradiction in terms to me.'

'In what way?' asks the Don.

'Well, I would suggest that all of the, what might loosely be called, family business activities you listed can only be described as essentially sinful, and we know that unfettered indulgence in sin alienates us from God. Your position is one that I just can't countenance. I fail to see how the suffering of so many people, through bestial criminality, can be justified or explained away when placed in the context of marginal benefits for a relative few. It may help to salve your conscience, Don Calogero, but, and I hope you will forgive my bluntness, it is a moral and theological position with which I am extremely uncomfortable. Were I your confessor I would guide you to repent.'

'So you would make a moral and spiritual distinction, would you, between the school you established on Grande Batture, with stolen money I might add, and my patronage of the St Pancras orphanage right here in Sicily? Both institutions aim to help vulnerable children; both are funded with monies that have been acquired illicitly; but my orphanage somehow is sinfully corrupt, while yours, no doubt, is a shining beacon of philanthropic Christian charity. Personally, and I hope you will forgive my bluntness, I'm not sure that I can see the distinction.'

The pope is nonplussed. There is absolutely no doubting the logic of the Don's argument. While the black-suited flunky refills his glass, Timothy endeavours to formulate a response.

'But surely there is a question of motivation?' he suggests.

The Don's hawk-like eyes narrow. 'Are you saying that, somehow, my motivation is lesser than yours?'

The pontiff is treading on eggshells. 'I can't know what motivates you,' he says. 'Only God can look into your soul, and only you can reconcile yourself with your Creator.'

The Don is silent. Timothy tries a different tack. 'You said earlier in our conversation that your primary function in life was to protect your family.'

'Yes.'

'And in your time you have ordered and sanctioned the murder of men.'

'Yes.'

'Can I ask: what about their families; their wives and children; their mothers and fathers, not to mention their brothers and sisters? What about them?'

There is no response from the Don.

'I would urge you to make your peace, not only with your Creator but with yourself. I can do nothing for you. It is wholly down to you and your conscience.'

'How very convenient,' Calogero replies. There is a moment's silence. And then he changes the subject abruptly. 'I take it that you have always believed that God had a plan for your life, that in a very real sense He planned your vocation...'

'If you mean, was it predestined, then yes, I think what happened to me was intrinsically part of a Divine Plan.'

'So why then is my, if you will, path in life not part of a similar plan? From what you're saying, I appear to have been "wired" for damnation. He created me. I am what I am. How am I, a mere "lump of clay", going to have any control over what the Potter has planned for me, especially if it has been predestined from the dawn of time?' Calogero pauses. 'It seems to me that God must have a quite remarkable sense of humour.'

'What makes you say that?' responds the pope.

'Well, it would appear that my "plan", if there is one, is bizarre in the eccentricity of its design.'

'How so?'

'I was born the fifth of five sons. As such there was no

real pressure on me to enter the family business. Of course, there would always be a place for me, that goes without saying, but it would always have been in "frontline services", if you see what I mean, rather than in "senior management". It was not an option that appealed. Since childhood I had been drawn, almost inexorably, towards the majesty and grandeur of the Church. Does that surprise you, Father?'

The pope shrugs his shoulders; nothing surprises him anymore.

'The Family were not at all opposed to my entering the priesthood. After all, it opened up a whole new range of contacts and opportunities. So I enrolled in a seminary here in Sicily, but, and this is why I find God's so-called Plan intriguing, it was because I was there for only a matter of weeks. One night, St Celia's Day to be precise, the Amberetes, our bitterest rivals, entered this very house late in the evening, where my grandfather was celebrating his birthday with all the members of the family, apart from me. The Amberetes were armed to the teeth and intent on blood. My relatives were taken totally by surprise and had no chance to fight back. All the men were murdered in cold blood. The women were stripped, gang raped and then slaughtered in front of the children, who were informed that this would be the fate of any Escatores who crossed them in the future.

'So, Your Holiness, what was I to do? I left the seminary, vowed revenge and took over the leadership of what was left of the family. The result is what you see today.' He pauses, lost in thought. 'For the life of me, I fail to see how God gave me much choice. As far as I can see, all I can do is live the life that has been set out for me. I am trapped. It is clear that I am destined for hell.'

'God does not create men in order to consign them to hell,' says the pope gently.

'I find that hard to believe.'

'If you seek forgiveness and truly repent of all your sins, you can restore that intimate relationship with the Almighty you appear to have had as a child. In your heart of hearts you know that surely.'

'I may know it, Father,' says the Don with a smile. 'The question is: do I believe it?'

Timothy looks sadly at the old man. 'God gives us choices, Don Calogero. I could have rejected His plan for my life but I didn't. For a time I embraced it wholeheartedly…'

'… and look where it got you,' interjects Calogero.

'I admit that things have not worked out quite as I expected, but, despite everything, even now I believe that God is working a plan for my life.'

'So it was all part of the Plan,' mocks the Don, 'that you became an embezzler, a fugitive and a recluse, living on a remote tropical island in the company of two young, highly attractive and, no doubt, accommodating nymphets?'

Now it is the pope's turn to lose his temper. 'Leave the girls out of it. They were totally innocent victims of this whole insane exercise,' he snaps.

'Innocent?'

'Yes!'

'You mean you never…?' The Mafia boss raises his eyebrows.

Pope Timothy glares at him, as if Calogero has just crawled out from under a stone in an extremely barren, arid desert. The look is sufficient; the Don knows better than to pursue the matter.

'At least they're safe now,' he murmurs. The pope stares at him quizzically. Calogero elaborates: 'Currently they are both at St Elena's, admittedly incarcerated, under the watchful eye of Francesca. But the women have been luckier than some of the other misguided members of your coterie…'

The pope jumps, sits bolt upright in his chair, and grips the arms so tightly that his knuckles turn the colour of pure alabaster.

Calogero continues: 'I fear you must prepare yourself for bad news, Your Holiness. Luigi Pedrosa phoned me from Grande Batture a few weeks ago. He told me that the local constabulary had found the bodies of two men at the compound you occupied. They had been murdered. Their bodies were not easy to identify – decomposition is always accelerated by tropical heat – but there was enough to ascertain that they were Peter Franklin and Enrico Marquez. I am sorry, Your Holiness, I can well imagine that this will come as a terrible shock. Pity really, Luigi had devised an ingenious plan to get them both off the island and to a place of safety. Such a pity…'

But the pope is not listening. He is stunned. He is distraught. He has been totally responsible for the death of two good men; men who had placed their complete trust in him – and he has failed them miserably. It takes him several minutes to compose himself. Calogero waits patiently; he appreciates the impact such devastating news must be having on his prisoner.

Finally the pope asks, 'Who is Francesca?'
'My granddaughter. She is the girls' mother superior.'
'And she told you…'

'Yes. I suspect that there will be some in the Curia who might well be displeased if they knew of Francesca's indiscretion.'

The pope is certain that there would be a number of high-ranking clerics, in the corridors of power, who would be absolutely appalled if they knew. However, that is for another time; the most pressing concern now is how to extricate himself from his current predicament. But even in his hour of difficulty, it is impossible to take the priest out of the man.

'Don Calogero, I am intrigued as to why you have gone to so much trouble to bring me here, and what it is exactly that you expect from me. I would say, however, that should you wish me to hear your confession, in order that you can be reconciled with your Maker, I would be happy to oblige. Of course, it goes without saying that repentance of sin and subsequent absolution would be only the first step. Rather like the blessed St Francis: a complete change in lifestyle would be an ongoing prerequisite for salvation.'

The Don laughs. 'That's very kind of you, Father, but I suspect that I am far too far gone for that,' he says. 'I cannot see me spending what time I have left ministering to the very particular needs of dumb animals.'

'The orphanage?' suggests the pope.

'I have staff for that, Your Holiness. I fear that I must prepare myself for an eternity in the inferno.' He pauses. 'I shall answer your first question with another question and, if I get the answer I expect, I shall make you an offer you may well find irresistible – think of it as a business proposition.'

The pope is not sure that he likes the sound of this, but he settles back in his chair, endeavouring to maintain an appearance of serenity, and waits for the Don to make his pitch. However, before his captor can begin his presentation, a faint buzzer sounds from somewhere near the trap door entrance.

'Ah,' says Calogero with a smile, 'our guests have arrived. We often get visitations from the local *politi* around this time of day. Suffice it to say that we usually get a couple of hours' notice from our friends at Headquarters. I fear that we shall have to maintain, what our friends in the submarine service call, radio silence for half an hour or so. Do I have your word that you will not utter a sound during that time?'

Timothy has not a lot of choice in the matter. He nods his head in assent.

'Good. Let's have another glass of *piersica* and make ourselves comfortable. It should not take too long.'

They sit back in surprisingly companionable silence. It gives the pope time to think, but he's not really sure what to think. He cannot begin to imagine what the Don is about to propose; whatever it is it will almost certainly involve paying a price for his release. He doubts whether the price will be financial, but it is bound to be costly in some form or other. The room becomes hot and stuffy, as the air conditioning has been turned off; then, after about three quarters of an hour, the buzzer sounds again.

Calogero breaks the silence: 'It would appear that our guests, rather like Elvis, have left the building,' he chuckles. 'Their tenacity is admirable but rather misplaced. Sadly they never learn but I suppose they are only following orders. I don't know about you but I could do with some fresh air.'

He goes over to an electronic keypad on the wall, punches in a series of numbers and the trap door rises slowly, bringing at least some light into the subterranean sanctuary. The pope follows the old man up the stairs, showing due deference for his seniority in years, then on through the office and warehouse, in the general direction of the sweeping verandah at the side of the house. There they find a long, pine kitchen table which has been set for breakfast. It is obviously going to be a simple affair: coffee, brioche and fruit, all beautifully arranged on brightly coloured platters. After the long journey, and subsequent interview with Calogero, Timothy suddenly finds that he is ravenous.

The Don waits patiently while the pope eats; he does not consume anything himself but sips occasionally at a thick black espresso, enjoying the stunning panorama. He loves his precious moments of *otium*. It is a time when he can allow his thoughts to roam freely, away from the oppressive burden of the day-to-day duties imposed upon him by his *negotium*, which, all too often, have consequences too terrible to contemplate. So he sits back, allows his mind to 'go here and there', and basks in the sublime glories of the landscape that sprawls before him. It is a view of which he never tires, especially the sight of Leonforte in the distance, perched precariously on top of a steep hill, shimmering in the heat haze of a late summer's day. It has been a very dry summer with barely any rain, and the ground is brown and parched. He breathes in the heady smells of marjoram, rosemary and sage, flourishing in large wooden beds dotted around the terrace. Above his head hang huge bunches of purple grapes, almost ready for harvest, which have been trained along the wooden latticework of the roof.

When the pope has finished his meal, Calogero takes up the conversation started in the cellar: 'May I start by asking you a question?' he says. In all honesty, his guest has no alternative but to reply in the affirmative.

'It's the sort of question that shallow, unimaginative employers often ask prospective employees at job interviews, but I shall be somewhat more specific. It is this: where would you like to be in five years' time? Still on the run from the criminals who run the Curia, or back in harness fulfilling God's mission and your vocation?'

Given all that has happened to him in the last couple of months, it is not really a question that the pope has ever considered; others have been shaping his destiny and he has been powerless to influence events. To be perfectly honest, he would have been quite content to spend the rest of his life at the hermitage in the Dolomites, devoting his time to prayer and contemplation, but this, evidently, is no longer an option. Right at the moment he does not have an answer to the Don's question. Surely, after all the horrendous events of recent times, it is inconceivable that he could return to the Vatican and take up from where he left off. If he were to do so it would mean having to battle Cuella and his henchmen all over again; it is not at all an appealing prospect.

Calogero waits; yet again he can sense the turmoil and confusion in the other man's mind. He offers some elaboration: 'Don't concern yourself with the mechanics of your return,' he says. 'If you want to go back, it can be arranged. I have been devising a plan to facilitate your restoration which, I believe, has every chance of success.'

The pope does not doubt for a single minute that the Don has a plan; men like Calogero always have a plan. The only problem is, what would he want in return for the implementation of the plan? What would be the price?

What would the Mafia boss expect in return? The old man appears to read his mind.

'Very little,' he says. 'Obviously I would appreciate, shall we say, some privileged information from time to time, and I would like Francesca to enjoy your patronage in order to secure her advancement, but, apart from that, I would leave you in peace.' He pauses. 'However, I do have one very specific request.'

Alarm bells ring out stridently in Timothy's mind. 'And what would that be?' he asks.

'You would bring down, destroy, humiliate and disgrace Cardinal Basil Alfonso Cuella!'

The pope stares at him in amazement. The old man's voice is suddenly filled with venom, his eyes flash in anger and his hands are clasped together like a vice. It is easy to see why this man is so feared, even by those who could be classed to be within his immediate circle of friends and acquaintances.

'Why?' mouths the shocked priest.

Calogero pauses for a moment, and then begins to speak very softly: 'You remember that I told you I spent several months in a seminary as a young man?' The pope nods. 'Cuella was there at the same time. It was obvious to everyone in the institution that he was destined (there's that word again),' Calogero smiles, 'for high office in the Church. He was by far and away the top dog in the seminary: intellectually brilliant, a gifted theologian, an outstanding communicator and clearly demonstrated the potential to become a highly competent administrator. But he was also a bully; a vicious, sadistic, unremittingly cruel bully. He made my life a misery.

'Things culminated one night in my cell. I was alone, deep in contemplation and reflection, when some of his associates turned up unannounced. He was with them. They grabbed me, pushed me face down onto the bed, virtually stripped me and then Cuella sodomised me. The bastard actually sodomised me. When he was finished he taunted me, laughing into my face. "What price your precious family now?" he hissed. Oh yes, he knew about my background but was not afraid. He was not afraid of anything.

'Since then I have, as teachers are prone to say, watched his career with interest, and have waited for and planned my revenge. I could have had him killed many times over, but that was just not enough. I want the bastard to suffer, really suffer. It has always seemed to me that the best way to accomplish this would be to take away everything for which he has worked and striven over the years, to reduce him to nothing. I want him broken and now, almost as if my prayers have been answered, God has sent you to me. He has sent me the instrument for my revenge.'

Revenge is neither a word nor a concept which finds much favour within the pope's philosophy and world view, but he can fully understand, and in some ways empathise with, the Don's anger and bitterness, even though the priest in him baulks at the notion of divine vengeance. Nevertheless, he is appalled by Calogero's revelation. Timothy has always struggled not to despise Cuella; the man has consistently undermined his attempts to reform the Curia, but now, to his horror and his shame, he finds that he has an overpowering urge to bring the wretched man to his knees. This, for a priest, is not exactly a good place to be, let alone a man in his exalted position.

'How would you intend to return me to the fold?' he asks quietly.

Calogero looks at him intently. It is almost as if the anger in his eyes has been replaced by much-longed-for anticipation.

'I have a tame cardinal, whom I would use to help effect your restoration,' he says.

Oh good God, thinks the pontiff. *First, we have a sodomising secretary of state, and now a tame cardinal under the control of the Mafia – what next?* But he says nothing and waits for the old man to continue.

The Don begins to outline the plan. In the background, in the groves and orchards of the estate, legions of jet black and orange cicadas emit a cacophony of sound, even though it is the middle of the day. As Calogero continues, the noise grows to a crescendo that is almost deafening; it is as if they are applauding the audacity, but yet simplicity, of the plan. It is a work of pure genius.

'You know,' says the pope thoughtfully, 'it might just work.'

VI

RESTITUTIO

VI:I

C ardinal Basil Alfonso Cuella looks down at the sea, or perhaps more appropriately sees, of expectant faces in front of him and experiences a moment of self-satisfaction and self-congratulation. He loves it when a plan comes together! There are forty-five cardinals in the room; each has been hand picked by him specifically for the purpose he has in mind. They have been contacted individually by telephone, bound to a code of absolute secrecy, and invited to an extraordinary convocation at a luxurious cliff-top hotel in Sorrento, looking out over the clear blue waters of the Gulf of Naples. Vesuvius glowers in the background, casting a menacing shadow over the surrounding landscape – dormant, yes, but still potentially devastating. It is a highly appropriate setting for the meeting because, if Cuella has his way, the consequences for the Church could well be equally as explosive as the eruption of 79AD.

The secretary of state has gone to quite extraordinary lengths to ensure that the tame cardinals enjoy their stay; he sees it as a sort of 'loyalty reward' scheme. The message is that 'if you cooperate' you can certainly expect 'more of the same' in the future. The Bellevue Syrene is a luxury five-star hotel, which can trace its origins back to Roman times, and has forty-eight sumptuous bedrooms and suites, all with balconies giving the most wonderful views of the bay and the city of Naples in the distance. A lucky handful of the, more 'significant', cardinals even have rooms with whirlpools and spas. Although one cannot be sure that the ascetic St Francis would have approved of such decadence, it is undeniable, as far as Basil is concerned, that the 'ends justify the means'! The restaurant, set on a terrace to one side of the hotel, serves some of the most fabulous seafood in the country and boasts a superb wine list, guaranteed to please even the most discerning ecclesiastical palate. Above all, the management is circumspect and can be relied upon to maintain the highest standard of professional confidentiality.

The whole hotel has been taken over for the week by the cardinals; there are no other guests as the hotel is closed in the winter months, but discretion is still the order of the day. All the men, gathered together in the Winter Garden, are dressed in casual clothes, and, in order to avoid raising even the merest hint of suspicion, their travel itineraries to the hotel have been staggered, so that they have arrived over a three-day period. In several of the cases 'staggered' being the operative word, as some of the more notorious prelates are well known for their partiality to the noble grape; which may help to explain why they tack gracefully through reception, somewhat like Spanish galleons under full sail in a choppy sea. And therein lies the genius of the plan: every one of the cardinals in the meeting either owes their elevated position to Cuella's patronage, or has something more sinister to hide. Now in the secrecy of a luxury hotel, it is time for the Secretary of State to the Vatican to call in some long-overdue favours.

At the back of the room he picks out a well-known cardinal, whom he knows has a somewhat unhealthy predilection for adolescent altar boys and girls. Next to him is an Asian archbishop who, it is rumoured, has substantial pecuniary interests in a number of Hong Kong-based Triad gangs. Cuella suspects that getting such men to support his enterprise will be, in the common parlance of the great unwashed, a 'piece of cake'. He takes a sip of iced water from a tall crystal glass resting on the top table, gets to his feet, rings a small bell and brings the meeting to order. There is almost immediate silence.

'Welcome, gentlemen,' he begins, 'to this quite extraordinary congregation. Before we begin, may I take the opportunity to remind you once again that what goes on in this room stays in this room. You have all agreed to treat our deliberations with complete confidentiality, and I expect you to maintain the vow of silence you made to me in our individual conversations. Any disclosure to third parties of the content of, and outcome from, our discussions will be met with consequences of the utmost severity.' He pauses. From the looks on the faces of his colleagues, the secretary of state is reassured that the point has been made. Some of the cardinals are genuinely petrified.

Cuella, with theatrical gravity, continues: 'What I am about to share with you has the most profound ramifications for the future of our beloved Church...' He pauses as if overcome with great emotion. 'Gentlemen, I find this very hard to say, and I fear that I must ask you to prepare yourselves for some terrible news... but I have to inform you that Pope Timothy is dead.'

To those who remember the rather mindless response of

the cardinals at the meeting in the Vatican offices, when they received the news of Timothy's disappearance, the reaction of their fellow clerics in the Sorrento hotel will not be at all surprising. There is no unbridled outpouring of grief and distress; it must be remembered that these men, by and large, are essentially career politicians, who have risen through the ranks as a result of factional alliances, devious strategic manoeuvring and political intrigue. This is not to say that they are not outwardly pious and devout, but these qualities tend to be on display only at weekends and on Holy Days; for the rest of the time they are political animals, governed by naked ambition. Their response to the news is muted and, yet again, largely confined to immediate considerations of 'what's in it for me?' The only person who appears to be visibly upset is Maurice Jean-Paul de Lange, former Bishop of Limoges, who Cuella has invited to the meeting because of his widely known homosexuality, and is therefore perceived to be a legitimate target for blackmail and manipulation. Of course, in the half hour that follows, there are large numbers of pious platitudes of regret and sadness articulated by a number of the cardinals, but these are largely only window dressing for the benefit of the wider audience. Sadly the late departed pontiff will not be missed at all by his Brothers in Christ.

The observant reader will no doubt note that Cuella is labouring under the misapprehension that the pope is very much alive, and still incarcerated in the friars' lair, high up in the Dolomites. From this it must be deduced that Bruno is doing a sterling job, although one has to be concerned that, by now, he is bound to have run out of preferred reading material; it is doubtful whether Aquinas will be very much to his taste. On Cuella's part, the announcement is something of a calculated risk; the pope would be of much more value to him if he were actually dead, but Cuella, even with his recent history of facilitating the termination of opponents, baulks at the idea of assassinating a pope. After all, is nothing sacred? Having said that, if things go badly wrong, he does have one agent planted among the ferocious friars, who has agreed to remove the pontiff from the equation – permanently if necessary.

Cuella is about to bring the meeting to a close by suggesting that the rest of the day is spent in prayer, meditation and thanksgiving for the life of Pope Timothy, when a hand is raised at the back of the room; it is the Archbishop of Palermo.

'May I enquire how the pope died?' he asks pointedly. 'After all, we knew he was unwell, but you must appreciate that the news has come as a considerable shock for all of us.'

'I'm afraid that he had a series of strokes after the initial one. Each was minor in nature, but their cumulative effect eventually proved fatal. The last one, a month ago, killed him.'

There is a moment's stunned silence in the room and then all hell breaks out. 'A month ago?' shouts a disembodied voice from somewhere in the audience. 'Why were we not informed?' Other voices are raised in agreement; the concept seems preposterous.

Before Cuella can reply, the Archbishop of Palermo sets another cat among the pigeons. 'I want to see the body,' he says. 'I simply do not believe that what you are telling us is possible.' As a friend and confidant of Calogero, he is well aware that the pope is currently residing with the Don in the bastion at Leonforte.

Cuella is well prepared for all such questions. 'It was

Timothy's wish, especially when he realised that his days were numbered that, in the event of his demise, the matter be kept secret from the wider community as he wished his remains to be returned to his beloved Andalusia and there cremated…'

Cuella does not finish the sentence; there is uproar in the room.

'Cremated?'

'Never!'

'Inconceivable!'

'… must be joking…'

'… the Lying in State and the funeral?'

'Has to be buried with his predecessors…'

The noise level is deafening, and Cuella is obliged to ring the hand bell for a full minute in order to regain some semblance of control in the room, which is, by now, seething with discontent.

'Gentlemen, gentlemen,' he says, 'you place me in an invidious position. I was torn between my loyalty to the Mother Church and my personal loyalty to the man I had promised to serve and obey. Timothy was, in so many ways, a very unpretentious and humble man. He could not abide a lot of the trappings and traditions which have been passed down to us through the generations. It was all I could do to persuade him not to be buried in a pauper's grave! He often commented that our Lord was a simple man from a humble background, and so he found a lot of what we do to be inconsistent with the Truth, even, on occasions, distasteful. So, Your Eminence, you see I cannot produce the body, because it no longer exists.'

He pauses for a moment. 'Your disbelief is quite understandable,' he continues, 'but I believe that I have devised a possible solution which, in some way, will help to appease my conscience, as well as provide a workable outcome to the somewhat bizarre circumstances in which we find ourselves.' He pauses again and takes a sip of water.

'Throughout his brief pontificate I did everything I could to assist and support Timothy…'

Liar, thinks Maurice de Lange.

'… because he was the man who had been anointed to lead us and so I demurred to his wishes and requests. In the matter of his death, I am relieved of such onerous obligations and have been able to devote my energies, such as they are, to consider ways in which there might be an acceptable resolution to our predicament. Therefore, I propose that there is a full state funeral, but that the casket remains closed rather than open. The mourners will still file past at the Lying in State, and may pay their respects in the normal way. As usual the whole process will be replete with symbolism, even if the main participant is, in actual fact, fertilising some olive grove in an isolated part of rural Spain. This solution, while not exactly the Wisdom of Solomon, I grant you, does give us a way out of the dilemma we face.

'My friends,' Cuella concludes, 'for many of you I know it has been a harrowing and trying few hours. I suggest that we retire, reflect on the situation, pray for guidance and convene tomorrow at ten o'clock. Thank you for your patience and forbearance. God bless you all.'

With that, Cuella draws the meeting to a close and the shocked cardinals file silently out of the room. Tomorrow, thinks Basil, should be a lot less complicated – or so he anticipates. One hopes, for his sake, that his optimism is not misplaced.

VI:II

On the evening of the meeting at the hotel in Sorrento, Calogero and Pope Timothy are having dinner in the Don's sumptuous dining room at Leonforte. The walls are littered with priceless works of art by some of the great masters, but these are arranged rather idiosyncratically, for example, Gauguin hangs next to Van Dyke, while Monet competes for wall space with Vermeer. It is all something of a dog's dinner and would, no doubt, not pass muster within the hallowed confines of the Uffizi. They are eating *caponata*, a peasant stew consisting mainly of aubergines, tomatoes, shallots and pine nuts; this will be followed by *manicotti* filled with cheese, and then locally caught swordfish. They are using heavy gold cutlery, which must be worth a small fortune, and each course is served on plates of fine oriental porcelain. The thick, earthy red wine they are drinking is poured from an ornate crystal decanter in the middle of the table, but, rather oddly, it is discharged into plain glasses that could easily have come from IKEA. The Don is a man of many contradictions. It is not until the swordfish has been served, and they are alone, that he initiates a conversation:

'Things are beginning to move on,' he says. 'Cuella has convened a meeting of hand-picked cardinals in Sorrento. He must be getting ready to make a move. Just before dinner I had a brief conversation with *my friend* who's at the meeting.'

'Who?' responds the pope.

'Do you really want to know?'

Timothy realises that the Don must be referring to the tame cardinal. 'No,' he says hurriedly.

'Thought that might be the case,' grins Calogero. 'I sent him to keep an eye on things. Like me he loathes Cuella but, unlike me, he is a consummate diplomat, which, I suppose, is why he is where he is today. Anyway, I have some interesting news for you.'

The pope waits patiently, while his host milks the moment to the maximum possible extent: 'I am sorry to inform you, Your Holiness, that you are dead.'

'What?' exclaims Timothy. Does this mean that he is eating his last supper – will he be taken outside and shot? If it is the case then at least it has been an outstanding meal; but no, the Don clarifies the situation almost immediately.

'Apparently you died from a fresh stroke last month. I have to confess that I find it all rather amusing. Yes, dear old Basil broke the news at the meeting this morning. It caused quite a stir.'

'I imagine it did – but it's preposterous. What about the formal announcement of my death? To take a month over it is unheard of, and then there's the question of the funeral. How on earth are they going to bury me without a body – my body?'

'According to my source, they are going to make the formal announcement tomorrow,' says a grinning Calogero. 'Cuella said that it was your dying wish to delay it so that your body...' he looks directly at the pope, 'could be taken back to Spain to be cremated...'

'What?' shouts the Timothy, leaping out of his chair,

flecks of half-chewed swordfish and salad tomato flying from his open mouth.

By this stage Calogero is beside himself. He is thoroughly enjoying the pope's obvious discomfort. Tears of laughter stream down his face. 'They're talking about having a closed casket – you'll probably be nothing more than a few used house bricks. The people filing past may well be paying homage to a building site. It's priceless.'

'It's a bloody obscenity,' screams Timothy, forgetting himself in the heat of the moment. 'It's blasphemous. It's sacrilegious…'

'… It's hilarious,' laughs the Don.

Timothy stops suddenly, and looks at the laughing Calogero. He is struck by the quite ludicrous nature of the situation. It is totally preposterous that here he is, theoretically at least, a force for good in the world, having a quite excellent dinner, in an impregnable fortress in the wilds of Sicily, with one of the most feared, murderous men in the whole of Italy. It's completely nuts. And yet José is forced to admit that the two men, after a less than propitious start, have forged a close bond over the days and weeks they have been together. It is something of a shock to realise that he has become rather fond of the Don. The smiling, mirth-filled Calogero he sees before him is totally at odds with the barbarity the man exhibits in pursuit of his profession. Is this the real Don Calogero?

Calogero displays, once again, the uncanny knack of reading the pope's mind: 'Yes,' he says, 'this is the real me, the man I would like to be, but the man I can never be outside these walls. Surely by now you don't need to ask why? It's not difficult, is it? If I show any weakness in public, not only am I a dead man but so is the whole of my family. Our enemies would annihilate us in an instant given the chance – look at what happened to my father and brothers. José, I have no choice in the matter. Mercy is a virtue I just cannot afford to display – I have to protect my family, even if it means doing and sanctioning things that, in my darkest hours, I find abhorrent. Come on, sit down, have a drink and let's get back to the matter in hand.'

Timothy is speechless, but complies with the instructions. He goes back to the table, takes a small sip of his wine, composes himself and then asks a question that has intrigued him ever since he first met the Don. 'Before we move on,' he says, 'there's something I would like to ask you.'

'If you must,' replies the Don. 'I suppose that I must have asked enough personal questions of my own during the last couple of weeks.' He sits back and lights a cigar.

'Just now,' begins José, 'you said something about your darkest hours – what I want to know is, how do you cope with the things that you have done? The pain and hurt and yes, the torment that your actions have caused? In essence, Calogero, how the hell do you sleep at night?'

'Do you really want to know?' asks the Don rhetorically, but the pope still nods. 'The simple answer is that I don't. I lie awake for hours burdened, oppressed and beaten down by the evil that I have inflicted on the world.' He pauses. 'I am an old man, José. The grim reaper is knocking on the door for my soul and I fear death and its consequences. Every night I fear death coming in the bleak, dark hours. I ask God for forgiveness but I can't believe that he hears me. Surely He can't forgive me?'

There is another pause while Calogero takes a meditative puff on his cigar. The pope waits patiently. There is obviously more to come.

'The legacy from my time on earth will be suffering, hatred and animosity, and when I die many people will rejoice. So I lie awake and reflect on the unfairness of it all – it is not what I wanted to do all those years ago. My life history has not demonstrated who I believe I am.' There is another pause. 'My dear José, since you arrived you have seen a side of me that I have never revealed to anybody else, least of all my family.'

He smiles. 'You may be a turbulent priest, José, but you are a good man; a good man who has found himself in a ridiculous position, brought about by his passionate, some might argue insane, desire to change the world. Idealism, I fear, has no place in the twenty-first century.' He stops.

The pope is, yet again, rendered speechless. In the blink of an eye his view of the Don is transformed. He knows that he is in the presence of an incredible man: is it at all possible that he is a good man? Surely not; Calogero has been involved in acts of unspeakable savagery and brutality – surely any form of compassion and understanding is totally misplaced? It is inconceivable that he could be considered a good man. And yet he is; deep down, in the innermost recesses of his being, he is a good man, a man who has been trapped into a life not of his choosing, but one which circumstances have forced upon him. The priest in Timothy; the man in him; the spirit of the Living God in him, screams out to him to help the Don; to save him; to love him; to tell him that not all is lost and that he is not forsaken or abandoned…

'Do you…?' he begins.

'No, Your Holiness,' says Calogero calmly. 'I do not want you to hear my confession. Frankly, I am not sure that we would have enough time, and anyway, there are much more pressing maters which require our attention at this time.'

Timothy very much doubts whether there is anything more important than saving the immortal soul of Don Calogero Escatores, but he has come to learn that the Don, rather like the Iron Lady, is not for turning once he has decided on a course of action.

The pope takes a few moments to gather his thoughts. 'What are we going to do?' he asks.

Calogero pauses before replying. If he does not handle the next five minutes well, many of his hopes and aspirations for the future will be dashed.

'It seems to me,' he begins, 'that fundamentally, you have two courses of action open to you: you may continue to have the freedom you have enjoyed over the last few months, or you can return to your vocation and endeavour to bring about the change you so passionately desire. Your "death" gives you the opportunity to remain anonymous and start a new life wherever you choose. On the other hand, you can activate the plan we discussed in the event of your demise being announced. My friendly cardinal has given us the head's start we need to ensure that you are able to return to the papacy, and take up where you left off. I suspect that the latter course of action will involve considerable sacrifices in a number of ways, but it also could be incredibly fulfilling. I hope you'll forgive me for appearing to lecture you, but one appears to be a selfish option, the other seems to me to be a selfless option. It is a choice not easily made. As I have said to you many times recently, the decision is yours and yours alone, but it is a choice that must be made right here and now – tonight. Once made there can be no going back. What'll it be, Papa?'

José looks across the table at the Don and, in that instant, makes a decision that will transform their lives forever.

VI:III

The meeting at the Sorrento hotel reconvenes promptly at ten o'clock the following morning. Many of the cardinals have spent a rather uncomfortable night; advisers and secretaries have been banned from attending the conference, and so the prelates have been obliged to make do with each other's company. Given that there is a history of dislike, bad blood and petty feuding between large numbers of the attending participants, quite a few of them have had a rather lonely twenty-one hours.

Cuella brings the meeting to order: 'Gentlemen, I think that we need to move on from the recriminations and disagreements which dogged a large part of yesterday's discussions. It is my contention that we focus our minds on the future, and consider what needs to be done in the short, medium and long term. May I take it that this is the general view of the meeting?'

There is a mumble of assent to this proposition from the majority of the prelates, although an archbishop from Colombia does inject a minor qualification: 'Just as long as there is a full investigation into what has happened when the dust, generated by this farce, has settled. Somebody,' he looks pointedly at Cuella, 'must be held to account for the seemingly chaotic way in which the whole matter has been handled by the Curia.'

Cuella is sorely tempted to reply by invoking Matthew chapter 7:1-5 and talking about 'motes and beams' or, equally as appropriate, John 8:7 and discussing 'sin and first stones'; the cardinal in question being suspected of having close links to a number of drug cartels in his homeland; but common sense prevails and he refrains. That particular score can, and most certainly will, be settled at a later date.

'You may rest assured that your concerns will be noted,' he says evenly. 'Let us proceed. First, I propose that a formal announcement of Pope Timothy's sad demise is made tomorrow. I fear we shall have to be somewhat economical with the truth as to the timing of his death, but that is a cross we shall all have to bear with fortitude.'

There is a murmur of agreement.

The Archbishop of Palermo interjects: '... provided, of course, that he really is dead. We only have your word for all of this, Cardinal Cuella.'

Cuella ignores him. 'Secondly, that the funeral mass be held in ten days' time.'

This meets with general approval, because it does give time for the candidates who wish to stand for the vacant papacy to get their campaigns underway.

'... And finally, that the Conclave take place two days after the funeral.'

It's a very tight timeframe and will give Cuella an enormous advantage, but there seems to be no reasonable alternative, so the cardinals agree once again.

Cuella then outlines the method for the official announcement of the death of the pope, as well as the processes to be engaged for the organisation of the funeral. There are tried and tested procedures for such matters; the cardinals pay hardly any attention at all. They know that things will swing into action within a few hours. Cuella already has a team of senior clergy in the Vatican ready to telephone the cardinals across the world, who have not been invited to the Sorrento meeting, so that they are informed before the public announcement is made. However, he is much more preoccupied with one other vital issue that is closest to his heart: the election of a new pope – his election, naturally.

'Let us now turn to a matter that, quite possibly, concerns us more than making the necessary funeral arrangements for a leader who has left us, and consider the matter of who will be elected to succeed him.'

The whole atmosphere in the room changes; tension fills the air. This is what the assembled gathering has come to hear; it will directly affect all their futures. Cuella knows that he has their full attention; nevertheless he feels that it is still important to remind the cardinals about their duty of silence.

'This is a matter of the utmost importance and delicacy. Again I am obliged to remind you of the need for total, absolute and utter discretion. What I am about to share with you would, no doubt in some circles, be seen as controversial at best and institutionally seditious at worst.

'I am sure all of you would agree with me that, in recent times, the pace of reform and change within the Church has been too rapid and, all too often, ill-considered. I believe you share my view, and this is why you have been chosen by me to be here today. It is my contention that we all have a vested interest in a return to the status quo which existed before the recent batch of so-called reformist popes were elected. We have been dominated, at times hounded, by a bunch of liberal reformist zealots who, I would argue, have no place within our religious community.'

There is a buzz of approval in the room; far too many of the 'delegates' have something to hide, something to protect, something to avoid or something to fear. Cuella is talking their sort of language; he is one of them. The secretary of state continues:

'Therefore, it is my sincerely held belief that we need a return to orthodoxy, to conformity, to the protection of those values and traditions which we all hold so dear, and which have served us so well in the past. This, my brothers, is why I summoned you here in such secrecy because I believe that with your help we can engineer a solution which will lead to the election of a leader who shares our aspirations, hopes and dreams. To be brutally honest, I am saying that someone in this room should be our preferred candidate to be the next pope, and that we should all work together to achieve that end.'

There is a burst of applause in the room. Cuella raises his hands for silence.

'You all know the situation: forty-five votes would not be nearly enough to win in Conclave but, my friends, were all of you to go out and win a single convert to our cause, then we would win convincingly and we would all have the man we deserve. What do you say? Are you with me?'

Oh yes, they are totally with him, they agree wholeheartedly with everything he says; all these men have a great deal to lose if yet another meddling, interfering priest is elevated to the position of ultimate authority in their organisation. They also understand the deal on offer. What Cuella is asking them to do is to support his candidacy for the papacy; in return they will be left in peace to carry on as usual. Given Cuella's reputation as a dangerous, almost deadly, political operator it is not a totally appealing prospect, but what the hell: *meglio il diavolo che sai*!

There is one person in the room who is neither applauding nor talking animatedly with his neighbour, and that is Maurice de Lange. He is appalled, but not surprised, by the way Cuella has used such a tragic event to facilitate his own personal advancement. All the work Timothy, and his immediate predecessors, initiated in an attempt to bring about change will be undone in an instant if the secretary of state takes over the reins. He is tempted to leap to his feet and launch a diatribe of righteous invective in the general direction of the overbearing bastard at the top table, but no, it will be better to wait. There has to be a way to thwart Cuella's naked ambition, so he says nothing, sits quietly with his arms folded and bides his time.

Later, in the limousine on the way back to Rome, Cardinal Basil Alfonso Cuella is jubilant; he has won, there is nothing that can possibly stop him. He will not be halted at the gates of the Eternal City and denied the Triumph that is rightfully his. He is the all-powerful conqueror and has secured a victory of epic proportions. He understands that the full story will never be told; but, quite frankly, he couldn't give a damn.

VI:IV

VIS: VATICAN INFORMATION SERVICE

This morning around half past five, the Pope's private secretary entered his apartment and found him dead in bed. The death was confirmed by Dr Abramo Caldi.

After confirming his death, the doctor stated that it almost certainly occurred sometime in the early hours of the morning. He also stated that the sudden death might well have been caused by another cerebrovascular accident or CVA (stroke).

A further statement will be made in due course.

VI:V

O n the Via del Lincei, in one of Rome's poorer suburbs, a fit, tanned, early-middle-aged cyclist, dressed in red and gold lycra, stops a man in the street and asks for directions to the Church of Santa Maria dei Monte.

FRIDAY 13 30

Giuseppe Panatone arrives home for lunch at his modest two-bedroom apartment in San Lorenzo. Lunch is the highlight of his day, not just because of the mouth-watering food prepared by his wife, Lucia; oh no, it is because of what, on good days, follows the food. He and Lucia have the apartment to themselves; their two 'adorable' children are safely at school. This state of blissful freedom enables other blissful activities to take place – that is, if the mood takes her. But today, even the prospect of an hour or so of connubial ecstasy pales into insignificance in comparison with the news he wishes to impart to his wife. He bursts in through the front door, impervious to the wonderful smell of *ragù alla salsiccia* emanating from the kitchen.

'Lucia,' he shouts. 'Lucia, you'll never guess who I saw this morning... he asked me directions to Santa Maria dei Monte... I couldn't believe it... I can't believe it! Lucia, I spoke to him... the pope... I spoke to the pope... I actually spoke to the pope. Lucia, I've met the pope! It's incredible!'

There is no response. Moments pass. His long-suffering wife looks at him blankly. Then she turns her head in the direction of a small television in the corner of the tiny living room. It is carrying wall-to-wall coverage of Timothy's death. His eyes follow hers. He stares at the screen. He turns up the sound. He changes the channel to CNN. The news is exactly the same. Giuseppe shakes his head again and again and again.

'Impossible,' he says. 'It's just not possible...'

FRIDAY 17 30

A gloriously good-looking man, his facial features somewhat obscured behind an expensive pair of Gucci sunglasses, is seen drinking a Campari and soda outside the Restaurant Di Rienzo, in the Piazza della Rotunda near the Pantheon.

FRIDAY 18 00

'Hi mom.'

'Hi Mary-Lou, how's Rome?'

'Hot, noisy, crowded but absolutely fantastic.'

'Where you been today?'

'Started at the Coliseum this morning; walked through the Forum; had lunch; paid our respects to good old Victor Emmanuel; took in the Trevi, and we're now having cocktails at a restaurant opposite the Pantheon which, I have to say, is one really weird building.'

'Wow, you've been busy. How are the feet holding up?'

'Sore and weary. Boy, I could really use an ice cold shower.'

'That's what comes from mixing with the rich and famous.'

'Sure does an' I reckon I am. Know you really won't believe this, but I reckon the pope is sitting a couple of tables away from us.'

'The pope?'

'Yup. Looks like he is drinking a Campari and soda.'

'Honey, you've either been in the sun too long or you've had a cocktail too many.'

'Huh?'

'For one, the pope would not be seen drinking at a public café, especially a Campari soda, and two, the poor man is dead!'

'You're kidding. Are you sure?'

'Yup. Heard it on Fox and Friends just now.'

'Gee whizz! Must be true then. Reckon that might explain why it's been so quiet today, why people are looking so strange and dejected but, boy oh boy, it really does look like him.'

'Well, it's not. His death is all over the news. Get right back to the hotel and take that shower. It may help to stop the hallucinations.'

VI:VI

O n the bridge crossing the Tiber in front of the imposing fortress of Castel Sant'Angelo, an extremely tall male, dressed in a blazingly white shirt and black trousers, is seen gazing down at the placid river below.

A nervous-looking gentleman, dressed in a dark suit and brown loafers, approaches a priest in the nave of Don Giovanni in Laterano on the Piazza di San Giovanni. The cathedral is the oldest of the four papal basilicas in the city. Its rich, ornate baroque style is a must-see for tourists, who are drawn to its glorious frescos and awe-inspiring altars. It is also the seat of the Bishop of Rome, in other words the pope, and so is a place with which Timothy would have been well acquainted. Today it is crowded with sightseers: some in large groups, following guides brandishing a range of brightly coloured flags and placards; others are more likely to be independent travellers, because they wander around, heads buried in guide books, taking in the majesty of the building. The man in the suit is obviously not a tourist; he looks rather worried and apprehensive.

'Father, may I have a word?' he asks. 'I am not of this parish but am in urgent need of help and guidance and, quite frankly, I did not know who else to ask.'

Father Mario Coppela, one of the mass of clergy attached to the cathedral, is still stunned by the news of the pope's death, but he is a sympathetic, empathetic priest and, seeing the man's obvious discomfort, immediately offers his support.

'Let's see if we can find a quiet place away from all these people,' he says sensitively. 'The cloisters are usually not too busy at this time of day. What is your name, my son?'

'Alessandro.'

'Come, Alessandro,' says the priest, 'follow me.'

Coppela leads the man through a large wooden door and away from the gaggle of tourists, who remain behind, dutifully inspecting the remains and relics of centuries of ecclesiastical history. The two men sit on a low wall separating a small square lawn, dotted with beautifully manicured shrubs, from the covered cloisters, the walls of which are covered with intricate inlaid marble mosaics.

'How can I be of assistance?' he asks.

There is a long pause; Alessandro does not appear to know how to begin. After a while he speaks: 'Father, do you believe in people having visions or even seeing ghosts?'

Thank you God, thinks Mario, *on today, of all days, you choose to send me another fruitcake!*

'Well, strictly speaking, my son,' he says gently, 'they are not actually the same thing. No, I don't believe that there are such things as ghosts, but God does elect, from time to time, whenever He so pleases, often through the Blessed Virgin or one of the saints, to reveal certain mysteries to us through the medium of visions.'

'Then if, as you say, I can't have seen a ghost, it means that I must have had a vision.'

'What do you mean?'

'I was crossing the Ponte Sant'Angelo just before lunch today, and I swear that I saw the pope.'

'He's dead, my son, shocking though it must seem. Sadly, Pope Timothy is no longer with us.'

'I know... I know... but I saw him, I actually saw him with my own eyes. It was him... I know it was him.'

Father Mario thinks it totally unreasonable of God to test his sanctity so sorely on such a terrible day – after all, he's not really a saint – but for the next hour or so, he tries his level best to persuade the frightened man that he is mistaken. Mario really is a sympathetic, empathetic priest, but he fails miserably in his endeavours.

SATURDAY 21 00

Basil Cuella is working late when there is a loud knock on his office door.

'Come,' he bawls. He does not appreciate being disturbed, especially when he is constructing his homily for the nine o'clock Mass in St Peter's the following day. He seriously regards leading services in the Basilica as an unnecessary intrusion into more important work, particularly when the work in question involves securing the papacy. Monseigneur Rossi enters the room. Rossi is Cuella's private secretary. He is a rather portly, bald, middle-aged man from Piedmont, who gives every impression of someone unable to resist the temptations that arise from the sin of gluttony.

'What is it, Rossi?' barks the belligerent bureaucrat.

'I don't know how to express this...' says the ever-hesitant Rossi.

'Then come back when you do!'

'But... but...'

'Get on with it.'

'It seems there have been a number of sightings of the pope, right here in Rome.'

Cuella's heart skips a beat. 'What?' he whispers.

'I know it's impossible, because he's dead, we all know he's dead,' mumbles Rossi, 'but the police have told us that at least five people have contacted them today to say that they saw him on the Ponte Castel Sant'Angelo just before lunchtime...'

'Imbecile...'

'... and that others saw him outside the Restaurant Di Rienzo in the Piazza della Rotunda yesterday afternoon...'

'... no doubt drinking prosecco in the company of a high class whore,' sneers the secretary of state.

'Oh no,' says Rossi. 'It wasn't prosecco. Most of them said that it looked like Campari and soda.'

Cuella jumps like a cat that has just had an unpleasant interface with boiling liquid. Campari soda is the pope's tipple of choice; effeminate maybe, but the information is plausible – it is exactly what the pope would choose to drink. It can't be him; surely it can't be him. He's tucked away with the mad friars in the Dolomites. He looks at his watch. It will be too late to contact them now; they will have shut down totally for the night. He will have to wait until morning. A feeling of the most intense foreboding comes over him.

Cuella dismisses Rossi, lights a Corona, pours a huge brandy, and begins to pace up and down the room muttering virtually inaudible profanities. It looks like it is going to be a long, sleepless night.

VI : VII

It is time for the members of the congregation to receive the Body and Blood of Christ at the nine o'clock Mass in St Peter's Basilica. Cuella has just made the pronouncement: *Ecco l'agnello di Dio, che toglie il peccati del mondo*, and the worshippers have descended on the Altar of the Chair, like a football crowd leaving a home match after a particularly good win; Italians are not known for their capacity to form an orderly queue.

Earlier in the service the secretary of state delivered his homily on the subject of Forgiveness. He has told the assembled gathering, most of whom are on their smartphones or tablets, that God loves to forgive; He always forgives; He never becomes tired of forgiving, but that an essential pre-condition is that the sinner acknowledges their sins and repents. Cuella tells the flock that the Lamb of God was sent to take away the sins of the world but, in a rare moment of insight, he does ask himself whether he can ever be forgiven for some of the things he has sanctioned in the recent past. To say that the sermon was somewhat dreary and uninspiring would be to give it more credit than is due. Frankly it was dreadful, but no one was really listening, and Cuella has other more important matters on his mind. Anyway, he is on the last leg of the service; all he has to do is dish out the bread (a priest is following him with the wine); sign off with the concluding rites; chew the fat with a few important members of the congregation, and then he can get back to things that really matter. Unfortunately he has been unable to make contact with the friars of San Giacomo Distruttore Del Mori but, thankfully, there have been no further sightings of the 'dead' pope reported to the authorities. This, for obvious reasons, is something of a relief.

The first members of the congregation are kneeling before the High Altar waiting to receive the sacrament. Cuella moves absently down the line, placing the wafers of 'bread' on some absolutely ghastly tongues, set in mouths that exude foul, fetid breath – garlic and nicotine are a noxious combination. It is all too apparent that the government's injunctions to abstain from smoking are falling on deaf ears. He murmurs 'Body of Christ' as he dispenses a morsel to each supplicant. Finally, he reaches the person second from the end of the row. A very, very, very familiar face stares up at him.

'Good morning, Basil,' says a very, very, very familiar voice. 'I wonder if we could have a little chat at the end of the service.' It is not a question, but a command.

Cardinal Basil Alfonso Cuella, Secretary of State to the Vatican, looks down at the beatific face of the man he has tried so hard to bring down. He then looks at the two hard-nosed thugs flanking him, and comes to the certain conclusion that his days in high office are numbered, most probably in the singular.

'Breaking news right here on CNN: Vatican sources have just revealed that, contrary to earlier reports, Pope Timothy is not dead. If you're confused at home then join the queue. Joe Bairstow, reporting for us in Rome, can you spread any further light on the situation?'

'Not sure I can, Alastair. Confusion reigns here in the Eternal City. This morning they were planning for a funeral, and this afternoon they are planning for the mother and father of all press conferences. Rumours abound: the pope went walkabout, there was an attempted coup d'état by a handful of recalcitrant cardinals, or even that he was kidnapped by ISIS and rescued by a team of Special Forces from the US and Great Britain.

You name it the list of scenarios going the rounds ranges from the ludicrous to the incredible. One Vatican insider told me, in all seriousness, that: the pope absconded with a couple of young nuns and a considerable amount of money to a tropical island in the Caribbean; was recaptured by some hit men, authorised from right here in the Vatican; was subsequently incarcerated in an isolated mountaintop monastery run by a religious order of fanatical, militaristic hermits, and was finally rescued from their clutches by one of the most vicious Mafia families in Sicily, who have somehow engineered his return to power. Honestly, Alastair, you couldn't make that one up if you tried.

If there are any further developments you'll hear it first on CNN.

This is Joe Bairstow in Rome handing you back to the studio.'

VI: VIII

The Mass is over. The congregation has dispersed and is now probably outside in the piazza, inhaling copious quantities of nicotine, or in one of the many nearby bars enjoying a pre-prandial aperitif. Cuella has changed out of his episcopal regalia and is back in the majesty of the basilica, peering furtively around, no doubt hoping that the ghastly apparition he witnessed back at the High Altar was a chimerical fantasy. It appears initially that he is in luck; there is no sign of the elusive pontiff, but he then sees a sight that makes his blood run cold: the two goons who had flanked Timothy at the rail are heading directly towards him. He turns and waddles away as fast as he can but it is no use; he is easily caught and is discreetly frogmarched through the now nearly deserted building. They leave the cathedral by a side door, and head towards the gate which leads out onto the Via della Stazione Vaticana. It is made perfectly clear to the clearly terrified cardinal that, if he attempts to alert the policeman on duty at the gate to his predicament, it will be the last thing he does on Earth. Just to emphasise the point one of the kidnappers rams what feels like a gun hard into the middle of his back. They pass onto the street; Cuella is thrust unceremoniously into a waiting car with blacked-out windows, and it pulls away heading east out of Rome.

They drive for what seems like hours, but Cuella has no idea as to where he is because the darkened glass precludes any view of the passing countryside. Not a word is said for the whole of the journey. His captors are intimidating to say the least. One of the monsters sports a seriously misshapen nose, which suggests a lifetime of unsuccessful pugilistic endeavour at some rather insalubrious sporting venues, where medical assistance has not always been readily available. Finally they arrive at their destination, which turns out to be a large, rambling, single-storey farmhouse, in the midst of flourishing vineyards set among rolling hills. It appears to be in the middle of nowhere. The priest is dragged from the car and commanded to lead the way into the building.

Entering the farmhouse, Cuella is taken into a rustic-style living room with a huge open brick fireplace, grey tiled floor and gigantic picture windows looking out over the rural landscape. He is made to sit on a hard wooden chair in the centre of the room, and his arms are tied tightly to the back, while his captors sit opposite him on a luxurious sofa and stare intently at him. It is all most disturbing because still not a word has been said since they left the basilica. Time passes.

The lull in proceedings gives the former secretary of state, or at least Cuella assumes that he is the former secretary of state, time to think. On the basis of the single-sentence conversation he had with Timothy in the cathedral, he presumed that he would be meeting the pope, somewhere in the Vatican, to account for his recent actions; but the pontiff does not appear to be present in the farmhouse. Which leads Cuella to wonder why on earth he has been transported to this out-of-the-way location. Is there a more sinister explanation? He begins to feel increasingly uncomfortable.

His feeling of unease is heightened further when, after about half an hour, he hears footsteps coming along the hall that leads into the lounge. The door opens slowly and a wizened, elderly man walks into the room. He is immaculately dressed in a charcoal grey suit, black shirt and bright yellow tie. There is something familiar about him, but Cuella cannot place exactly what it is. The old man glares at the trembling prelate, his piercingly blue eyes full of malevolence and pure hatred.

'I take it, Basil, that you don't remember me,' he says.

'I feel we have met before, but I can't remember where or when,' replies the priest nervously; the old man looks disconcertingly dangerous. He walks round the room, circling the chair, the sound of his shoes echoing menacingly on the hard floor, like a metronome stuck on *adagio*.

'So you can't remember your seminarian days then?' hisses the voice.

Cuella looks at him closely, and then the penny drops with all the resonance of, as St Paul might have said, *aes sonans aut cymbalum tinniens*. Fear drives into the very core of his being.

It is as if the elderly man in front of him can read his mind. 'Yes, Basil, it's your old friend Calogero. I would like to say that it is a pleasure to see you again after all this time, but that would be dishonest. I have dreamt of this moment every day of my life for nearly fifty years. I have plotted, schemed and fantasised about what I would say and do to you, but I have had to learn patience. I have bided my time. Today, vengeance is mine! Your day of reckoning is at hand.'

It is an eloquent opening gambit but, as he speaks, the words sound hollow and meaningless to the Don. He has waited decades for revenge, but now that the hour has come, is this what he really wants? What, in the name of all that is sacred, has the pope done to him?

If Calogero finds his speech underwhelming, it has exactly the opposite effect on the cardinal: Cuella blanches visibly. Calogero Escatores has a formidable reputation, which has spread far from the confines of his Sicilian home. He is brutal. He is merciless. He does not forgive. Above all, he does not exactly have an exemplary track record in returning his victims to the bosom of their family unscathed. Basil Cuella is convinced that he is a dead man. But how the hell did this terrible ogre end up in league with Timothy? It is inconceivable!

'It's a long story, Cuella,' says his nemesis, pacing up and down across the room, the soles of his shoes tap, tap, tapping on the unforgiving tiles. 'I shall not bore you with the rather bizarre way José and I have come to be joined in an alliance. Suffice it to say that, in return for my assistance in facilitating his return to Rome, he has given me you as a reward. So, Basil, I intend to make you pay, make you pay; for consigning me to a life of introspection, of regret, of guilt...' But does he really mean what he says? In the light of his recent experiences, the desire for revenge no longer holds the same sway that it did.

Cuella, by now certain that he has not long to live, is emboldened to respond. His eyes narrow. 'So you're blaming me for all your shortcomings; blaming me for everything you've done wrong in your life? I know all about you, you bastard! You've killed, maimed, tortured and destroyed countless lives. You're just a common criminal from the sewers of Palermo. So what are you going to do with me, you *figlio de puttana*? Are you going to torture me? Murder me? Perhaps even crucify me? If so, get on with it, especially if it makes you feel better, if it appeases your conscience. But it won't, Calogero, it really won't. You won't find the peace you crave, you pathetic, miserable little man.'

'Bravo!' says the Don, clapping his hands in mock appreciation. 'A fine performance of defiance. And you're right, Basil, if it was left up to me, I would damn well crucify you or, better still, submit you to death by a thousand cuts. Believe you me, Cuella, I would apply every cut myself, making sure that each slow, lingering slice caused you the utmost agony. But it is not up to me. I am subject to a higher authority…'

'A higher authority?' ridicules Cuella. 'A higher authority than that of the all-powerful Don Calogero Escatores: the most feared man in The Kingdom of the Two Sicilies? I can't believe it. Tell me, please tell me: who on earth could possibly be more pre-eminent than you?'

Calogero looks at him incredulously. 'You really don't know, do you?'

'No,' says Cuella, 'I really have no idea at all.'

'Amazing,' says Calogero, shaking his head in surprise. 'We shall see how long it takes you to work it out. Let me ask you a question,' he continues. 'Do you regret anything at all that you have done in the last eighteen months?'

'No,' answers Cuella.

'Not anything?' repeats the Don.

'Not a single thing, and don't start to lecture me about having sanctioned murder and violence. For God's sake, man, look at the brutality that can be traced directly to your door; look at the blood dripping from your own hands. I'm sorry if this disappoints you, but I won't be reprimanded by a homicidally insane gangster.'

'All that I did was to protect my family…'

'And all that I did was in order to protect my Church. Look, Calogero, admit it, there is very little to choose between us. We are both as bad as each other. Let's stop going round in circles…'

But Calogero is like a dog with a rabbit: he just won't let go. 'No, Basil, we are totally different. You did your evil to feed your ambition, your advancement, your success! Even at the bloody seminary it was blindingly obvious that you were a driven man; a man who would do anything in order to rise to the top. We are not the same at all. I did my evil to protect those I loved because, if I hadn't, they could easily have been slaughtered…'

'Like your dear old grandfather,' laughs Cuella. 'I remember it well. Don Eugenio got everything he deserved. At least the Amberetes saved the Church from the trauma that would have come from admitting scum like you into the priesthood.'

The Don takes a deep breath and pauses; he is not going to be riled by this vile creature. He still wants answers to the questions that have haunted him for decades.

'Why did you sodomise me, Cuella? Why did you humiliate me? Why did you make me a laughing stock in front of my peers?'

'Because I detest everything that you and your hideous family stand for; because you lord it over the rest of us; because you think you are untouchable and above the law; because you have the arrogance to believe that you can have anything you want, with no concern for the consequences.'

'So I am the scum and you are the cream,' says Calogero. He has moved away from the cardinal, and is standing at the largest of the picture windows, looking out over the vineyards which stretch far in to the distance.

'Yes.'

'And so, you are totally blameless?'

'Yes.'

'Do you sleep at night?'

'Yes.'

'I wonder if the cream curdles by dawn,' says the Don.

'Most amusing,' laughs Cuella. He takes a deep breath. 'Come on, let's get on with it…'

'What do you mean?' replies Calogero.

'You're obviously going to kill me,' says the cardinal. 'Let's get it over and done with. Have your revenge.'

Calogero sniggers. 'Oh, my poor misguided Basil, you have got it so totally wrong. The last thing on God's created Earth I am going to do is kill you, although I admit that there's a very real part of me that would love to do just that. However, José would not condone such an action. José is the "higher authority" to which I referred, by the way. He carries out our good Lord's injunction to "turn the other cheek" to a quite extraordinary degree. He really is a "most forgiving man". Having said that, I do intend to make you suffer for a long, long time, just as you made me suffer, as a result of your despicable actions, all those years ago. There is a very real sense, and I think José is probably right in this, in which your death would be far too easy a solution. I want you to know what it is to endure years of anguish and pain, day after day after day, hour after hour, minute after minute. You never know, Basil, it might even help you on your path towards sanctification.'

Cuella does not know whether to be relieved or petrified.

Calogero continues: 'Timothy made it perfectly clear to me that you are not to be harmed physically, but he did give me the freedom to devise your punishment. He, of course, sees it in terms of penance, but I suspect that the possibility of you actually repenting of your "sins" is about as likely as A.P.D. Leonfortese winning Serie A. Let's face it, Basil, you have been remarkably disloyal, intensely devious and, almost certainly, horrendously criminal. So there is an awful lot to take on board before you can really have been said to repent.

'Being a generous man, I have devised two alternatives for you to consider. To be brutally honest I suspect that, whatever you choose, there will be times when you, and I sincerely hope that I am right in this, will actually wish that you were dead. So, my *bête noire* let me tell you about your options. The choice will be yours and yours alone. There will be nobody to blame but yourself. Come, let us begin...'

VII

ONE YEAR LATER
SERENITATEM?

VII:I

If a week is a long time in politics, then a year stuck on Kintana and New Lyon, in the middle of the Pacific Ocean, is akin to an eternity in purgatory; or so thinks the former cardinal Basil Alfonso Cuella. It is a nightmare that seems to have no end. As a man used to the finer things in life, he is heartily sick of his staple diet of tinned fish and rice. He hates taro and cassava with an all-consuming passion – unless, that is, one has actually been exposed to the hideous stuff! He has not had a decent cup of coffee for over a year, and the only alcoholic beverages regularly available to him are Foster's and Jacob's Creek. He has had malaria, dengue fever and giardia, is covered with tropical sores and lesions, and his hair is host to a colony of lice in a size of biblical proportions. It is just all too much for a cultured, refined gentleman of his class to bear.

To make matters worse, the two parishes under his jurisdiction are four hundred miles apart. In order to celebrate Mass in each community he has to: make a weekly round trip through the turbulent air above the Pacific; in a battered old Twin Otter; piloted by a pock-marked, gnarled, blasphemous, elderly Frenchman, who is quite plainly an alcoholic. Cuella, who shares his former boss's aversion to flying, is nearly always sick and constantly petrified as the plane lurches, pitches and drops alarmingly in the unpredictable thermals.

The irony of ending up in a place very similar to that where he found the runaway pope is not lost on him, but he really had no choice. The Don's options were stark and unappealing: it was either end up as a virtual prisoner of the insane friars in the Dolomites, or work as a priest in one of the most remote parishes in the Catholic diaspora. The decision, as they might well say in the tabloid press, was a 'no brainer'; and so now he finds himself thousands of miles from civilisation, ministering to a group of Pacific islanders as well as the misfits and mercenaries which make up the expatriate community. To ensure that he fulfils his priestly obligations in a responsible and conscientious manner, he is subject to regular, unannounced visitations from an officious, pompous, overbearing, narrow-minded monseigneur from New Caledonia, who delights in making his life a misery. After all, it is not every day that one gets to 'boss' the former boss. It also has the effect of negating any possible nefarious activity with the delectable, and readily available, Polynesian beauties that inhabit the islands. It is all very frustrating. Basil Cuella is seriously depressed.

His is a seven-year term of office, after which time he will be free to retire to Valencia; by then, it is to be hoped that he will have completed his penance and learnt from the error of his ways.

VII:II

Much to his amazement, Maurice Jean-Paul de Lange, Secretary of State to the Vatican and formerly Bishop of Limoges, is invited to the pope's private apartment in Prati, a relatively affluent suburb of Rome to the north west of the Vatican City. All their previous meetings have been within the confines of the Vatican itself, most usually in the papal apartments. It is extremely unusual for a pope to have a residence outside the Vatican, but Timothy says that he needs his own 'space' to reflect, to be able to think, to be his own man. There are times, he argues, when he just has to be alone. Until today de Lange did not even know the location of this personal Shangri-La, so he can only speculate that the matter to be discussed is either intensely private or that the pope is undergoing some form of spiritual crisis.

The flat is located on the top floor of a nineteenth-century building in the Via Cicerone; anyone who is intent on doing the pope harm will have to climb five flights of stairs to get to him, by which time, it is assumed, they will be positively exhausted. The front door is opened by Antonio, one of the pope's three bodyguards. As former employees of Don Calogero Escatores, who no longer has need of their services, it goes without saying that they are not to be trifled with; they are also fiercely loyal to their new master. However, they are not the only security feature associated with the apartment: the entrance is monitored by

CCTV, the front door is armour-plated, and all the windows are reinforced to withstand the impact of bullets and bomb blasts. There is also an internal 'safe' room where the pope can take refuge if the flat comes under attack. One cannot be too careful.

'He's in there,' growls Antonio, motioning towards a door at the end of a long narrow corridor. Maurice walks down the hall, past framed pictures of a much younger José in his cycling days, knocks on the door and enters a spacious room filled from floor to ceiling with books; the only wall spaces not fully lined with shelves are in each corner, where four giant Bang & Olufsen speakers bear testament to the occupant's love of loud music. One hopes, for his neighbour's sake, that the room is fully soundproofed. The pope is sitting in one of two dark blue Brufani armchairs facing each other across a pine coffee table. He is dressed in well-worn jeans and a T-shirt bearing the logo 'I ♥ Tereza's Hotel Corfu'. In his right hand he is cradling a large brandy glass, half full of golden, amber fluid.

'Good to see you, Maurice,' says the pope, smiling inanely. 'Help yourself to a Metaxa. It's a little early for Rioja. Take a seat and, for heaven's sake, don't bother with any of that ridiculous ring-kissing business.'

It is certainly a little early; it's barely half past ten in the morning and it is obvious from the pope's demeanour that this is not his first Metaxa of the day. Maurice picks up the bottle on the table – it is only half full – pours himself a discreet measure and sits down opposite Timothy. Silence reigns. Maurice tries to break the ice.

'Going on holiday?' he jokes.

The pope looks at him vacantly and then the light

dawns. 'Very funny,' he says looking down at the T-shirt. 'Mind you, had some wonderful holidays there when I was a boy and dad was Cultural Attaché at the embassy in London. We'd go for a couple of weeks every year. Still keep in touch with Thanasis and Leo... used to play with them when we were kids... but obviously now I can never go back there as a guest...' He takes a deep draft of brandy. '... bloody job... I hate the bloody job.'

Timothy stares into the distance, perhaps reliving some happy memories from childhood, but then he sees his secretary of state looking at him with concern on his face.

'Don't worry, Maurice, I'm not about to go on my travels again. I've learnt my lesson. I've just got to get on with it – bloody job.' He takes another slurp.

'Never wanted to be a priest, you know, never. Wanted to be a professional cyclist – ride the Grand Tours and perhaps win one, but I was never good enough. Had a few races, even in the Vuelta once, but it was soon obvious that I'd never make the grade at the highest level. The best I could hope for was to be back in the peloton riding as a domestique, working my balls off for some other sod, who would probably be full to the gunnels of performance-enhancing drugs, so that he could get all the glory.

'... so the family got on my case. "Get a job," they said. "Get a proper job." On and on and on they went, and finally I capt... capilut... gave up.

'Every choice seemed too ghastly to contemplate: I could work on the family farm breeding bulls for the ring, but I found the notion of raising fine animals for eventual slaughter in the name of entertainment nauseating; lawyer

– lying to protect the guilty; banker – cheating people of their hard-earned money; teacher – delivering irrelevant knowledge to clients with no interest in the subject matter. It was not until I got to priest that an option seemed vaguely appealing: one day a week, no set hours, do as little or as much as necessary, status and respect. Seemed as good a choice as any and so I sort of drifted into the priesthood…'

He refills his glass and knocks back a healthy slurp.

'… was top of my class at the seminary, was attached to a parish in Malaga, did a bit of university teaching, was "noticed" by the local archbishop – I think he fancied me – and rose rapidly through the ranks… not through ambition, you understand… just right place at the right time, combined with the woeful incompetence of my contemporaries.

'And where did I end up? Standing on that bloody balcony… in front of all those bloody people… with that arsehole Cuella behind me… promising me his full support in my "reforming" endeavours… and then shafting me at every possible opportunity…

'Somebody once told me, can't remember who for the life of me, that I am an idealist and that there is no place for idealism in the twenty-first century. But there is, Maurice, isn't there? Surely there must be… otherwise, what's the point of it all? What's the point of it all?' He tips more Metaxa down his throat.

'Do you know what, Maurice? We're lucky, we're so very lucky. We have a wonderful, liberating message to share with the world. It's a message that can transform lives; bring hope to the desolate and needy; make a real difference, but at every stage we are blocked by "friends" like Cuella who are interested solely in their own selfaggg… selfarrr… power…'

José stares blankly into the distance and then turns towards his friend.

'Been meaning to ask you for some time, how's dear old Gustave... dear old Gustave... lovely, long-suffering old Gustave? I never see the sod, are you still together?'

'He stayed in Paris when you moved me here,' says de Lange. 'We both felt that it would be for the good. He would have felt trapped in Rome and, anyway, tongues would have been bound to wag. You know what our colleagues are like! Then there was Hercules to consider.'

'Who's Hercules?'

'He's Gustave's cat – our cat.'

'You mean Gustave stayed in Paris, principally to look after a cat?'

'Yes.'

'*Incroyable*!' exclaims an incredulous pope. 'People never cease to surprise me. I find it hard to believe that anyone could become deeply attached to such aloof, arrogant and selfish creatures. Mind you,' he rambles on, 'did once have some friends in Madrid who were moving to Beijing and wanted to take their cat with them. They actually went into the Chinese Embassy on Arturo Soria and enquired, from a bewildered consular official, what formalities they would have to go through in order to transport the *gata* to China. He was amazed: "You wanna take cat Beijing? Why? Plenty cats in China!"' Timothy smiles at the memory. 'Anyway it didn't work out and they ended up getting DHL to transport the animal to friends in Alfaz del Pi, where, I believe, it had a much better life than it would have done on the thirteenth floor of a high-rise apartment block in the centre of the city. So you've lost touch with Gustave then?'

'Oh no,' says Maurice, 'I manage to get to Paris every couple of months – incognito of course.'

'Must be hard,' says the pope.

'It is, but we both believe that the sacrifice, such as it is, is worth it. After all, somebody has got to keep an eye on you.'

'Hmmm,' responds José.

There is another long break in the conversation. In the background Freddie Mercury is trying to 'break free' which, de Lange thinks, is not a totally inappropriate track in the light of what has gone on in the recent past. José, his eyes increasingly bloodshot, starts babbling again:

'Did I ever tell you, Moe my old friend, that Cuella shafted me... shafted me at every opportunity... the bastard... every possible opportunity...'

He peers intently at Maurice, his eyes glassy and increasingly bloodshot. 'You won't shaft me, will you, Maurice? You'll support me. You won't shaft me like that bastard Cuella, will you?'

If his secretary of state is shocked by the remarkable change in tone of the pope's didactic exegesis he does not show it, after all he is a consummate diplomat.

'No, José. I won't betray you. You have my absolute support. One hundred percent.'

The pope appears not to have heard him and blathers on: 'Do you know why there are times when I hate this job, Moe? Have I told you that I hate the job? I hate it because nobody knows who I am, nobody at all. Oh yes, they all see me when I'm wheeled out in that bloody mechanical contraption, they cheer and wave and give me their babies to bless – but they don't know me. They just see a figurehead, an icon, a reassurance of continuity and meaning in their lives. They see the veneer but not the chipboard inside. When I administer the Sacraments I don't know the people I am serving except, of course, the bloody cardinals and all too often I find myself wishing that I did not know them at all.'

He looks at de Lange. 'Do you know me, Moe? Can you say that you really know me?' Maurice says nothing because, in all truth, he has come to appreciate that, even with the long history between them, he really does not know the pope at all. He admires, respects and likes the person he has come to think of as his friend, but does he understand him as a man? No, he does not. He is ashamed to say that he has never given the matter any thought, after all, the pope is the pope is the pope – end of story. It appals him to think he has never realised that the man in front of him is very much alone and friendless, weighed down by enormous burdens which he can never shake off. Timothy looks at him, nods slowly and then takes another deep, deep draft of brandy. He changes the subject:

'I heard from Calogero this morning. I envy that man. He's doing fantastic work. Wish I were in his shoes – great guy!'

Maurice nods. 'I never did quite work out how that happened,' he says.

'Didn't I tell you?'

'No.'

'Must have done…'

'No, I don't think you did.'

The pope smiles broadly and takes another drink.

'I sent a party of those crazy ninja friars down to Leonforte. They cleared out the old man's bodyguards, even my old friend Antonio here, in under half an hour – they did not know what hit them – don't worry, nobody was seriously hurt. They brought the Don to me at Castel Gandolfo in the middle of the night. We had a bit of a chat – well to be honest it was more than a chat – lasted over forty-eight hours. In the end he confessed, repented of all the harm he had done and turned around. He begged for forgiveness. I absolved him and, as part of his penance, sent him for three months' prayer and contemplation at San Isidro… tough place San Isidro… good for him… they sorted him out… really sorted him out… and that's how he ended up where he is today… great guy… great guy…'

He is almost drifting off to sleep and is quite clearly in a world of his own.

'… not like me – look at the mayhem I created – if it was not for me Jackson and Flanagan would still be alive… God only knows how many other people I hurt… I can't sleep at night Moe… I lie awake for hours… thinking of all the harm my selfishness has caused… the hurt… the terrible pain… the agony…'

His eyes close. Maurice wonders if it is time to take his leave, but then:

'Don't worry Moe… good old Moe. I won't let you down in public. I'll wave. I'll deliver inspiring homilies and speeches. I'll travel. I'll preach the Gospel across the world. I'll even kiss bloody babies for you…

'… but I must have somewhere for me… somewhere where I can read pulp… somewhere where I can watch crap TV and listen to Queen with the sound turned full blast… somewhere where I can fart without people thinking I've got bowel cancer…

'… we'll get those bastards, won't we, Moe? We must root out the bastards…'

He is almost asleep but then he says something that both surprises and touches Maurice:

'… pity about Carmen… so sad… I love that girl… really, really love her… so much… so very much…'

He begins to snore. The glass is angled precariously. Maurice takes it from the pope's hand and places it on the coffee table. He looks down at José. His heart is breaking for his old friend. He bends down, kisses José gently on the forehead, and then, very quietly, lets himself out of the room.

VII:III

They call him Papa Don: the children in the orphanage in Aleppo. Traumatised by war; bereft from bereavement; ground down by poverty – he is their rock; their strength, and their shield from harm. He is loved and respected and admired.

He is their Saviour.

Don Calogero is at peace.

END PEACE

FORTY YEARS ON

In the papal apartments high above St Peter's Square, on a blazingly hot day in June, an old man is dying; a good man is dying. The usually hyperactive pigeons are not menacing the tourists thronging the square; rather they stand mute and silent on the statues of the long-dead saints surrounding the piazza – as if in homage to the passing of a man who is universally loved and admired.

In the bedroom of the apartment, high up above the piazza, those closest to Timothy wait in anticipation of the dreaded, but in some ways hoped for, event; he has suffered enough. His hands are held by two elderly, distraught nuns who are weeping uncontrollably; the man they have loved unconditionally for decades is leaving them. They are inconsolable.

But it is noticeable that, between shallow laboured breaths, He is almost smiling. It is not the rictus of death. He seems to be in a place beyond all of them.

José is on the wooden decking at the Sanctuary...

the sun is shining...

that bloody bird is making a hell of a racket as usual...

the girls are sunbathing and look so beautiful......

surf is pounding......

trees...... smell of frangipani......

what.........

what.........

what.........

a............

beautiful............

beautiful............

way............

way............

to....................

to....................

GLOSSARY

Gehenna	Ancient equivalent for hell.
Lepus in lumina	Rabbit in the headlights!
Osso Bucco d'Agneau aux Cèpes	Slow cooked lamb shanks with mushrooms.
'Docere autem mulieri nom permitte neque dominari in virum sed esse in silento.' (Neo Vulgata))	"But I suffer not a woman to teach, nor to usurp authority over the man, but to be in silence". 1 Timothy 2:12 .
Oblata arripe! Rapiamus, amici, occasionem de die!	Take what is given! Let us snatch our opportunity from the passing day! (Horace)
Hemidactylus Mabouias	Tropical house gecko.
Mia bella bocca di Leone.	My beautiful snapdragon.
Bellum sacrum	Holy war
Milites Christi	Soldiers of Christ
Cavalli per I corsi	Horses for courses
Otium	A time for leisure and contemplation. The opposite of negotium – work and business.
Meglio il diavolo che sai!	Better the devil you know.
Ecco l'agnello di Dio, che toglie il peccati del mondo	Behold the Lamb of God who takes away the sins of the world.

aes sonans aut cymbalum tinniens (Vulgate)	A noisy gong or a clanging cymbal. 1 Corinthians 1:13:1
Taro	A root vegetable, whose leaves can also be consumed, common in Asia and islands in the Pacific Ocean.
Cassava	A root vegetable that, if not correctly prepared, can be poisonous.

ACKNOWLEDGEMENTS

I would like to thank Joanne Fiona Tait and Brenda Flanagan for reading the manuscript. The suggestions and advice they offered were invaluable. I would also like to thank my wife, Geraldine, for the emotional and secretarial support she gave me – but, as usual, she does not want to be acknowledged.